Death Department

DEATH DEPARTMENT

Bill Knox

Constable · London

First published in Great Britain 1959
Copyright © 1959 Bill Knox
This edition published in Great Britain 1998
by Constable & Company Ltd., 3 The Lanchesters,
162 Fulham Palace Road, London W6 9ER
The right of Bill Knox to be identified
as the author of this work has been
asserted by him in accordance with
the Copyright, Designs and Patents Act 1988
ISBN 0 094 79090 6
Printed and bound in Great Britain by
MGP Books Ltd, Bodmin

A CIP catalogue record for this book
is available from the British Library

For Michael

I

SEVEN proud storeys high stood the monolithic bulk of the building, a man-made landmark in the sunbaked city, its polished blue brick facings winking and sparkling in the harsh, glaring light. Tall, yet made squat by its very bulk, Hillman's Store was almost a self-contained town, serviced by its own small army of workers. It was a place of money-spending pilgrimage for the masses of people who every day passed its display windows— windows that cried in carefully pitched and controlled tones of the wondrous attractions that lay waiting within this twentieth-century, cash-or-credit Aladdin's Cave. These broad sweeps of glass were front-line weapons in the commercial jungle, served ammunition by a squad of experts to whom display was a scientific study and victory won when a passer-by broke step to glance at the attractions they displayed.

Lesser adversaries cursed or admired Hillman's, unashamedly copied its sales technique or wept tears of rage at the cut-rate prices its fantastic turnover made possible.

The combined floor-space of those seven storeys would have absorbed Wembley or Hampden with ease. The store had its own doctor, nurses, lawyer, "police", electricians, plumbers. Painting was a job that had begun the day the store first opened, and would keep a full-time squad of tradesmen occupied until the unlikely day it closed.

In the hot, still atmosphere of the rare June heatwave, a constant tide of cotton-frocked customers flowed through the entrances, passing the huge "Summer Sale Starts Saturday" posters that covered every vantage-point—vantage points

7

scientifically selected for maximum consumer-impact, as indeed were the very colours and type faces of the posters themselves.

Inside, where the temperature was only a few degrees cooler than in hot, dusty Sauchiehall Street, cash registers chimed and banged a cheery moneyed chorus, while assistants, perspiring in their uniform black-and-red outfits, envied the cooler clothing of their customers and used wrapping paper at the rate of a mile an hour. The total effect of this mid-morning activity should have brought joy to any company official. But, in a penthouse office on the roof of the bustling concrete hive, a worried scowl creased the broad, sweat-beaded face of Hillman's managing director, Charles Farringdon. He thumped the smooth mahogany desk top with a heavy fist and declared, 'These damn sneak-thieves are taking us for a small fortune each week—and all you can do is ask stupid ruddy questions. It's action, action I want, not gossiping!'

Farringdon, a bald, corpulent individual of about sixty, unattractive to the eye, might at first glance have been dismissed as a strong man gone completely to seed.

But if the stranger looked again, and more especially if he heard that harsh, compelling voice barking commands, then would come realization that this was a power-house of a man whose sole driving purpose was the establishment of bigger and better sales figures. His flabbiness was almost an occupational condition—because the mahogany-topped desk was operational headquarters, and strolling the store, or for that matter the golf course, was so much time wasted from his relentless figurework and planning.

Right now, his little gimlet eyes were a hard and angry grey as he glared round the other men seated in the richly furnished office. Jerry Watford, his young assistant manager, met the gaze, stared back for a moment, then, his blue eyes half-shut, lowered his close-cropped blonde head and scuffed his feet in the thick pile of the dark blue carpet. The head store detective, James Rose, flushed at the implied criticism in Farringdon's tone and shifted uncomfortably in his chair as he remembered the sharp dressing-down he had had from the same source just before the conference

8

had begun. Henry Allen, the head buyer, gently cleared his throat, and gazed over the managing director's head, trying to ignore the gross figure before him and concentrate on the antics of the lazy, drifting specks of dust caught and magnified by the bright sunlight pouring through the window.

Scowling more fiercely than ever, Farringdon turned his gaze on the two other men in the room. His outburst seemed to have produced only a studied expression of bored disinterest on their faces. The taller man met and held his gaze, and for once it was Farringdon who turned away first, to flip open a silver box and, with deliberate discourtesy, take out a cigarette and light it. Chief Detective Inspector Colin Thane, head of Millside Division of Glasgow C.I.D., waited equally deliberately until Farringdon had blown a long cloud of blue tobacco smoke skywards, then, firmly and quietly, said, 'Trying to bully us won't help, sir. We know you're in trouble. That's why we are here. But . . .' he gestured to the slimmer figure by his side, 'Inspector Moss and I can only make progress if we have your real co-operation. And that means answering questions if and when we ask them. We'll try and provide the action soon enough.'

Farringdon's face became more thunderous than ever, twitched with rage . . . and just as suddenly a grudging hint of a smile appeared in one corner of his mouth and he gave a faint suspicion of an approving nod. He left the cigarette smouldering, forgotten, in the big glass ashtray on the desk top, his voice, still hard and brisk, but somehow more tolerant, demanded, 'Well, what else do you want to know, anyway—not that I see what good it's doing.'

Thane gave a faint sigh. 'I was asking why you had any reason to suppose that this wave of thefts from Hillman's was anything other than a normal seasonal increase. Remember, the summer holidays are starting, and plenty of people who are tight for cash may be tempted to help themselves.'

'Seasonal increase,' growled Farringdon. 'Seasonal be damned. Watford'—the assistant manager jerked back from his contemplation of the carpet—'give them the figures we've drawn up.'

Jerry Watford picked up the top sheet from the sheaf of papers balanced on his knee. He gave a friendly smile across the room and explained, 'We keep a monthly return on stock believed stolen, its value, people caught, all that sort of thing. Part of normal business procedure. Well, in the normal year, we lose something like thirty thousand pounds' worth of stock by shoplifting.' Thane gave a faint whistle of surprise as Watford, glancing apologetically at the store detective beside him, went on, 'Mr. Rose and his staff keep busy of course, and we'd lose a lot more but for their efforts. They catch maybe nine or ten shoplifters a week. But the fact still remains that about six hundred pounds' worth of goods disappear out of here every normal week without being paid for.

'That's a normal trading loss—every store has to contend with a certain amount of theft. But this is different.' He stabbed one finger at the paper before him. 'For the past three months our shoplifting losses have been steadily rising each week— rocketing, in fact. They started jumping the first week in April— to seven hundred and fifty pounds. By the beginning of May they were over eight hundred a week, and still rising. This month'—he shrugged—'it's been running at just over a thousand a week. Yet over the past five years the June shoplifting average has been seven hundred.'

Thane leaned forward, thumb rubbing gently along his chin. 'The final total?' he asked.

'Four thousand pounds above normal over the three months,' growled Farringdon, taking over the reins again, 'and you ask about seasonal increases.' He thumped the desk top again. 'There's an organized gang at work, I tell you, hammering our stock. Our ruddy store detectives can do nothing. They're worse than useless. The first time we complained, you gave us two policemen. Up till now they've done precisely damn-all to help. That's why we asked you to this meeting today. You're the head of Millside Division C.I.D. This store's in Millside . . . and we need something done and done quickly.'

Thane sat silent for a moment. When, a few weeks before, Hillman's had complained of increased pilfering from their store, he had detailed a detective sergeant and constable to investigate. They had picked up a couple of well-known small operators, both women, but had found no other unusual activity.

'My men weren't given these figures,' he protested angrily. 'Why did you keep those totals back from them? How were we to know how serious the position had become?'

'Blame me,' said Farringdon. 'We thought at first it was just chance, a run of bad luck. But then we saw we were wrong, that some people were getting easy pickings. Of course we didn't give details . . . do you think we wanted the story to be picked up by the newspapers? Do you think we wanted all of Glasgow to know that you can "knock" anything from a cake of soap to a coat at Hillman's and get away with it? We kept quiet and hoped your men could sort things out. They couldn't—and now we're having to come out into the open.' He glanced at his watch, a slim gold disc dwarfed by his huge, hairy wrist. 'We've told you the hand that's been dealt us, and now we're asking you to play it for us. I've another appointment in five minutes. These three,' he scowled at his assistants, 'will help any way you need. I'm too busy to get involved unless it becomes vital.' He took another cigarette from the box, nodded, lit it, picked up some letters from the desk. The conference was obviously over.

Escorted by the three store executives, Thane and Moss left the office, each boiling inwardly at the brusque treatment they had received. Out in the tiny corridor, walking towards the lift gate, Jerry Watford was first to break the silence. 'Don't mind him,' he said. 'Growls like a bear with a sore head half the time, but he's never done anybody any real harm and we've a smaller turnover of staff than any other store in the City of Glasgow. He's rude, crude and tough on the surface, but he's all right underneath. And he's the best in his line when it comes to cold cash returns.'

Thane nodded. 'With a set-up like this, that's obvious. Ignoring personal opinions, your chief's idea of a general get-together is pretty sound, I think. Let's see, it's coming up for noon now, and I've got one or two things to do that can't wait.

Could all three of you be available after lunch so that we can get down to fine detail about the whole matter?'

'I've a better idea,' said Watford. 'Come back here for your meal, both of you. I'll arrange a table in a quiet corner of our restaurant floor, and all five of us can get together over lunch.'

Both the store detective and head buyer nodded their approval of the idea. 'Suits me,' agreed Thane.

.   .   .   .   .

The slight difficulty in dealing with a couple of Scottish "home rule" enthusiasts, caught the night before trying to paint rude words across the entrance to the premises of an "invading" English firm, meant that it was a few minutes after one before Thane and Moss were free to leave Millside police station. They said good-bye to the Special Branch man who had wandered over from Headquarters to have a look at the Nationalists, now rather forlorn in their drab station cell, then stepped into the waiting C.I.D. duty car.

The police driver took the Jaguar gently but swiftly through the dusty streets, his uniform cap and the prominent radio aerial causing two street football matches and a pavement bookie's "pitch" to break up in sudden disorder. It was a ten-minute journey towards Hillman's, and the division's latest problem.

'This looks like being a bit of a stinker, Phil,' said Thane, relaxing back on the roomy rear seat. He settled his grey soft hat more comfortably on the back of his head and went on. 'By Farringdon's figures, it looks as though he's right in thinking this is a well-organized attack on his store rather than just a chance wave of casual shoplifting. We know "lifting" follows a pattern—before Christmas and just prior to the summer season count as peak points. But this outbreak is too big to fit the pattern.'

With an easy air born of long personal friendship, Detective Inspector Phillip Moss gloomily agreed. 'I started the boys

12

digging out that list from "records" as you asked, Colin,' he reported. 'All known shoplifters, petty thieves and "neds" who might fit our bill, male or female, city regulars or country half-day visitors. Photographs and notes on how they operate will be ready by this evening, tomorrow at the latest.' Moss slipped a hand into one pocket of his heavy tweed suit, worn in defiance of the rare heat-wave conditions hitting the whole Clyde coast, and pulled out a round tin box. 'No knowing what those restaurant meals are like,' he muttered, popping a small tablet from the box into his mouth. 'This is a medical sample pack, got it from my cousin's husband—he's a quack, you know. Chalk extract, they're made of . . . gives a lining to the stomach.'

Colin Thane smiled and shook his head. Phil Moss had been his friend and colleague for several years now . . . and all that time the Inspector had been trying a never-ending stream of pills, bottles and diet-sheets in a constant battle with his trouble-some stomach. Phil was nursing a duodenal . . . sometimes painfully real despite the tender care lavished on it. The ulcer and its treatment constituted one of Moss's major interests in life . . . though Thane was convinced the trouble had become as much psychological as physical. Still, despite it all, Moss, small, wiry, remained a first-class officer. He might lack that spark of long-distance deduction which had lifted Thane over his head. But they remained an inseparable team, with a long record of kills.

Thane, in his early forties, was tall, dark-haired, a burly, clean-shaven man carrying perhaps a stone more weight than fifteen years back when he had been a top-line amateur athlete. His powerful physique was still close to maximum efficiency, his name almost a household word in a city where crime was regular front-page news. Leaning back in the car, however, he smiled like a schoolboy as he suddenly recalled, 'You know, Phil, my wife had our two kids at Hillman's a few days back. She was taking a prowl round looking at carpets, but decided to wait and see how the prices come down in this summer sale they're having. We need a new carpet badly in the living-room. That red thing we've got is getting near to the coal-bag stage. Don't ask me

13

where the money's coming from, though . . . Mary's probably busy juggling with the housekeeping money right now to raise the necessary!'

Moss gave a superior, bachelor grin. 'Watch she doesn't knock one off from the store,' he chortled. 'Imagine the result to that ruddy managing director's fat face . . . it would almost be worth trying it just to see him explode!'

'Don't under-rate Farringdon,' warned Thane. 'I remember hearing about him once. Started off as a young counter assistant when old man Hillman first began in business—a wee two-roomed shop was all he had in those days. Farringdon rose up the ladder as fast as the firm grew—in fact some people say it was Farringdon's drive that made many of the old man's ideas succeed. Anyway, when old Hillman died a few years back Farringdon took over. He may not be the majority shareholder, but for all practical purposes he can run things as he likes as long as the store keeps paying good dividends.'

'And shoplifting goes on the debit account—which cuts into Mr. F.'s profit figures,' mused Moss.

'Exactly—and so he tries to put the heat on us,' grimaced Thane as the police car slowed outside the distinctive blue building. The blazing sun was sending the temperature panting upwards through the eighties—the polished surface of the car body was warm to the touch; they felt the baked heat of the pavement soaking through the soles of their shoes as they left the Jaguar and walked across to the store's wide main door. A uniformed doorman had been watching for their arrival. He stepped forward as they approached.

' 'Afternoon, sir,' he greeted. 'Remember me?'

Thane gave a surprised glance, recognized the long-jawed face before him. 'Andy Richards . . . so this is where you got to. Bit of a change from pounding the beat, eh?'

The doorman, until a scant eighteen months before a beat constable in the Millside division, shook his head. 'Not as big a change as you might think, Mr. Thane. By the time I've spent a day pounding these floors my poor feet know all about it. Still, the pay's good, hours aren't long, there's a canteen, good

14

holidays, nice bunch of people to work with—and no night shift. Put all that on top of my police pension, and I'm doing very nicely, thanks.' As he talked, he led them inside the building, through the maze of busy counters and over to one of the battery of express lifts. 'Mr. Watford asked me to bring you up to the Sycamore Restaurant on the third floor,' he explained. 'They're waiting on you there—he and Mr. Allen and Rose, the store dick.'

'What are they like to work for?' asked Thane.

'Rose is a bit of a—och, let's just say he likes to think he's a helluva lot smarter than he is, and likes throwing his weight about. He's an amateur . . . no police training,' said the doorman with supreme contempt. 'The other two are all right. Watford's a bright boy if ever I saw one. Allen keeps himself to himself, but he seems all right. I suppose you are over about the flogging that's been going on?'

'Uh-huh,' Thane nodded. 'What do you know about it, Richards?'

'Nothing much, sir.' The doorman commandeered a lift that had just come down and was emptying. He held back a tide of shoppers intent on getting aboard, shepherded his two charges inside, and nodded to the lift attendant. He whistled quietly to himself while the lift hummed up to the third floor, then, once they were outside again and in a broad, sycamore-panelled corridor from which the restaurant got its name, said, 'There's something queer about it all, Mr. Thane. Whoever's doing it is up to something pretty clever. All the staff know about the losses—they couldn't help it with Mr. "Sherlock" Rose running around foaming at the mouth and stock checks being made every other day. The departmental managers are on the verge of nervous breakdowns over it all.' He gave a knowing wink.

'I've been keeping my eyes open . . . and it's none of the old gang that I know. Och, there's a few of the regulars coming in—Detective-Sergeant MacLean caught Long Lizzie working the message-bag trick. You know, dumping her hold-all on the counter and scooping up stuff through a cut in the bottom of it. Another bloke tried to get away wearing two coats, and then

15

there were the usual small-time operators and amateurs. But there's a real professional at work somewhere, and I'm darned if I see how it's being done. For, mind you, general security isn't too bad, despite old Rose.'

'Will you keep your ears open for us, Richards?' asked Moss.

'Aye, sure, Inspector. It'll be a pleasure,' agreed the ex-policeman in a confident voice. He swung open the glass door of the restaurant. 'They are over in the corner,' he pointed. 'I'll need to get back now—but I'll contact you the moment I find out anything,' he promised, turning away.

Jerry Watford came to greet Thane and Moss as the two policemen threaded their way through the restaurant's busy tables. 'Glad to see you,' he exclaimed. 'We're all ready and waiting . . . and there's one extra member of the party.'

They moved over to the table, set close to a large window overlooking bustling Sauchiehall Street, far below. The head buyer and store detective were already seated, in quiet conversation with a small, attractive woman in her forties whose neat, close-cut hair showed faint traces of grey. She looked up and gave a pleasant smile as they approached.

'This is Miss Marchand,' introduced Watford. 'Judith's our women's buyer, and in charge of the fashion department. We thought she should come along, seeing her section of the store is easily the worst hit.' They exchanged greetings and settled down. Conversation kept to generalities throughout the meal by mutual consent. Only when the table was cleared and the waitress had brought coffee—extra-white for Moss's ulcer— did Watford lean forward and declare: 'Let's get down to business, Mr. Thane. You shoot the questions and we'll contribute the answers.'

Thane accepted the cigarette offered by Allen and a light from Watford then said, 'First thing seems to be, are you sure the stock disappears here? Couldn't some of it go before it reaches the store—while it is in transit from the maker or wholesaler?'

'Impossible,' retorted Henry Allen. The head buyer, a small,

16

stout man in his forties, thinning hair spread carefully over his heavy forehead to give maximum coverage, gave a stifled belch. 'Impossible. All goods come straight to our receiving room, and every item is checked against invoices before we accept delivery. And there's another check after that, made by each department before they receive the consignment into their own stockroom.'

Thane shrugged. 'Fair enough. Now, what are the security measures taken inside the store? Mr. Rose?'

Rose, thin, sharp-featured, an R.A.F. tie blending with his well-cut, double-breasted suit, let his cigarette dangle carelessly from one corner of his mouth as he sketched his security system. 'I've got four people—two men, two women—constantly circulating through the departments. They've all done the job for years, completely satisfactorily until now, The shop assistants and supervisors are really our front line—they're well briefed to keep their eyes open. I've another assistant "on call" in our office. We carry out the usual technique required by law—we wait until the suspect's leaving the store, then ask them to come back to the office and account for any goods they have on their person. If they don't, we call the police.'

'You've never actually been in the police yourself, have you, Mr. Rose?' asked Thane gently.

'Heavens, no,' exclaimed Rose. 'But what's that got to do with the matter . . . are you trying to hint I don't know my job?'

'No—not for a moment,' soothed Thane. 'It was pure curiosity on my part, nothing more.'

'Hmpph. Anyway, that's our situation. I could use more staff, I keep telling Watford. That's all I need, more staff. There's no real mystery here, Mr. Thane. Simply lack of staff to tackle the problem, and perhaps dishonesty on the part of employees. Some of these girl assistants are probably helping the thieves.'

'That's hardly fair,' protested Judith Marchand. 'The heaviest losses and most of the increases over normal have been in my department. And I assure you, Mr. Thane, I trust my girls implicitly. Besides, there's the Agency check to remember—and they've reported nothing adverse.'

'The Agency?' queried Thane.

Jerry Watford explained. 'It's like this,' said the assistant manager. 'Most big stores like our own employ an outside agency to make test purchases. We use the Apex Agency, over in Argyle Street. They send investigators into the store from time to time to make test purchases. They watch the assistant doesn't overcharge, make sure they get a bill for the right amount and the correct change, and report on things like the service and courtesy they receive. If any assistant acts suspiciously they play her along . . . then tell us all about it.'

Inspector Moss let a slow, lazy trickle of smoke come down his nostrils, then asked, 'What size of a staff do you need to run a place as big as this?'

Watford grimaced. 'One of the features of modern merchandizing is that, like the Army, we need as many people in behind the scenes as we need in the front line. We've got a staff of just over a thousand—five hundred actually selling to the public, the rest in the office, accounting, despatch and other back-room billets. The boss is always complaining about it—that's one of the reasons why Rose can't have his extra bodies.'

'A thousand staff,' whistled Thane.

'Sounds a lot,' agreed the assistant manager. 'We have to make them eat in a shift system. They've got their own canteen, of course.'

'Any inquiries made into their background before they're hired?'

'None worth speaking about. But most of them have been with us for years.'

'I still say some of them are in on these thefts,' growled Rose. 'And that holds especially good for your department, Miss Marchand. You've one or two high-and-mighty pieces of goods in there I wouldn't trust an inch.'

The woman's eyes flashed, twin spots of red appeared on her cheeks, 'Maybe that's because they feel the same way about you,' she retorted. 'I know some things that have happened after hours, even if others don't.'

Thane hurriedly stopped what might have developed into a

18

minor war. 'A place like Hillman's must have a fantastic number of people going through it every day—and a turn over to match.'

Henry Allen nodded, and, in a satisfied tone, said, 'One hundred thousand people come into the store every week. On an average they make about forty thousand purchases—though,' he smirked, 'we hope to have a big increase on those figures next week with the summer sale we are running.'

Watford, stubbing out his cigarette in his saucer, oblivious of the ashtray inches away, declared, 'And that's my big worry right now. If the losses are running around the thousand pound mark on a normal week, what'll they be like on a sale week, when the place is crammed with customers from the moment it opens? You can't keep even a normal watch under those conditions.'

'Tell me more about the stock check,' demanded Thane. 'You told me that was how losses were found . . . but how often is it carried out?'

'Usually once a week,' said Watford. The assistant manager went into a long explanation of the system. Each department carried out a mid-week stock check, usually on a Thursday— 'That's the quietest day of the week—nobody's got money left to go shopping.' Goods on counters, in drawers or departmental stockrooms were checked against drawn quantities and known sales. Any difference between the two usually meant another shoplifting.

'And the women's departments, dresses and underwear, that kind of thing, have been the worst hit? Are any others badly affected?' asked Thane.

'Children's wear, men's haberdashery—ties, shirts, handkerchiefs,' said Allen. 'The stationery department loses a bit, the tobacconist's stall has some trouble. Hardware and food are only a little bothered—mostly for small items that can be slipped in the pocket. Of course, you can forget furniture, carpets, and other heavy items.'

Thane felt a faint nudge from Moss and restrained a smile.

'I'd like to have a look around the store,' he declared.

19

'Particularly in your department, Miss Marchand. And in the meantime, until we get a slightly better idea of what's happening, I'd like a full list of the stock found missing at the end of last week's check. The next one should be due in—let's see, this is Monday—three days' time. Right, I'd like a similar list from that one. Mr. Rose, your people probably know most of the really familiar faces in the shoplifting racket, but at any rate the police are preparing a selection of photographs and descriptions. We'll get them over as soon as we can, and your staff can study them. I'll draft some plain-clothes men in—two or three women as well, if Headquarters can spare them. We'll have other men outside, watching the entrances. I'm not suggesting simple methods like those will break the epidemic, but they represent a start.'

They rose from the table. Henry Allen excused himself. He had to confer with Farringdon and the publicity manager on some final details for the coming sale. The store detective also had other business. Jerry Watford, however, glanced at his watch and said, 'I'll come along with you to the fashion department, if you like. Give you a bit of moral support in a women's world . . . eh, Miss Marchand?'

The woman smiled. 'I won't question your motives,' she declared. 'Though I know someone who might.'

.   .   .   .   .

Women's fashions occupied the whole of the second floor. Busy and bustling round the hat and blouse counters, crowded at the cosmetic section, where a demonstrator from one of the main manufacturers was displaying the merits of a new brush-on lipstick to some sixty shoppers, mostly office typists ending their lunch-hour, it shaded into calmer conditions in the far-away section, devoted to coats and costumes. Judith Marchand led the three men through her realm with assured grace, throwing a quick greeting here, answering a question there, while her staff dealt with the flow of custom.

A tall, slim girl moved to intercept them, a worried look on

20

her attractive, sun-tanned face. 'Could you spare a moment?' she murmured to Judith Marchand.

One of the supervisors, guessed Thane, glancing at her tailored green corduroy suit, an assortment of pins stuck in one lapel. All the rank and file in Hillman's seemed to wear some variety or other of that black-and-red uniform.

'I was looking for you anyway, Pat,' declared the woman buyer. 'Miss Miller, my second-in-command—this is Chief Inspector Thane and Inspector Moss. They're going to try to solve our mystery, Pat.'

The girl gave a pleasant but worried smile to the two detectives, one hand playing with the pins on her lapel. Her eyes brightened a little as she said, 'Hello, Jerry . . . you might as well be here too. I've had some rather nasty news—perhaps your police friends will take it off my plate.'

'Bad news?' Judith Marchand frowned. 'Not more stock gone?'

'I'm afraid so.' The girl pursed her cupid's-bow mouth and gave her dark, wavy hair a despairing little shake. 'A customer wanted a tailored two-piece, and one of the girls went to fetch the dark blue gabardine costume with the white piquet edging. It was there last night. . . . I saw it on the rack myself. Now it's gone. There seems to be another missing too, a Lovat tweed costume. I've checked with the girls. They haven't sold either.'

'Couldn't they be in the stock-room, Pat?' asked Watford. 'Maybe they were put away by mistake?'

The girl slowly shook her head again. 'The gaberdine was on its size rack last night. I'll swear it. A woman came in late yesterday evening, just before we closed, and took a fancy to it. But she decided to come in again, and left. I saw the assistant put the gaberdine back on the rack. The suit was there when we locked up . . . and nothing has been put back in the stock-room since. I'm having a check made there, of course, but I'm sure it's gone.'

'How much were the two costumes worth, miss?' asked Moss.

'The blue retailed at eighteen pounds, the tweed at twenty,' said the girl. She sighed. 'I'm afraid this department's going to be at the head of the points table when it comes to losses this month. And the worst bit of all is, the girl who discovered the gaberdine missing says she thinks she knows who took it. . . . Jenny Rey, another of our staff. She says she saw Jenny bundling something into her locker just after the shop opened this morning; something dark that could be the costume, Whatever's going on, it looks as though Jenny's up to her neck in it.'

2

JENNY REY was sullen and white-faced, a spotty-complexioned girl of about nineteen with dyed blonde hair and late-night dancing shadows under her eyes. She stood beside a table in the fashion department office, eyes fixed on the blue gaberdine costume lying before her.

Rose, the store detective, had just thrown the two-piece on the table after bringing it from the girl's locker. Inspector Moss, who had gone with Rose to carry out the search, pursed his lips and thought on the eternal stupidity of the vast majority of petty thieves, whose punishment was not just a court sentence, but loss of job, of friends—and often of future. The store detective, however, was untrammelled by any such thoughts. A jubilant sneer on his rat-trap of a mouth, he declared, 'I told you all, but you wouldn't listen. The girl's just one of them . . . the trouble lies among the staff. I'll show you.' He seized the shopgirl by the shoulder of her black-and-red jacket. 'Speak up, girl. Who's in it with you—come on, come on, speak up.' He shook her with such force that she teetered back on her high-heeled sandals and almost overbalanced. Only the harsh grip on her shoulder stopped her from falling. Jenny Rey's heavily-painted lips quivered. But she said nothing.

'Leave her be,' snapped Thane, angered at the needless violence in Rose's action. 'We'll question her at the proper time and place—after she's been formally cautioned and charged at the police station.' He lifted the bright red telephone from its wall-rest beside him and got the store switchboard to pass a call to Millside station. When the police operator answered, the

23

Chief Inspector ordered a car to be sent round to the store. 'Send a policewoman with it,' he instructed. 'There's a female prisoner. What? Oh . . . never mind, then, but make sure the car comes round as soon as possible.' He replaced the phone and turned to the waiting group. Jenny Rey was no longer quiet. She was weeping noisily into a wisp of handkerchief. 'There's a slight snag,' said Thane. 'We usually want a policewoman along when we're running-in a girl—obvious reasons. There isn't one free just now. I wonder—Mr. Watford, could Miss Miller come along with us to play gooseberry?'

'Sure, that's all right,' nodded Watford. 'That is, unless Pat has any objections.'

The girl shook her dark head. 'Anything I can do to help,' she declared, looking round for her handbag and sparing time for an almost pitying glance at the still-weeping thief.

Judith Marchand followed her gaze, and stepped softly forward to lay a gentle hand on the young shopgirl's arm. 'It's all right, Jenny,' she soothed. 'Whatever you did, just tell the truth—I'll do all I can to make things easier for you.'

The girl stopped weeping as suddenly as if a tap had been jammed shut. Her watering eyes became hard, bitter. There was an hysterical, savage undertone in her voice as she snapped back, 'Take your hand off me . . . you sanctimonious old bitch. You're in no position to lecture anyone.'

The woman buyer flushed scarlet. She took an involuntary step backward, bewildered. 'Jenny!' she protested. 'Be sensible . . . you need your friends now. Don't make things more unpleasant than they are.'

But the sullen look was back on the girl's face again. Her eyes dropped. James Rose opened his mouth, words ready on his tongue, then decided against what he had been about to say. But his mind was toying with a strange new idea . . . one which he thought it wise not to launch himself. It could keep, he decided. Meantime, he could savour the possibilities . . . and the sweet future prospect of humiliating the hurt, bewildered Judith Marchand.

24

'I'll come down to the station with you, Chief Inspector,' he volunteered. 'You'll want a statement, I presume.'

'No need,' said Thane. 'We'll collect that from you later.' He was frankly puzzled by the girl's outburst. Just where this 'teenager fitted in the pattern of thefts . . . if she did at all . . . was a mystery. He spent the next few minutes collecting witnesses' names and other details and was barely finished when the internal phone rang to announce the car's arrival at the main door of the store. He gestured to Moss. The latter took a practised, deceptively casual finger-and-thumb grip of Jenny Rey's sleeve and quietly told her, 'Come on, lass.'

Slowly, soberly, they left the room in procession out into the busy clamour of the fashion department. Thane and Pat Miller led the way, Moss and the shopgirl behind, Rose, the shop detective, tagging on at the rear. Judith Marchand stood at the door of her office, watching as they walked through the racks of coats and dresses and out past the counters to the battery of lift gates beyond. Pat had the blue gaberdine costume over one arm. Several shoppers glanced at them as they passed, but few, if any, realized the significance of what they saw.

They travelled down from the second floor by lift, past hardware and foodstuffs on the first, and stopped with the slightest of jars on the ground floor. The little party let the other occupants of the lift, two young mothers and their chattering children, head towards the medley of "taster" counters carrying selections of the goods available on the floors above. Then they, too, moved off, over towards the main exit.

The inevitable "grapevine" had carried a rumour of what had happened round most of Hillman's staff. Frankly curious assistants took a moment off from serving customers to watch with raised eyebrows as the group, Moss's hand still unobtrusively gripping the girl's sleeve, threaded their way through the crowds. Andy Richards, the ex-policeman turned doorman, was at his usual post. 'Car's outside,' he reported.

He shook his head as he gazed at the little shopgirl. 'Small fry,' he muttered, standing close to Thane. The latter shrugged.

'Probably, but she may know something,' he said equally quietly. 'I rather think she does.'

.   .   .   .   .

Jenny Rey was sullen as ever when she left the car at the police station. She climbed listlessly up the flight of worn concrete stairs to Thane's first-floor office. The girl broke step only once—as they passed a massive grilled door on the half-landing leading to the station cells. She gave a faint shiver as the antiseptic smell of carbolic wafted to her nostrils, then trudged on.

Thane's office had drab cream walls, brown rubber floor covering and plain wooden fittings, with a divisional map on one wall and a "crime chart" beside it. The only relief from austerity was a photograph hanging in one corner showing a group of smiling American airmen round a jeep—a memento of one of Thane's grimmest cases.* The girl gave a flicker of interest at the sight of the American uniforms, then sat down in the straight-backed chair she was given. Thane waited till Pat Miller was also settled then, as Moss closed the door and quietly took out a notebook and pencil, began a slow, kindly, yet relentless series of questions.

Jenny answered easily at first. She had been at Hillman's for exactly eight months, three of them in the stationery department before being transferred at her own request. She lived with her parents in a council house in Millside. Her father was a corporation bus driver.

'You know that suit was found in your locker, Jenny,' said Thane. 'How did it get there?'

She was silent.

'Did you put it there, Jenny? You did, didn't you?'

'Yes, I took the thing,' she admitted reluctantly. 'But it's the first time I've ever taken anything, mister, honest. Wasn't me had anything to do with all the rest of the stuff.'

'Nobody said you had,' soothed Thane. 'Tell me, Jenny, how were you planning to get the suit out?'

* *Deadline for a Dream*

'Under my coat at the end of the day,' sulked the girl. 'Wouldn't be the first time it's been done in there. I know . . .' She stopped.

'Go on,' Thane leaned forward. 'You know . . . what do you know, Jenny?'

'Nothing. I don't know anything.'

'Jenny, you'd better tell him,' chimed in Pat. 'Look, dear, you've landed in a silly mess. The best way out is to tell the police all you can.'

Jenny gave a quivering sneer. 'Tell them?' she answered the older girl. 'Who's likely to believe anything I say? My word counts for nothing.' The tears began to roll down her cheeks again. She wiped them with the cuff of her jacket, sending a long smear of lipstick from her mouth up across her cheek in the process.

'Why did you take the suit, Jenny?' asked Thane.

'Because . . . because I couldn't afford to buy one, Mum needs most of my pay to help run the house. And my boy-friend's coming home on leave from the Army at the end of the month. I . . . I wanted to look smashin' for him. Other people were getting away with it, more important people. I didn't think I'd be caught.'

'What other people?' Thane's tone was sterner. 'Look, Jenny, you don't really want to land in prison, do you? You could be in for quite a little while; long enough to miss the boy-friend when he's home. It isn't very pleasant "inside" you know. Now, no more nonsense. What—do—you—know? Out with it.' His voice ended like a whipcrack.

Jenny broke down in a flood of tears. Pat Miller began to rise from her chair to comfort the girl, but a quick, emphatic shake of the head from Phil Moss, standing behind the shopgirl, held her back.

Jenny, still sniffling, raised her head again. 'All . . . all right,' she wept. 'Why don't you bully Miss Marchand for a change, and really do yourself some good? Why don't you ask her what she knows about the stuff that's disappearing?'

Pat gave a startled gasp. Even Thane was shaken by the

27

shopgirl's reply, But as Moss scribbled furious shorthand in his note-book, his chief persisted. 'What about Miss Marchand?'

Slowly, tenously, the girl's story was dragged out.

'It was about two weeks ago. . . . I'd been working a wee bit late, sorting out stuff for a special counter display. Then we all went home, except for Miss Marchand. She said she had some invoice work to do in her office. Well, I was away out, and getting on the bus to go home when I remembered I'd left a parcel in my locker at the store. It was a prescription for my mum from the chemist—ointment for her hands, you see, she gets terrible hacks. So I ran all the way back. The place was really closed up, but Andy the doorman let me in when I explained about the prescription. I went straight up to the fashion department. The floor was deserted, but there was still a light on in Miss Marchand's office. It was bright enough outside, you see, but it's always a bit gloomy in the store . . . we always have the lights on during the day. Well, I just tapped on her door and barged in to tell her why I was back after hours. She's a stickler for that sort of thing.

'She was standing at her desk. There were two blouses lying on it.' Jenny gave a faint twisted smile at the recollection. 'She got an awful shock . . . she couldn't have heard me coming. Then, sudden like, she bundled the blouses into her desk drawer, face red as a beetroot, and bawled me out for not knocking more loudly. Said I shouldn't have got back in. That she'd get me and the doorman into trouble if it happened again.'

The girl paused, looked round to see what effect her story was having. Pat was white and tense. Thane, imperturbable, took his cigarettes out from his jacket pocket and offered them to the girl.

'Ta.' Her grubby hand with bright red, chipped nail-polish pulled a cigarette from the packet. She cupped her hand in expert fashion for a light, took a quick, nervous puff. 'Well, I knew right away, see? It was flogged stuff. It had disappeared the week before. I knew, all right. I was on the blouse counter, and that weed Rosey—I mean Mr. Rose the store detective—he quizzed me up and down. There were about a dozen blouses whipped . . . and the two on Miss ruddy Marchand's desk were among them.'

'You could have been mistaken,' suggested Thane.

'Not me, mister.' Jenny was becoming more anxious than ever to give maximum effect to her tale. 'Look, mister, believe me, we didn't have more than half a dozen of this particular kind of blouse. They were a queer yellow colour, with red embroidery all over them—you couldn't mistake them. In fact, I fancied them myself at the time. And the lot were flogged the day after they were put out on the counter. So I thought to myself, "That's what the game is, is it?" But I didn't say anything, just went and got mum's prescription, and left. Well, I got in early the next morning, in fact, I was one of the first in the building to clock in. I went straight to Miss Marchand's office . . . the door isn't locked. And I sneaked a quick look in her desk. But the stuff wasn't there. Then I nipped out again, and checked the storeroom, and the counter . . . but there had been no fresh delivery, And . . . and well, after that I just thought . . .' Jenny began to blubber again. 'I thought if that old witch can get away with it, so can I.'

Hands in his pockets, Thane sat back on the edge of his desk and gave a silent whistle. Things were certainly happening. If he'd been asked to consider any of the Hillman top brass as possible suspects, Judith Marchand would have been about last on his list. Moss had shut his note-book. Later, a transcribed copy of the girl's statement would be given to her to sign. Right now—Thane picked up the phone, and gave some quiet orders. In a couple of minutes a woman turnkey appeared and led Jenny Rey off to the cells.

'We'll be sending for her people, of course,' he told Pat Miller. 'She'll be held in custody for a couple of days, then it's up to the court to decide.'

Pat bit her lip in worried fashion. 'Surely you don't believe her story . . . about Miss Marchand, I mean? Even if there were blouses on her desk, why, she could have bought them elsewhere, or . . . or they might have been samples for a new order,' she finished lamely.

A strictly neutral expression had slid across Thane's face. In equally colourless tones he replied, 'Of course not—but even if just to assure Miss Marchand's reputation against that story being spread by the girl we'll need to make a few check inquiries. You'll keep completely quiet about it ... even to Miss Marchand?'

The girl nodded. 'You can trust me . . . because I don't believe a word of it,' she declared. 'And now, I'd better be getting back to the store, I think. We've a lot of work on our hands at the moment.'

'Summer sale?' grinned Moss from the corner of the room. 'The Chief Inspector's looking for a carpet, miss . . . or at least, his wife is, and he's looking for the money to pay for it.'

A faint smile crossed Pat's face. But she obviously was in no mood to appreciate Moss's banter. That worried, puzzled look once more clouded across her clear hazel eyes as with a last, not unfriendly, nod she left the office.

.   .   .   .   .

When the two men were once more alone in the room, Thane slid down into a comfortable slouch in his wooden-armed swivel chair. Judith Marchand—brisk, intelligent, bright-eyed—could the, he wondered, have any possible link with what, the more he thought of it, might well be a definite, well-organized raiding scheme?

'You know, Phil,' he growled, 'what keeps niggling at the back of my mind is not who is doing it, but why. Somebody's got a nice foolproof scheme—so they think—for dipping the store's goods. How foolproof is up to us. But what are they doing with all the stuff they get away with? How many of them are there? This isn't just the Marchand woman . . . even if that little brat's story is to be believed, and the woman is involved. Imagine the quantity of stuff being "knocked". You can always get rid of a certain amount through back-street traders. But you can't go on doing that for too long without being caught, especially if you're trying to unload any quantity, And there isn't such a hell of a lot of money in it. Anybody that gets a sniff that the stuff's stolen will offer less than a third of its value to "take it off your hands as a favour, mate'!"

'So they must have some regular organized outlet?' questioned Moss. 'Is that what you're getting at?'

Thane nodded. 'A regular outlet, and a regular, profitable arrangement about money. Look, most shoplifters we come across take goods for one of two reasons—if you ignore the "kleptos". Either they want the stuff for themselves or their family because they're broke, or they are small-time crooks raising some "ready". None of them make a really wholesale business of it— none until now, that is,' he wryly corrected himself.

Moss munched absent-mindedly at a tea-biscuit, a favourite palliative for his friend the ulcer. 'And Jenny Rey?' he asked, brushing some crumbs from his lap. 'She's a brassy little bit of stuff, but you know, I think she was scared enough to be telling the truth . . . simply because it seemed the best way out of her own troubles.'

'I'm with you there,' agreed Thane, tapping a thoughtful finger on the desk top. 'Stuffing a costume into her locker was too clumsy, stupid in fact, to even suggest the kid is connected with the main thefts. And as far as we know, little Jenny's got no reason to have it in for Judith Marchand. That's what makes her story seem real—even if a puzzle, We'll have to handle the next bit with kid gloves.'

'Mmm . . .' Moss finished chewing, gave a last, cud-like motion with his mouth, and fumbled in the pocket of his tweed suit for his cigarettes. He tossed one across the desk and, as Thane scooped it up, demanded, 'What do we do? Barge in and put Judith Marchand through the hoop? We haven't enough to go on for that, have we?'

Thane shook his head, tapped the cigarette firm on one thumbnail. 'These ruddy tobacco firms are packing their fags looser than ever. No, we run the rule quietly over her background. We make a thorough check into Hillman's Store—especially what goes on after it closes to customers. And you, when you can stagger to your feet, will start knocking up some of those alleged

31

contacts you have on the dark side of the city and see if they know anything about clothing being unloaded.'

'I was going to the pictures tonight,' wailed Moss. 'There's a cowboy on—and it's the last night.'

'Pretend you're playing at policemen instead,' coaxed Thane with a grin. 'Don't worry, I'll be working too. I'm nipping home for a quick meal, then I'm going to pay a little social call on Miss Marchand. I'll go alone. She'll probably feel more at ease that way than if a squad of us marched in like a Russian peace delegation.'

.   .   .   .   .

Judith Marchand's flat was two stairs up in a good-class tenement in the Hillhead district. Thane glanced at his watch as he rang the doorbell. It was just after seven thirty, a reasonable time of night to catch most people at home. The sun, still high in the sky, filtered through the dusty window of the tenement landing, and sparkled on the well-polished brass nameplate on the door. He heard a woman's voice humming softly, then the door opened. In off-duty dress . . . an old pair of slacks and a heavy fisherman-knit sweater . . . the middle-aged woman still contrived to be neat and attractive. A look of surprise crossed her face, but quickly she invited the detective to come in. Hat in hand, Thane followed her through the tiny hallway and into an equally small lounge, decorated in a bright, pseudo-Regency style. His eyes fastened on the two photographs prominently displayed on the white-painted mantlepiece: a bearded man in naval uniform and a grinning, leather-jacketed boy of about sixteen.

The woman noticed his glance. 'My husband and my son,' she explained in a quiet, proud voice. 'I'm really Mrs. Marchand. Most people know it, but for business the "Miss" is easier. My husband was on landing craft . . . he was drowned off the Normandy beachheads in the Normandy invasion. Billy, my boy, is named after him. Billy's out in Canada now, living with my sister and her husband. They've got a 'teenage family of their own.' She gave a small, apologetic gesture with her hands. 'I thought it would be better for Billy to have the chance to grow up with a normal family background, rather than to just stay with a mother who has to go out to work.'

'Never feel like emigrating yourself?' asked Thane. 'Wouldn't you like to go out to join him?'

'Some day,' promised the woman, her eyes softening. 'In about another two years, to be exact. I'm saving up enough to open a small business, then I'll go over to join him . . . he should have finished his education by then. When I do go, Pat Miller will probably take over my job at Hillman's. . . .' she stopped, laughed. 'But that's by the way. Do you always have this effect on people, Chief Inspector, making them pour out their personal hopes? Sit down, please . . . and what brings you here anyway? Has little Jenny Rey given you more trouble?'

Thane shook his head, and took the arm-chair she indicated. He sank down into its comfort with a sigh. 'No . . . she's probably crying to herself in a cell right now,' he said. 'It'll do her a lot of good, too, maybe make her think twice before she "knocks" anything again. But I did want your help to clear up one or two points about the stock that's gone missing. I thought you might be able to guide me, perhaps even find that you had some private theory about what's happening.'

There was the faintest flicker of hesitation on Judith Marchand's part. Then she nodded slowly, and padded on slippered feet over to the small oak sideboard. 'A drink first, Mr. Thane?' she invited, opening the sideboard door and disclosing a slim, but choice, array of bottles. 'Whisky, or a sherry? I'm sorry, there's no beer.'

Thane shook his head. 'Nothing for me,' he declared. 'It's agin' the rules. Miss Marchand, how can all those stolen goods get out of the store? Do you really think it's merely a gang of shoplifters at work?'

The woman selected a delicately shaped glass, half filled it with sherry, and took a sip from the pale liquid before she replied. 'I wish I knew,' she said with false brightness. 'Then I could solve the whole mystery, and maybe get a bonus from

Mr. Farringdon. He's not such a bad old ogre really, you know. I've worked with him for over twenty years . . . since before I was married. As it is, though,' she shrugged, 'I'm as much in the dark as anyone. We're all relying on you. Still, fire ahead with your questions, Chief Inspector, and I'll do my best.'

'The stuff taken then, the clothing from your department at any rate. Could any of it be traced by its particular style, or by the labels on it . . . anything like that?'

The woman became more serious. 'Definitely not, as far as clothing taken from the fashion floor is concerned. None of the really exclusive designs are ever really brought into the store. We deal with the ordinary housewife, and she can't afford to pay extra money just for the sake of a fancy couturier's label—even if she had the nerve to wear some of the queer things they turn out. Any articles taken are, with a few exceptions, things that you could buy almost anywhere. In fact——' She stopped, appeared about to say more, then flushed a little and stood looking into the fireplace, its carefully set coal and sticks unlit on that warm summer's night.

'How did you get on with Jenny Rey?' asked Thane. 'Ever have any trouble with her?'

'None . . . none whatever,' said Judith emphatically. 'I'm sure she's got nothing to do with all this business. That was just an hysterical outburst she had at the store, I'm sure. She's just a silly child. I've always found her a good, hard worker, a bit empty-headed perhaps, and talking about nothing but boys. But then, most girls her age do. She's silly, not bad.'

Thane shifted uncomfortably. He could sense, without being able to put a finger on it, something very wrong in Judith Marchand's demeanour . . . as out of character as the tight, tense way in which she gripped her glass. She seemed unconscious of the fact that her other hand was clenched knuckle-white by her side.

Time to drop a depth-charge, he decided, taking a long, deep breath, Slowly, in almost conversational tones, he asked, 'Purely as a matter of interest, how much more money do you need to save before you can go to Canada?'

34

The stem of the wineglass snapped with a sudden tinkle. The sherry splashed to the carpet, spreading in a small, dark stain. Judith Marchand, the broken glass still held in her hand, flushed scarlet with anger. 'If you're trying to suggest in a clumsy, policemanish way that I'm building up my bank account by stealing, you're much less intelligent than I thought,' she snapped.

'Nothing like that at all,' protested Thane, rising to his feet The expected explosion had taken place all right: he followed it up hard and fast. 'But I think I'm right in believing that you could say more, about something you either know or suspect.'

'I . . . I know nothing,' replied the woman. 'Now, if you don't mind, Chief Inspector, I suggest you leave. You'll find me at the store any time you want to ask me any sensible questions, but right now I don't feel like continuing this conversation.'

Thane nodded silently, and followed her from the room. The door slammed behind him as he left the flat. Puzzled, and not a little disgusted at his own behaviour, he walked down the stairway, wondering at the almost pleading expression that he was sure had been lurking on the woman's worried, angry face.

He swore to himself, rammed his hat on his head, and walked through the close and out into the sunlight. Youngsters in multi-coloured open-necked shirts were teasing a group of giggling girls at the corner of the street, too busy to notice as he walked past them and on down the long row of red sandstone tenements. At the corner, a flash of green caught his eye and, drawn to its coolness like a parched man to water, he crossed over, deciding on a short-cut through the Botanic Gardens. Hands in pockets, he slouched along the shrub-fringed pathway, kicking a pebble before him. A band was playing somewhere in the distance. A magnificent blaze of colour, the red, whites and pinks of a bank of rhododendron, caught his eye and held his admiration. He was reminded of his own gardening problem—should he scrap that bed of gladioli under the front window at home, and replace them at the end of the season with that offer he had had of a job lot of roses? The soil would suit the roses, he mused.

Reluctantly, he returned to the problem in hand. Judith

Marchand was hiding something. Why? What other reason than that she herself was involved? She had the motive . . . wanting to get to her son in Canada. There could be no stronger factor than mother-love. She had the opportunity . . . she would know what goods could be taken and, if he was right in thinking that there was a definite channel of disposal, could easily decide the articles hardest to trace. And, most important of all, as a store executive she could remain after hours in Hillman's without attracting suspicion.

He walked on, idly kicking the pebble ahead of him. 'Getting some fresh air, Mr. Thane?' he heard a familiar voice ask from just ahead, and, looking up, he let an answering grin spread slowly over his broad, tanned face. Another few steps and he would have bumped into Hillman's assistant manager, Jerry Watford, and, arm-in-arm with him, Pat Miller. They were obviously a little embarrassed at the unexpected encounter, but amused at the policeman's reverie. There was a radiant glow about the girl, a glow that took Thane back some fifteen years to his own courting days.

The twinkle was back in his eyes as he said, 'This sort of summer night's meant for loafing about. . . . But I didn't count on bumping into you two.'

'We're heading for a long, quiet drink,' said Watford. 'Care to join us?'

Thane hesitated a moment, then agreed. 'Just one, though,' he warned. 'My wife's expecting me home reasonably early . . . expecting isn't the right word, exactly. It's more of a threat of wrath to come if I don't.'

'You'll have pretty odd hours in your line of business, I suppose,' said Watford. 'No nine till five routine.'

' 'Fraid not. "Neds" don't work a five-day week. Not in this city, anyway. Our best times are when the rain is lashing down or when it's freezing cold. Thugs would rather stay by the fireside with a bottle than be out and about causing trouble.'

He fell into step with the couple, noting with pleased approval the girl's neat-fitting grey skirt, topped by a tailored white blouse, a baby-blue woollen cardigan slung casually over her

36

shoulders. She was a perfect picture of natural grace as well as being as pretty as they came.

Watford was whistling a lazy tune to himself, obviously feeling very pleased with the world. The girl, walking between them, suddenly asked, 'Anything fresh, Mr. Thane?' Her happy look momentarily faded. 'Have you been seeing . . . anybody?'

'I have,' said Thane, in friendly but cryptic tones. 'But it's still too early to say we've established anything. Detection boils down to hard work more often than not. We haven't the glamorous life most people imagine. At the moment we're just digging. There's really nothing I can tell you, I'm afraid.' He gave an apologetic grin to the girl.

'Quite right, too,' said Watford. 'Forget Hillman's for a bit, Pat . . . look, there's the main gate. Now there's a little pub just across the road, Chief Inspector, with a nice quiet lounge bar. . . .'

The little pub served an ice-cold lager that was sheer delight. Thane took a long, appreciative drink, and told the two seated at the table beside him: 'Coming here's about the best idea I've had today. You know, this is one pub I've never been in before. Don't get me wrong, a glass of beer now and again's my stretch, but there's a lot of calls under that ancient phrase "in line of duty".'

'We discovered it some weeks back,' confessed Pat. 'That is . . . well, Jerry and I came across it.'

'Pat and I see quite a bit of each other,' said Watford, stepping into the gap. 'But we'd get our legs pulled like nobody's business back at the store, and so we don't broadcast the fact that we're going around together. Judith Marchand knows, of course, but not many of the others.'

'Trust me,' promised Thane. He drained the rest of the lager from his glass, pushed back his chair, and got up. 'Time to move,' he apologized. 'But you'll be seeing enough of me over the next few days, don't worry. I'll be looking in at Hillman's tomorrow, for a start. We've got some "Rogues Gallery" photographs to hand over to your store detectives, and I want to find out a bit more about your security system.'

'Hope you nail whoever's doing it,' said Watford, giving a friendly wave. 'The old man's hopping mad about the whole business, and that means we've all got to creep around on tip-toe.'

.   .   .   .   .

Tuesday morning dawned bright and filled with the promise of another warm day. In his bungalow home at Southwood, a still-green suburb of smoky Glasgow, Colin Thane washed, dressed, ran his electric razor quickly over his stubble beard, then, after rubbing a quick trace of after-shave lotion on his face, came whistling through to the kitchenette. His wife Mary was already bustling about, setting breakfast at the alcove table where four red-plastic-topped stools were lined in readiness. Sounds of activity from elsewhere in the house showed that the children were having their usual sleepy-headed rush to dress for school.

' 'Morning,' yawned the policeman, kissing his wife lightly on the mouth. He glanced at the table. 'That cereal again,' he groaned. 'How much longer?'

'Only another four packets,' promised his wife. 'Then your son will have his nine box-tops and can get that model supersonic jet plane.'

'Huh.' He peered out the window. 'Sweet peas need watering.'

'Going back to Hillman's again today, dear?' asked his wife busy with the teapot and caddy. 'If you are, Colin, could you maybe take a quick look at the carpet department? The one I think we should get is a deep blue self-coloured with a centre medallion.'

'Have a heart,' protested Thane, perching his bulk on one of the stools. 'Can you imagine me saying to their managing director, "Excuse me, Mr. Farringdon, I can't bother about your shop thefts right now . . . Mary wants me to look at a carpet for her?" We can take a look in together later in the week, before the sale begins.' He opened out the morning newspaper, took a quick look at the page one news, shuddered and, turned quickly to the back-page comic strips.

38

A police car with Phil Moss aboard arrived at his house at 8.30 a.m. 'There's been a spot of housebreaking three avenues away from you,' explained Moss. 'One of the detective constables was getting a run out, so I thought I'd come along for the ride and pick you up on the way back.' As he spoke, the inspector wandered through the hall, a slightly indignant Thane following behind him.

'Hello, Mary,' said Moss. 'Hello, you kids . . . you'll be late for school.' He gazed at the breakfast table. 'Er . . . Mary, I . . .'

'Sit down,' she said in mock resignation. 'We'll find a cup of tea in the pot. Help yourself to toast.'

'No, no . . . not tea, thanks. A nice glass of milk perhaps, but I'm off tea. My tummy, you know . . . when I was out doing the rounds last night about that stuff stolen from Hillman's, I bumped into a bloke I haven't seen in years. We used to be in the same darts team at the local—that was before my tummy, you understand. Anyway, turns out he's had the same trouble. But it hasn't bothered him since he stopped drinking tea. He believes the tannin in the tea causes all the bother. I don't know, myself . . . but it's worth trying.'

'Here's your milk,' sighed Mary, planking a glass before the new arrival.

'How'd you get on anyway, Phil?' asked Thane, buttering a last piece of toast. 'Get anywhere?'

The older man shook his head in gloomy fashion. 'No luck. I did a full round of the usual places—pass that marmalade, will you, Colin—but I just couldn't get a line. I even got hold of old Benny and "greased" him with a quid. But he says there's nothing out of the ordinary coming on to their market at all— and he's a bit peeved that, if all that stuff's going, the thieves should be by-passing the regular channels for getting rid of it.'

'We'll go into the station now,' said Thane, folding his newspaper, 'I want to pick up those shoplifter photographs, then we can move on to Hillman's. Come on, Phil, pour it down.'

Obediently the inspector gulped the last of the milk, gave a friendly grin to Mary, and followed out on Thane's heels.

'Give me a cigarette, Phil, will you?' asked Thane as they walked down the short garden path towards the police car. 'I forgot to get any on the way home last night.'

Pulling a face, Moss brought out his packet and, as they both lit up, asked, 'How about Judith Marchand? Any joy there?'

'There's something damn funny about that woman, Phil. She was worried stiff when I saw her. But whether it was for herself or not . . .' Thane shrugged and walked to the car, a smart black Humber. The uniformed driver was sitting patiently at the wheel, listening to the two-way police radio.

'Morning, Mr. Thane,' he greeted. 'Things are quiet on the air for the moment.'

'Hush,' said Thane, scrambling in beside him while Moss climbed in the back. 'Even saying that's asking for trouble.'

The police car drew slowly away from the kerb. It had just reached the corner of the avenue, and was about to turn into the main road when Thane's prophesy came true.

'Calling any car in the vicinity of Millside docks, berth eight,' crackled the voice of the headquarters radio operator. 'Constable requiring assistance. Chasing man armed with knife. Ambulance summoned.'

Thane nodded. 'Head there fast.' As the car shot out on to the main road and began to roar past the morning traffic, travelling fast in the direction indicated, he told the man at the wheel, 'See what happens when you open your big mouth?'

The driver grinned, then concentrated on the task of controlling the speeding Humber.

.   .   .   .   .

At 8.30 a.m., just as Phil Moss had arrived at Thane's house, a policeman on quayside duty at No. 8 Berth at Millside Docks saw a Lascar seaman shuffle away from the quayside, obviously just off the big tramp steamer that had arrived from India two days before, and which was now lying waiting to discharge cargo. The ship had customs clearance all right. But the dock

40

cop, long wise in these matters, noticed a furtiveness in the Lascar's walk, an uncommon bulkiness about the old bus-driver's coat the native was wearing over his thin brown body.

He moved towards the seaman, beckoning. The Lascar, whites of his eyes rolling, broke into a run, heading in the opposite direction, the uniform man hard on his heels, tugging out his police whistle. At the first shrill blast, dockers working round the nearby sheds stopped to watch the chase, laughing. But their laughter froze as they saw the Lascar, still running, whip out a rusty but still wicked-looking knife. One man sprinted to the nearest phone-box, others began to follow the chase at a wary distance.

It ended with the little Lascar trapped in an alleyway crammed with wooden packing cases. The seaman took a wild knife-slash at the policeman, his rusted blade ripping through the blue serge uniform jacket and opening a deep gash in the man's shoulder. But, despite the stinging pain, the cop moved in, baton swinging. It fell . . . bash . . . in the regulation collar-bone-breaking blow recommended by the police instructors, then again, smash, in a strictly unofficial belt over the skull which seemed to send a ripple running downward through the little seaman before he dropped as if pole-axed.

The police found two pounds of hemp drug in the Lascar's pocket. Thane arrived in the Humber at 8.55 a.m. By 10 a.m. the Lascar was in the cells on a multitude of charges, the bobby was in hospital and squads of customs men were once more giving the tramp steamer the full treatment.

Two hours later, three other Lascars joined their shipmate in the cells. Another four pounds of hemp, all ready to be mixed into expensive "reefer" cigarettes, was lying on Colin Thane's desk at Millside.

A cup of tea standing beside the canvas bags, Thane scanned through the reports before him while Moss gazed gloomily at the clock on the wall. 'We've still got to get to Hillman's, Colin,' he reminded, 'and this is Tuesday, their half-day. They shut the shop at one o'clock, remember.'

'Blast it,' growled Thane. 'It's nearly noon now. Not much

41

sense in going at this time. Och, give them a ring, Phil, and explain what's happened. Better get hold of young Jerry Watford. Tell him we'll be along first thing tomorrow. Waiting till tomorrow won't make much difference.'

If he could have guessed what was waiting for him Colin Thane wouldn't have dismissed the department store puzzle so easily, even though, at that stage, it hardly rated as a major crime. And he would not have settled down to the necessary, but not particularly urgent job of making some long-distance telephone calls to Scotland Yard and a couple of South of England county headquarters regarding a suspected cheque fraud case that seemed to have links with those areas.

But then, as Phil Moss said later, 'If policemen could look into the future, why, there wouldn't be any . . . if you know what I mean.'

3

THE brief, typewritten note lay on the top of a pile of occurrence reports brought into Thane's office first thing on the Wednesday morning. He yawned his thanks to the young police messenger and glanced at the sheet. It answered a query he had passed to the Criminal Records Office the previous afternoon.

"No listing of a Judith Marchand on our files. Check with Admiralty shows a Lieutenant Marchand posted killed during Normandy invasion. Wife receives appropriate pension.'

He slid the note to one side, yawned again. . . . Why the heck had he had to stay up late last night reading that darned science fiction book . . .? and resignedly picked up the next report. A Section 15, Road Traffic Act case . . . a drunk driver who'd gone off the road, knocked down an equally drunk pedestrian, who was miraculously uninjured, then wrapped his car round a lamp-post. A faint grin slid across Thane's face as he read the final words of the report: "The man has been certified by a doctor as being under the influence of drink. In fact, he is still lying in a cell, too far gone to appear in court this morning."

Phil Moss wandered into the office, giving a brief, perfunctory knock on the door. The Detective Inspector had a cardboard-bound file in one hand, and laid it casually on the desk top before pulling a chair over from the wall. He swung the chair round and straddled it, arms folded on its wooden back. 'That's the Hillman store file, Colin—you know, photos and descriptions of shop-lifters, the gen we gathered yesterday but couldn't deliver. Want me to run round there this morning?'

'Mmh. Personally, I don't think they matter a damn, for all

43

the good they'll do.' Thane picked up a paper-clip from the desk and began to bend the wire between his fingers. 'I think we'll both take a trip over to Hillman's. I want to have another talk with Andy Richards . . . you know, the ex-cop on the main door. And I want to find out a little more about how the staff check out at night, and who's left around after the store closes. Incidentally, I suppose we got those extra men in all right yesterday?'

Moss gave a faint sniff, pulled out a grubby handkerchief, and gave a roaring blow to his nose. 'Think I've got a cold coming on,' he complained. 'The men . . . yes, we got them in all right, three plain-clothes and a couple of policewomen in civvies.' He grinned and went on, 'The boys tell me there was a minor barney. One of the store dicks who hadn't seen our people before became suspicious of the way one of the girls was hanging about, and tried to run her in. Then a customer—a big Marine who'd been running his eye over our lass for size—thought she was being pestered and got ready to wipe the floor with the Hillman man.'

'Who was the girl?' chortled Thane, settling back.

'Jean Arnoch—you know, the little dark-haired piece who's a judo expert.'

'I know the one,' agreed Thane. 'Slapped in an expense account for two pairs of nylons the last plain-clothes job she was on—claimed she ripped them dancing with a con-man she was keeping an eye on.'

The office door swung open, and a detective brought in two mugs of tea, expertly balanced on an old biscuit-tin lid. He laid the "tray" down on the table, and turned to leave.

'Hold it, Johnny,' said Thane. As the man faced him again, he asked, 'You were on the uniform beat in Millside before you were transferred, weren't you?'

'That's right,' said the young detective constable. 'I moved over about a year ago, sir.'

'Remember a cop called Richards? He's retired now.'

'Aye, I mind him all right, sir. . . . why?'

'Anything . . . unusual . . . about him that you can remember?' asked Thane. 'You know, was he square enough? Did he get on

44

with the rest of the men all right. It's an awkward question, I know, but it's maybe important.'

The D.C. shuffled his feet, obviously embarrassed. 'Seemed all right to me,' he declared. 'Mind you, he was never my mate on the beat. But he seemed a reasonable bloke.'

'Okay.' Thane gave a brief nod of dismissal, and the young policeman, more than a little puzzled, went out of the room.

'What was that in aid of?' quizzed Moss as the door closed. The detective inspector took a sip of tea from his mug, then lifted a pencil from Thane's desk and used it to stir the brown liquid. He speculated, 'Have you got a hunch Richards is mixed up in the Hillman robberies?'

Thane shrugged. 'Could be. After all, he wouldn't be the first man in the force to go wrong, and he's in a key position when it comes to knowing what goes on in the store . . . and, more important, who goes in and out and when. Have a poke around when you've got a chance, and see what you can find out about him.'

'I'd rather have a dig into Mr. James Rose's history,' declared Moss. 'He may be the head store 'tec, but for my money he's a no-gooder. I'd back Judith Marchand against him any day.'

'We'll take care of Mr. Rose,' promised Thane. 'He and one or two others—Allen, the head buyer, and a few others who're well placed. Maybe even young Watford, the assistant manager. We've a lot of ground to cover, Phil. Someone's milking that place for about three hundred pounds a week—and if my mental arithmetic's right, that could mean damn near sixteen thousand a year. This is anything but kid stuff—and we've got to kill the business as soon as we can.' He picked up the telephone and, as the police switchboard answered, ordered, 'Lay on a car for me, will you? Have it ready in, say another twenty minutes. We're going down to Hillman's if anyone phones, but we'll probably be back within a couple of hours.' He laid down the receiver, picked up his tea, and demanded, 'Come on Phil, get your fags out.'

.   .   .   .   .

The polished black of the police car sparkled like a mirror in the sunlight as it drifted through the city streets towards the department store. There were all the signs that another scorching day lay ahead. The uniformed driver whistled softly to himself as he steered through the traffic, which seemed to have taken a lazy mood in tune with the already warm, relaxing temperature. The weather, combined with the Wednesday country holiday, seemed to have brought plenty of out-of-town shoppers into the city centre. Sauchiehall Street had cars sitting on either side along the parts of its length still not hit by parking restrictions. They were jammed nose to tail at the pavement outside Hillman's and the black saloon had to draw up opposite a small red-painted tourer, the sole occupant of which was a large, nondescript dog.

'Squeeze the car in somewhere around,' Thane instructed the driver. 'Then stay by the radio. If there's a call for me, trot in and dig me out of the store.'

The driver acknowledged the order, then, as Thane and Moss got out and the doors slammed shut, gently slid the car into gear again and crept back into the traffic stream.

Richards, the ex-cop doorkeeper, was busy dealing with the questions of a couple of harrassed-looking women shoppers. He could only give a wave of his hand as Thane and Moss strolled past, heading across the vast, busy ground floor towards the lifts. The two detectives managed to jam into a packed, airless lift-cage, which slowly disgorged its occupants as it sped upwards until, at the sixth floor, they were the only remaining passengers. Conscious of the interested gaze of the young lift-girl, they got out and walked along the sixth-floor passageway to the main office block. A couple of minutes later they were shown into Jerry Watford's room, a bright, spacious office set in a corner of the Hillman building, On two sides, broad glass windows gave a bird's-eye view of the streets far below. On one of the walls, a Peter Scott watercolour copy, the wildfowl seemingly about to take-off through the glass, hung close beside the framed photograph of a sleek-looking motor gunboat. The air was cool and clean—a conditioner unit was purring quietly away at one window.

Watford gave the two men a friendly welcome and when they were seated, cigarettes burning, got quickly down to business.

'Back about the thefts, I suppose? There's nothing really fresh we can report at this end, I'm afraid,' said the young executive. 'Tomorrow, though, may be different. That's weekly stock-check day, and, believe me, the last few times it's been a major operation. The boss'—he pointed ceilingwards and gave a grimace—'has seen to that, all right. He's calling for a check down to the last pair of bootlaces!'

Thane flicked the grey tip on his cigarette into the broad glass ashtray. 'We brought this file along, pictures of shoplifters, things like that. Your store detectives can probably use it. But I really wanted to find out a bit more about the way the store's run from the workers' angle . . . how they clocked in and out, that sort of thing, We're interested in the customers too, of course. How do you know they all leave at night?'

'The customers, too . . .' echoed Watford, a slight frown on his face. 'I'm afraid I'm coming round to thinking the way you do, Chief Inspector. There may be more in this than meets the eye. Though I'm darned if I have the faintest idea what exactly is going on. How do they get the stuff out of the store, to start with?

'Anyway, this is the set-up. All our people, except the management, of course, have to clock in every morning and out again at night. We're strict about that. Oh, they can be a few minutes late now and again and it doesn't matter. They're not on a time rate, or anything like that. But it helps us to nail any persistent late-coming and, of course, it helps us to calculate any overtime.'

'Overtime?'

'Yes. The store closes at five-thirty. But there's often work to be done afterwards for an hour or so—arranging goods, doing books, stock work, you know the sort of thing. Then there's the transport people. Sometimes they get back pretty late from deliveries—we've our own garage in the basement, you know. The entrance is at the back of the store.'

47

'So quite a few people could be in the store after hours?' asked Thane.

'They could, and often are. But we know exactly who is in at any time, Each departmental head has to send down a daily list of any staff who'll be working late that night. And anyone working late has to check out with the night commissionaire at the rear door. He ticks their names off on his book as they leave. He keeps a pretty close eye on them—old Joe's an ex-C.S.M. and loves the job. Management types are supposed to let him know if they're going to be late, and he's got a board in his room that shows at a glance whether any of us are still in the store . . . though I'm afraid that bit doesn't always work out. If you're up to your ears in work you're sometimes inclined to ignore the red tape.'

'Supposing someone went into hiding just before the place closed? We'll say a customer fancies a roam around when the store's empty.'

'It could happen,' agreed Watford, 'but we watch that as well. The night watchmen—there's two of them under the night commissionaire—make a complete round of the building about seven o'clock and, believe me, it's a thorough search. They look everywhere . . . toilets, behind counters, odd corners, cupboards . . . you know the sort of thing. We've caught a few people at it over the years. One character hid in a wardrobe in the furniture department, and locked the door from the inside. The watchman heard a noise just after he'd tried the wardrobe door and found it locked. So he grabbed a ball of string from the nearest counter, and wrapped the lot round the wardrobe. Then he called the police. The fellow got six months if I remember rightly.' He gave a cheerful grin, and stubbed his cigarette-end in the ashtray.

'Hh-huh.' Thane sat silent for a moment, digesting the information, seeking weaknesses in the broad outline of the system. 'After that, do the watchmen keep up a patrol? Right through the night, I mean?'

'So—so. The place is stiff with automatic alarms and that sort of thing guarding every door and window. Once the seven

43

o'clock search is over we've got two patrol systems. The first is the most important. One watchman operates outside the store— that probably seems funny.'

Thane shook his head. 'No, I know that system all right. A regular outside patrol can spot trouble more quickly than any other.'

'That's it, Hillman's stands on its own. No other building joins on to it, there's pavement on all four sides. A man goes round every half-hour or so—I forget the exact drill. The two watchmen make another complete check of the store about midnight. The rest of the work's left to the automatic alarms. . . . Joe, the night commissionaire, is chairborne most of the time.'

'How long will the searches inside the store take, Mr. Watford?' asked Moss, who had begun taking a few sketchy notes on the back of an old envelope.

' 'Bout an hour, I'd say,' replied the assistant manager. 'It really depends on how thoroughly it's done.'

'And is it? Done thoroughly, I mean,' pressed Thane.

'Since this trouble started, yes,' said Watford, nodding ceilingwards again. 'The boss sees to that. He's got a small flat of his own up there, you know, besides his office. And quite often he stays overnight, working till Lord knows when in the morning. Sometimes he takes it into his head to make a swoop down in the middle of the night—and woe betide any watchman he caught dozing on the job.'

The two policemen grinned in sympathy. Charles Farringdon was hard-working without a doubt—and a managing director who expected just as hard work and loyalty to the store from his staff as he himself gave it. They could imagine that an employee caught on the hop would be in for a pretty rough time from the bulky, harsh-voiced store boss.

The buzzer on the intercom. set by Watford's side gave a discreet bleep. He flipped the switch and his secretary's voice announced, 'Miss Miller is here to see you.'

'Show her in,' said Watford, colouring slightly. 'It's a busy time of the day,' he apologized, while the two policemen nodded solemn agreement. They rose as Pat came into the room, wearing her green corduroy two-piece again, an order book in one hand.

''Morning, Jerry—oh . . .' Her voice faded as she saw Thane and Moss.

'Back bothering people again, I'm afraid,' said Thane pleasantly. 'In fact, I was planning to take a look down in your place shortly.'

'If it's to see Miss Marchand, you're out of luck,' said the girl. 'She hasn't come in this morning. I was wondering if you'd sign these,' she turned to Watford. 'They are confirmation orders for some extra sales stock, and they must go off this morning. I'd get Mr. Allen to sign them, but he's up in the penthouse in conference with Mr. Farringdon . . . something to do with the sale displays.' She laid the book on Watford's desk, her hand brushing gently against his in the process.

'Well, Allen should do it as head buyer, but, heck . . .' Watford pulled a ball-point from the inside pocket of his jacket, flicked the point down, and scrawled his signature where Pat indicated. 'Any idea what's wrong with the lady in question?' he asked, looking up with obvious pleasure at her nearness.

'No, not really.' The girl gave a determined glare towards Thane. 'But she was feeling a bit off-colour yesterday, I know. She said she had an awful headache. I . . . I think I'll take a quick look out at her flat at lunchtime.'

'I'll get the transport manager to lay on a car,' offered Watford.

'Thanks, but you needn't bother, Jerry,' smiled the girl. 'I can get a bus from just outside the door. It's only a fifteen-minute run each way. . . . I'll have plenty of time.'

'Couldn't you phone Miss Marchand?' suggested Thane.

Watford shook his head. 'She's not on the phone,' he explained. 'She's been trying to get one for years, she told me once, but the Post Office say there are no lines, or some such flannel.'

'Aye, it's a problem,' agreed Moss. 'My landlady's got a shared party line in the house. Mind you, she loves it. She spends half her time listening on it . . . the other party's the local corset-fitter, and she just loves listening to what's being laced up. Quite interesting too, some of them,' he admitted. Even Pat joined in the laughter. Then, picking up the order book, she turned to go.

'You'll let me know how Miss Marchand is keeping,' said Thane, quietly, meaningly.

'I will, Mr. Thane,' said the girl. 'But I can assure you now that it won't be anything you need worry about.' She swept from the room, that hurt, puzzled look back in her eyes again.

Watford whistled softly. 'Hey, Chief Inspector, you've certainly got Pat's back up for some reason . . . what's going on?'

'Maybe she isn't over-fond of policemen,' Thane tried to laugh the matter off. 'She's probably just a little upset about that young assistant getting into trouble, or maybe she's worried about Miss Marchand. They're pretty friendly, I gather.'

'It's not like Pat,' frowned Watford. 'It's funny . . . she was pretty quiet after you left us the other night, too.'

'Not to worry,' said Thane, rising. 'Well, we'll get on our way now. I want to have a look around the store before I go, and chat to a couple of people.'

'Help yourself,' said Watford. 'Oh, and if there's anything you fancy on the counters . . . well, I hope you don't mind me saying so, but just give me a buzz, and we'll chop our share of the profits from the price.'

Thane grinned his thanks, and the two detectives left. 'Carpet department?' asked Moss as they walked back towards the lifts.

'Carpet department,' agreed Thane, 'but not for what you think, you old miser. I just want a look at that blue carpet Mary was talking about. Watford's a nice enough fellow . . . but I wouldn't like to take a discount from him, then a few days later maybe have to pull in one of his pals on a major theft charge. Carpets . . . for a look only. Then we'll go down and have another word with Andy Richards at the front door. He should have shaken off those women by now.'

.   .   .   .   .

Richards, the ex-cop, was still by the main entrance to the store, hands clasped loosely in front of his brass-buttoned black uniform jacket with its red piping. He straightened the peaked cap on his head, and his sleepy, disinterested look vanished as the two detectives came towards him.

' 'Morning, Mr. Thane,' he greeted. 'Any luck yet?'

'That's what we came to ask you,' countered Thane. 'Heard anything at all which might be useful?'

'No, not yet,' said Richards, then, sidling closer and speaking little above a whisper, 'but I may be on to something. I don't want to say anything right now in case I'm wrong, but'—he gave a knowing grimace—'there's a wee chance I may turn up with something in the next day or so. Er . . . not that it makes any difference, of course, me being ex-force myself, but I suppose the boss'd probably give some reward?' He grinned in a not particularly pleasant way.

Thane felt a slight revulsion. 'There's been none mentioned as far as I know,' he replied. 'What's on your mind, Richards . . . ? You know better than to start playing detective on your own.'

The doorman seemed to squirm a little. 'I can't say yet, honestly, Mr. Thane. But I'll give you the buzz the moment I can. There's my job to consider . . . if I put my foot in it it wouldn't do me any good. You can see that,' he finished lamely.

Thane surveyed the flow of shoppers coming and going through the doors, all ages and sizes, some poorly dressed, others having cash and quality in every line of their dress. Their voices and accents lost all individual identity, became a babble of noise mixing with the clanging of cash registers, the soft "slap" of pneumatic messenger tubes and the persistent, musical, but penetrating, sound of bell chords. Some sort of signal system, he presumed.

Still not looking at Richards, he warned, 'Don't leave it too late, that's all. And don't try anything silly . . . remember you've a police pension to think of, Richards.' Even as the man began a hoarse protest Thane turned away, and looked round to find that Phil Moss had gone. Then he spotted him . . . Phil had drifted a few feet away to a tie counter, and was examining the rainbow-like range of neckwear on display.

With a sigh Thane walked across. 'Come on,' he persuaded. 'They don't stock approved school colours . . . at least, not the kind you went to.'

'Hang on a minute, Colin,' protested Moss, pulling a worn leather purse from his pocket. 'Miss—this one, please . . .' He handed over a sad-looking grey tie, and slowly counted out the necessary silver into the girl's outstretched palm.

'You're busy, I see,' said a sharp, sarcastic voice at Thane's elbow. Rose, the store detective, immaculate as usual from the tips of his pointed, highly polished black shoes to his sleek dark hair, stood watching, thin features set in a peevish frown. 'Chasing shoplifters, I presume?' he asked in the same acid tones.

'I thought you felt it was something different from shoplifting we had to find,' replied Thane innocently as Moss, the tie in a small brown paper bag, turned to join him. 'You seemed to disagree with Miss Marchand on the point, if I remember rightly.'

Rose stiffened like a ramrod. 'I still do, Mr. Thane,' he declared, with vehement eagerness. 'And I still feel sure that that little brat of an assistant who was caught the day before yesterday can confirm that . . . of course, I wasn't allowed to press the point with her, if you remember. I presume she is being interrogated on that issue? Or have you got her in a nice cosy room with a police-woman holding her hand and wiping her tears?' In a more confidential tone, coming close enough for Thane to catch the raw odour of tobacco-smoke on his breath, Rose went on, 'Do you remember what she said about the Marchand woman that day, Chief Inspector . . .? Have you thought what that could mean?'

Thane nodded imperturbably. 'We're keeping all these points in mind, don't worry. I suppose you know Miss Marchand's off sick today?'

Rose snorted. 'I wonder. I——' He checked himself suddenly, a cautious light in his eyes. 'Well, thank you for one thing,' he continued sardonically. 'Watford says you've left that file of shoplifters for me. And now, at any rate, my staff should be able to separate them from the police.'

Moss, toying with the bag containing his new tie, gave a faint cackle. Rose stiffened again, nodded a brief 'Good day, gentlemen,' and marched off up the crowded passageway, ovei towards the hardware department.

'Home to the station, Phil,' decided Thane. 'Mr. Rose doesn't seem to like us very much, does he?'

'Smooth ruddy . . .' muttered Moss.

'Don't be rude about the taxpayers,' grinned his chief. 'After all, think of the money they pay you.'

Detective Inspector Moss was still spluttering over his opinion of the taxpayers' contribution to his welfare when Thane gave him a good-natured shove into the sun-baked back seat of their waiting radio-car. Sucking a digestion tablet all the way back to the station—'getting angry always starts my juices going and gives me hell'—Moss continued his detailed summary of life in general and a policeman's lot in particular. He caught a grin puckering the corner of the police driver's mouth.

'What are you finding so flaming funny?' he demanded. 'Wait till you've been a few more years in the force like me, and see how you feel about life.' He grimaced as a faint twinge reminded him once more of his stomach. 'I started on the beat my lad, not sitting on my bottom on a soft car-seat polishing my issue serge trousers.'

'Knock it off, Phil,' sighed Thane. 'You remind me of a martyr looking for a bonfire . . . though the only way you'll see Heaven is on a day return ticket.'

.   .   .   .   .

Twenty minutes later, back in his office at Millside station, his jacket thrown over a chair, shirt sweat-stained under the armpits, Colin Thane stood by his desk, rubbing the faint stubble on his chin with one hand as he stared at the letter before him. It had been among the mail waiting on his return, in a plain, small envelope, bearing the address "Chief Inspector

54

Thane, Glasgow Police" in inked capitals. The letter had gone to city headquarters in St. Andrew's Square, and the morning despatch car had brought it round with the normal inter-divisional mail. It was a short note. Printed in the same inked letters as the envelope, it said, "Be in Hillman's on Wednesday night and you'll find what you want to know." Nothing else. No name, no address, not even a date. The postmark was a central one.

He pulled a cigarette from the packet lying on the desk, stuck it between his lips, then, the tobacco still unlit, went through next door, to Moss's room. The inspector, his heavy tweed jacket still on his shoulders in defiance of the temperature, was speaking on the phone, but Moss quickly closed the conversation and hung up.

'What's the matter?' he asked, wiping his perspiring forehead with one sleeve.

'This,' said Thane, tossing the note on to the desk. 'It was waiting for me when I got back.' He sank into a chair, feeling the wood cool and firm against his back through the thin cotton of the shirt. 'God, it's getting warm. . . . Read it, and tell me what you make of it all.'

Moss raised his eyebrows at Thane's obvious perturbation. But he picked the paper up carefully by one edge, glanced at its contents, and gave a sucking noise through his teeth. 'Someone's cracking,' he commented. 'Here . . .' He took a loose match from his pocket, struck it expertly on the worn edge of his desk, and held the flame towards Thane's cigarette.

'Huh . . .? Oh, thanks,' grunted Thane absent-mindedly, leaning over and drawing on his cigarette till the tip glowed bright. He let the smoke trickle slowly from his nostrils, then, the cigarette dangling loosely from his lips, admitted, 'This ruddy business is getting worse all the time, Phil. Who wrote the note . . . and why? Somebody on the inside of the robberies? And where the heck are they fencing the stuff once they take it?'

'You'll be sending the note to the fingerprint boys in the Scientific Bureau?' asked Moss. 'They might get some "dabs" if you're really lucky.'

Thane nodded. 'Envelope's postmarked 1.30 p.m. yesterday,' he commented. 'Pity it didn't come straight here, so that we could have known about it when we went to the store.'

'Will we go back again tonight?'

'Can't afford not to,' said Thane. 'Just how do we get in though, without anyone knowing . . . ? Wait a minute.' He leaned forward, a forefinger tapping the desk top for emphasis. 'Farringdon's our man. He can fix it so that we stay in that store tonight . . . all night if necessary. He can do it all right.' He relaxed back in the chair, then rose again almost as quickly. 'Hey, I can't sit here. I told Mary I'd try and get home for lunch for a change. Will you hold the fort till I get back?'

'Have I any option?' asked Moss in mock melancholy resignation. 'No . . . I thought not,' he added, as Thane disappeared out of the door. 'Oh well. . . .' He opened the big drawer of his desk and, with a shrug, lifted out a bottle of milk and a packet of sandwiches. He listened a moment, then dived into the desk drawer again and pulled out a brightly-covered Western.

.   .   .   .   .

'These kids are driving me crazy,' laughed Mary Thane as she waved good-bye to the two children in question, bustling from the house on their way back to school. 'And there's two whole months of school holidays to come. . . . I don't know which is worse, a policeman husband or a couple of juvenile delinquents as children.' She began to clear away the dishes from the table, and asked hopefully, 'Did you see our carpet this morning, dear?'

'Hey, less of the "our",' protested her husband. 'I got a look at it, yes, but it's a bit expensive, sale price or not.'

'Expensive? I'd say it was dirt cheap at——oh blast!' She dumped the pile of dishes back on the table as the phone rang out in the hallway. 'I'll get it, dear. . . .'

She came back into the room a minute later. 'It's for you, Colin, A Miss Miller. She says it's important.'

A few swift strides took Thane to the waiting receiver. 'What's up, Pat?' he demanded.

The girl's voice, faint over the wire, but obviously distressed, came through in a flood of words. 'It's Judith, Mr. Thane. I'm outside her flat. . . . I think there's something dreadfully wrong. I phoned the police station, and Mr. Moss said you were at home. He . . . I—I wanted to tell you, personally.'

'Go on,' said Thane tensely. 'Just take it slowly, and tell me what's the matter.'

There was a moment's silence, then the girl, speaking more coherently but still greatly agitated, said, 'I went to Judith's flat as soon as lunchtime came round. . . . I only got there a few minutes ago. The milk was lying outside the door, and her morning paper is still in the letter-box flap. I've rung and rung the bell, but there's no reply. I'm worried, terribly worried, Mr. Thane.'

'Where are you speaking from now?' snapped the policeman. 'The phone-box at the corner? Right, Stay where you are. We'll get over as quickly as we can, Now hang up.' He waited till the line went dead, pressed the receiver rest to get the dialling tone, and hurriedly spun the Millside number. 'Inspector Moss,' he barked, the moment the switchboard answered. There was a click, a buzz, and Phil Moss's voice came over the line. He had obviously been waiting for the call.

'Phil . . . Colin. The Miller girl's just been on,' rapped Thane.

'I know. She wouldn't tell me what——'

'Never mind that just now, Phil. Get on your way, but quick, to Judith Marchand's place—you know the address—and get another car out for me, at the double. The Miller girl says the milk's lying outside, and there's no reply.'

'Want to bet?' asked Moss, grimly.

'Could be. But get in that house any way you can, And if . . . if she's still inside, get an ambulance—or the police surgeon.'

.   .   .

The police Jaguar swept round the last corner in the road, roared down the straight and came to a screaming, braking halt beside the red telephone box. As Pat Miller hurried forward, the rear door was flung open and from inside Moss shouted, 'Jump in.' Then, as she scrambled aboard, they were off again, on a last three hundred yards, with the car braking to a standstill again before it had got into top gear. Led by the girl, Moss and the other two detectives pounded through the tiled close mouth and up the stairs to Judith Marchand's first-floor flat. For a long thirty seconds Moss pressed the door-bell. Then he stood back and whipped off his jacket. Bundling the cloth round his right hand, he swung his padded fist and smashed a hole in the upper glass panel of the door. The glass tinkled inwards, and with a grunt of satisfaction he stepped back. One of the other men thrust an expert arm through the jagged, star-shaped hole, felt behind the door for a second, then turned the lock handle from the inside. The door opened a fraction, and Moss nodded, 'In we go.' He led the way, keenly sniffing the air. 'No gas,' he remarked. 'Right, search the place.'

The house was empty. The girl gave a sob of relief. 'I . . . I thought . . .' she began.

'So did we,' nodded Moss grimly. 'But if she's not here, then where is she?' He turned to the two waiting D.C.s. 'Take another squint around, boys. See if there's any note, any signs of packing.' He was walking towards the kitchenette again as he spoke, and over towards the cooker, a fairly new gas model. He lifted the lids from the two cooking pans standing on it. The first was empty. The second was about a quarter full of already-peeled potatoes, topped with water. 'Helping for one,' he said. 'Funny . . . looks as if she meant to come back.'

'No sign of a note, Inspector,' said the first D.C., coming into the small room. The second policeman, just at his back, shook his head in agreement. Moss continued his inspection.

'Breakfast dishes left to drip'—he pointed to the draining board—'but they're dry enough now. Means nothing, though, in this heat. Milk . . .' Moss lifted up a half-filled bottle, took off the top, and sniffed the contents. 'Ugh . . .' He wrinkled his nose in distaste. 'Sour.' He turned to the girl by his side. 'Looks as though your pal's been away for quite a little time.'

'Bed hasn't been slept in,' volunteered one of the D.C.s.

'You mean it's still made up,' corrected Moss. 'You may just throw the covers back when you get up in the morning, and pull them back over you at night, son, but other people make them up as soon as they rise, Still . . .'

'What do you think has happened?' questioned Pat, her face troubled. 'Can't we do something? Phone the hospitals, anything like that?'

'Take it easy, lass,' soothed Moss. 'We can't automatically presume that anything serious has actually happened to her. She may have had a sudden call from relatives. Or she may even have decided that she wanted to get very far away from us all.'

'You mean . . . you mean that she may have run away because she's mixed up in the robberies? I can't . . . I just won't believe that.'

Moss shrugged. Then, as he heard the sound of a car drawing up outside, he left the kitchenette and went rapidly through the house to the front window. Looking down to the street below, he called back to her, 'Here's Mr. Thane now . . . he didn't waste much time, anyway.'

A minute later Thane was in the flat. Quickly, Moss told him what he had found. Thane nodded. 'They diverted a radio patrol to my house,' he said. 'Saved a lot of time. So she's gone.' He stood for a moment, silent, thinking quickly. Had the woman really "taken off" because she was tied up in the store robberies, and felt she might soon be arrested? Was his theory that she was protecting someone other than herself wrong? There could be an innocent explanation for her disappearance, but surely she would have contacted Hillman's. The potatoes in the pot, the paper in the door and the milk outside. Did that add up to her having been away since the previous day? Making up his mind, he turned to Moss again. 'Go back down to the car again, Phil. Put out a general call . . . no, wait a minute. If you use the radio there's just a chance some newspaper might pick it up. Take the car back to that phone-box, and pass the message over the wire to Headquarters. Tell them to keep the "lookout" off the air, but to send it on the teleprinter network . . .

and to brief every man as he goes on duty. Get them to pass it on to the county forces too . . . and they'd better tip off the airport and dock sections.'

Moss nodded, and left the house. Thane strode over to the front window and looked out. A small crowd of curious neighbours was already gathering in the street below.

'See if you can find a picture of her around anywhere,' he told the waiting D.C.s. Then, turning to Pat Miller, he said softly, almost apologetically, 'We've got to do it, you know. If we find her, there may be some simple explanation. But we can't take chances.'

The girl nodded dumbly, took a wisp of a handkerchief from her handbag, and dabbed at her eyes. 'I'm being damn silly,' she admitted. 'But Judith . . . I can't believe it, honestly I can't.'

'No pictures,' reported one of the policemen. 'We've had a look in all the rooms. Want us to go through the sideboard drawers and that sort of thing?'

Thane fished his cigarettes from one pocket, and gave a negative shake of his head. He offered the packet to the girl, who, trembling just a little, took one, accepted a light, and sat down in an easy chair.

Thane cleared his throat. 'Look, Pat . . .' She glanced up obediently. 'You can help us here, and save a lot of awkwardness. Take a look through her things, and see if you can find a photograph of her. Try and see if any clothes are missing, too. If Judith Marchand is still missing by tonight then we'll probably get a warrant and go through everything in the flat. But right now, well, she'd probably like it better if you did the looking. And, I'll admit, it'll be less awkward for us.' White-faced, the girl nodded silent agreement. 'Then I want you to go back to the store,' went on Thane. 'Just go back and try to act as if nothing has happened. It won't be easy, but pretend you didn't manage to get out here after all. You didn't contact the store, did you? You didn't phone Watford, or anyone else?'

Pat shook her head. 'I phoned the police station, then your home.' She laughed shakily. 'I was going to call up Jerry, but I hadn't any change left.'

'Good. And you'll play along with us? You may be helping your boss just as much as you'll be helping us,' said Thane.

'I'll do it,' agreed the girl. 'I'll do it . . . because I don't believe Judith's done anything wrong.'

'Thanks. Now I'll tell you something I didn't want to say before, in case you thought I was trying to soft-soap you into agreeing. Somehow I've still got a notion that, though Judith Marchand can probably tell something about the robberies, she's not involved in them herself.' He frowned. 'It's just possible that something may have happened because of that . . but don't worry too much on that yet.'

The girl looked up at the tall, heavily-built figure before her. Somehow she seemed to draw strength from the calm, purposeful air of the man, couldn't help accepting him as a friend. She got up from the chair. 'I'll try the bedroom first,' she declared.

Thane waited until Pat had left the living-room. Then, on an impulse, he went over to the small writing-table set in one corner and quietly opened the centre drawer. Letters, bills, a roll of sticky tape . . . he tried the left-hand drawer. Lying at the top was a small pad of cheap writing paper. Swiftly he lifted it and slipped the pad into his jacket pocket. Then he silently shut the drawer again, just as the girl came back into the room.

'Nothing in the bedroom or the lounge,' she declared. 'I'll try in here.'

Thane nodded, and watched without comment while she checked the writing-table and the sideboard. There was no picture.

'Can't be helped,' he shrugged. 'We'll get one somehow.' Then he glanced at his watch. 'Time's getting on. I'll give you a run back to the store. One of the men will stay here for the moment. We can't leave the door the way it is.' He gave a faint smile. 'You never know, someone might try to break in.'

4

THE slow, outwardly cumbersome but minutely thorough
machinery of search was already grumbling into action when,
a couple of hours later, Thane and Moss paid yet another visit
to the department store. A carefully worded teleprinter message
had clacked out to all police divisions, asking that a look-out be
kept for Judith Marchand, who was "missing from home".
Line by line, the message tapped out: "Brown hair, cut short and
greying, Hazel eyes. Height five foot three inches, medium build,
pale complexion. When last seen, wearing grey wool dress, long
white jacket, belted at back, blue nylon scarf and small grey felt
hat. White high-heel sandals. May be carrying large brown
leather handbag. Immediate information to Millside Division,
Glasgow."

Pat Miller had given the clothing description, based on what
Judith had been wearing on the Tuesday morning, At hospitals,
hotels, even the low, red-brick city mortuary, quiet-voiced
detectives or uniform men were making their rounds. At airports,
railway stations, docks, other men, outwardly idling about,
watched and waited, always ready for a woman whose features
and dress would match the description each carried in his mind.
To the outsider, the job might appear like looking for a needle
in a haystack. But the legmen, the watchers, the listeners,
between them, had proved times without number that success
could achieve a practical ratio.

A phone call had let Farringdon know that the two detectives
were coming. They crowded into the service lift on the ground
floor, stayed with it until it reached the sixth, then walked along

to the small private lift that led to the store chief's penthouse office. Thane pressed the single mother-of-pearl button, and the cage, a tiny four-man affair, purred silently down. They got in, the doors closed automatically, and the cage slid upwards again.

Sitting in his shirtsleeves, the fat man was in a more amiable mood than on their first interview. He waved them to chairs, opened a drawer of his huge mahogany desk, and produced a bottle and glasses, brushing aside their protests. Thane sipped his drink—a smooth, beautifully matured whisky. Phil Moss, remembering the 'no alcohol' clause written in capitals on his diet sheet, took an even more cautious taste, and, glass in hand, muttered a silent regret.

'I've just finished tying up a deal,' said Farringdon. 'A pretty big one. . . . I won't bore you with details, but it's something I've been angling after for about six months.' He drained his glass with an heretical disregard for the spirit's quality. 'Now . . .' he smacked his thick, fleshy lips, 'how about this thieving? What's the progress, Chief Inspector?'

With a warning glance at Moss, Thane replied slowly, 'Not very much . . . yet. That's why we're here. We need your help, in rather an unusual way.'

'Go on,' Farringdon nodded.

'We want to stay hidden somewhere up here, in your office, until after the store closes tonight. Perhaps all night, if necessary.'

'What the hell for?' demanded the fat man, loosening one button of his shirt, and scratching his chest with one hairy hand. 'You after someone on the staff?'

'It looks that way, I'm afraid,' said Thane. 'Between ourselves, we had a tip-off note which suggested something might be happening tonight.'

'That's settled, then,' said Farringdon. 'See that door in the corner? Go through. You'll find a small bedroom through there, and a kitchenette. I spend the night there when I'm working late. Anyone see you come in? Doesn't matter. . . .' He entered enthusiastically into the game. 'I'll buzz my secretary in a minute. When she comes up from the main office I'll dictate a note addressed to you . . . tell her you've not long left, and that it's the answer to an inquiry you made. For all anybody knows, you could have walked down the stairs and out into the street. Eh . . . mind if I stay tonight myself, and see what happens?'

Thane shook his head. 'I'd rather you didn't,' he said. 'From what I can gather, word would get around that you hadn't left and it's unlikely anyone would prowl around knowing the boss was still on the loose in the building.'

Farringdon chuckled, his heavy jowl quivering with mirth. 'Right, I'll go quietly. So it isn't shoplifters,' he mused. 'What, then?'

'Frankly, we haven't worked that out yet,' admitted the detective. 'I'm just playing hunches . . . plus the note. And I'd rather not say too much at the moment. You'll understand later, I hope.'

Farringdon was obviously disappointed. But the big man shrugged. 'Just nail the thieving swine, that's all I ask. Now'—he lowered his voice to a conspiratorial tone—'if you want to go through into the room, I'll buzz my secretary. I'll need to get on with this paperwork. Help yourself to any of the stuff in the kitchenette. . . . I'll look in before I go for the night.'

The two detectives went through. It was a bigger room than they had imagined, tastefully furnished. A telephone and a Dictaphone machine, lying side-by-side on a little table close by the bed, showed that Farringdon didn't believe in wasting a minute. Thane unlaced his shoes, took off his jacket, loosened his collar and tie, then stretched out on top of the bedspread with a groan of pleasure. 'Nothing to do but wait,' he declared. 'Take your shoes off, Phil. Quieter that way if you move around—but watch where you put them. The pile on that carpet's thick enough to bury anything short of army boots.'

Time crept by. They smoked in silence, glanced at the few magazines lying about the room—most of them dry-as-dust business publications. Phil investigated the tiny kitchen, and soon rustled up some sandwiches and coffee. From time to time, faint sounds of activity and the murmur of muffled voices reached them from the next-door office. It was six-fifteen by Thane's watch before there was a faint tap on the door, and Farringdon

64

came in, a Homburg hat on his head, a bulging brief-case under one arm.

'I'm going now,' he declared. 'The store shut three-quarters of an hour ago. Nearly everybody should be away, Anything else you need?'

Thane shook his head. 'Nothing,' he declared. 'Just as long as everyone thinks we've left.'

'They do,' chuckled Farringdon. 'I had Allen, the buyer, up just over an hour and a half ago, and told him you had called, then left again. He's an old wife at heart . . . biggest gossip in the place . . . and with any luck the whole damned store will know by now that you've been here, and that you left again.' He pointed towards the phone. 'That's a private line. Use it for any calls you want to make. The other phones, including the ones on my desk, are out of action now. Any ordinary incoming calls are switched through to the night commissionaire's box.'

'How about the watchmen? Do they come up here?' asked Moss. 'And the cleaners . . . do they come up in the morning?'

'Well, the lift up to here is switched off now, like all the others,' said Farringdon, 'and I lock the door at the foot of the private stairway. The commissionaire's got a key, of course, and uses it to let the cleaners in when they start work at six in the morning, But the night watchmen don't come up here on their patrol. They check the general office, and just make sure the door's locked at the foot of my stairway. You can open it from this side, of course. . . .' He took a last look around, then, reluctantly, added, 'I'll go now. Hope you catch them, whoever they are.'

Thane settled back on the bed again as the door closed. 'I'd like to call the station and find out if there's any progress in the hunt for the Marchand woman,' he declared, reaching out for one of the magazines. 'But that wouldn't be playing it smart. If it's someone really on the inside track, the odds are they'll know Farringdon's private phone number. And what better way to check if the boss is away than to call him up? They find the line engaged and . . . boom! We've wasted our time.'

E—DD   65

If the time had passed slowly before, it seemed to be positively stationary now. The long summer evening seemed to be reluctant to fade. Thane and Moss waited patiently . . . waiting comes easy to police after a while . . . waiting, watching, hoping for a "break". Below them, the six storeys of brick and concrete should be lonely and deserted except for the occasional tread of the night watchman on his evening round.

The phone rang at nine-thirty. The two men sat quiet but tensed, listening to its persistent note. Then it fell silent again. As it stopped, Thane hurriedly pulled his shoes on and struggled into his jacket.

'Down we go,' he said quietly. 'All set?'

Moss nodded as he finished tying his shoelaces, and stood up.

'Right,' said Thane. 'If Watford's time-table is right, the watchman should be downstairs now, sitting in the commissionaire's box. We'll "do" each floor from the sixth down—and for Heaven's sake keep the noise down.'

The door at the foot of Farringdon's private stairway opened with the faintest of creaks. Quietly, they inspected the main office, with its rows of desks, covered typewriters and empty, sentinel chairs. The canteen . . . grey and ghostly with its waiting, clean-scrubbed tables. Downstairs to the next floor—"Radios, TV, gramophones, record shop," recited Moss to himself. "Men's and children's clothing, toys to the left on the fourth. . . . Hell, I sound like a lift attendant! Still a blank, though. Rows and ruddy rows of dust-sheet covered counters. Silence everywhere. Nothing moving. Noth—no, only a cat." He relaxed as the furry shape miaoued, then flashed down one of the long aisles. Third floor . . . the Sycamore restaurant, with a faint, slightly stale smell of cooking still in the air. The flowers on the tables had wilted in the heat of the day. On over to the other side of the floor . . . hairdressing and shoes. Thane stopped to take a quick look at a display of boys' football boots in the shoe section, made a mental note of their price, then moved on again, to join Moss, already waiting by the stairway.

Just as they started down that stairway, down to the second

66

floor, it happened. A faint sound, so faint that only the vast, waiting quiet of the sleeping store could have transmitted it at all. It could have been a door closing, a drawer being slammed shut. The two men froze . . . and the sound was repeated.

"Second floor, women's fashions", recited Moss mentally 'Women's fashions . . .' Thane spoke, hardly above a whisper, 'Judith Marchand's department. This is it!'

They crept down the long flight of concrete steps, slid into cover at one side of the entrance archway. Cautiously, Thane inched forward until he could look round into the long, rack-cluttered floor. All was quiet again, nothing moved. He slid back into the cover of the archway. Lips close to Moss's ear, Thane told him, 'Go round by the left, Phil. I'll take the right. Shout if you come across anything . . . and use any cover you can find.'

Moss felt with a loving hand for the sawn-off baton he carried in his right-hand hip pocket, nodded, and slipped round the archway. Thane stopped for a second, to pad the handkerchief from his breast pocket round the loose change and keys in his trouser pocket and prevent them jingling. Then he stepped forward. Phil Moss had already vanished among the counters, like a tracking Indian in some exotic pastel-patterned under-growth. Thane bore quietly to the right, through long rows of close-hung coats.

And somewhere up ahead, a door creaked open. Up ahead . . . from where Judith Marchand's office lay. He heard quick, nervous footsteps coming down the length of the floor towards him.

Cat-like despite his bulk, Thane moved rapidly forward, still keeping to cover. The man was coming down the centre aisle, a good forty feet away . . . twice he caught a quick glimpse of the figure as it crossed the narrow spaces visible between racks, still moving diagonally towards him.

Now. . . . Thane quit his cover and sprinted across, giving a bull-like roar, 'Hold it . . .!'

The man ahead stopped short, gave a startled gasp of fear, and seemed ready to break into a run, But, before he could recover from the shock, James Rose, Hillman's store detective, had been seized tight and was helpless in a wrist-searing lock. He quivered with fear again . . . and fainted. Thane unceremoniously lowered the store detective to the floor, and looked around. Where the devil was Phil? He gave a hail, 'Hey, Phil, over here man . . . Come and see what we've landed.' His voice echoed back, but nothing moved, there was no answering shout from Moss. 'Phil!' he tried again, louder, suddenly, unaccountably anxious.

This time, the faint rumble of voices and the sound of heavy feet, feet pounding up the stairway, answered his hail. He looked towards the entrance to the floor, as two men, panting from their climbing rush, erupted through the archway. One, in civvies, swung a heavy baton. The other, the night commissionaire by his uniform, carried a short metal poker. They charged over, then, as they suddenly saw the huddled figure at Thane's feet, came to an uncertain halt a good ten feet away. 'Stay where you are,' gulped the commissionaire, waving the poker in an impotent threat, obviously reluctant to come closer, his baton-hugging friend hanging back a good yard to the rear.

'Police,' snapped Thane, shoving a hand into his jacket pocket. The two men raised their weapons in almost automatic reflex, then relaxed as he brought out a small leather wallet. 'There's my warrant card,' he told them. 'Here . . .' He tossed the wallet towards them. It landed on the concrete at their feet with a soft thud. The commissionaire picked it up, glanced at the framed card in the front envelope of the wallet, then gave a sigh of relief and walked forward.

'Sorry mate,' he apologized, nervously. 'Thought you were a burglar . . . here, what's up with him? How'd you get in anyway?'

At their feet, there was a moan as Rose, starting to come round, gave the first faint signs of returning consciousness.

'That's your store 'tec,' said Thane, as he kept looking anxiously around. 'Never mind him. Have you seen anyone else about?'

'Us?' queried the poker-wielder. 'No, sir. We hammered up the stairs when we heard the shouting. N'that right, Bert?' The watchman nodded agreement.

68

Thane's face went a shade paler under its tan. 'There's another cop around somewhere,' he said. 'Look, eh . . . ?'

'Deacon, Joe Deacon, sir,' said the commissionaire, still bewildered by the situation.

'Joe. You stay here with Rose. Watch him carefully . . . very carefully, you understand. Don't let him move away. Your pal can come with me, and we'll start looking for my mate.'

'Don't bother,' said a shaky voice behind him. 'I'm here, more or less, Colin.' Phil Moss stood a few feet away, dazed, holding on to the steel side-tube of a dress rack with one hand, while the other slowly, painfully explored the back of his head. 'Someone clobbered me, good and hard,' he went on. 'Sorry, Colin. I must have practically stood on his toes as I was creeping along. I just caught a vague, rushing move, and then I got thumped on the skull.' He winced as his searching fingers contacted a tender, throbbing patch of scalp. His hand came away red with surface blood. 'I must have gone out like a light . . . only for a minute or so, I suppose, but then I couldn't do anything but lie there on the deck, feeling woozy as hell. When I did manage to look around. . . .' He shrugged.

'You didn't see him?' asked Thane, going over and taking a close look at the inspector's bloodied scalp.

'Hey, easy . . .' protested Moss as Thane's prodding brought a fresh throb of pain. 'No, there wasn't a ruddy sausage to be seen, except what whoever it was had used to belt me.' He mustered a suspicion of a grin. 'It was a ruddy display stand— one of those plastic ones they use to display gloves. The bloke must have picked it up when he heard me coming.'

'You're born lucky,' said Thane. 'There's a small cut, but it isn't deep.' There was a louder groan from behind him as Rose began to move. 'I found him in a rush to get away from the place,' explained Thane.

'Rose?' whistled Moss. 'Who slugged him?'

'Nobody. He got a fright,' said Thane.

'Och, he'll be all right,' said Deacon, bending over the store 'tec. 'Look, sir, his eyes are opening, Funny, though, I didn't know he was still in the building.'

Rose started to sit up, helped by the commissionaire. He looked wildly round, 'What . . . who . . . what's happening?' he mumbled.

'That's what we want to know,' said Thane, in a hard voice. 'Get up.' Half-pulled by the comissionaire, the store 'tec got to his feet and, in an unsteady voice said shrilly, 'It was you, Thane . . . you attacked me!'

'We'll go into that later,' the chief inspector cut him short. 'Joe, is there anyone still on duty downstairs? Anyone watching the back door?'

'Aye,' nodded Deacon. 'The other watchman's standing by. He was just going out when we heard the shouts. He stayed on guard while we came up.'

'Whoever clobbered you, Phil, it wasn't Rose,' snapped Thane. 'That means there's someone else still prowling around. We'll get down to that back door, quick.'

'What's this ridiculous nonsense?' demanded Rose, then, as Thane seized his arm again, he protested, 'Let me go . . . you can't push me around.'

'Down,' ordered Thane. There was a hard undertone in his voice which stopped the store 'tec's further protests as, still glaring indignantly around, a flush of rage replacing the pallor on his cheeks, he was bundled towards the stairway. The little party clattered down the stairway and along a short passageway to where the second night watchman was waiting, a duplicate of his friend's baton in one hand, an anxious look on his face.

No, he emphasised, no one had come near him. 'He'd have got a dose o' this,' he declared, gripping the baton still tighter.

'Then whoever it is is still in the building, sir,' said the commissionaire. 'The store is burglar-alarmed like nobody's business. And they work just as well when somebody's trying to get out anywhere else as when somebody's trying to get in.'

Phil Moss leaned back weakly against the wall of the commissionaire's little office, a few yards away from the outer door. 'We'd better bring up reinforcements, Colin,' he suggested. 'Give us a fag . . . 'strewth, my head's aching.'

70

Thane lit a cigarette, took a puff, then placed it between Phil Moss's lips. Striking a match to light another cigarette for himself, he nodded agreement.

'Get your two men outside, Joe,' he ordered. 'I want them to keep patrolling round the building, non-stop. You watch that door. I'm going to use the phone in your office. Come on, Rose, you get in here too. You've a good few questions to answer.'

'And they'd better be good answers,' winced Moss as he followed the two men into the little bothy. 'They'd better be very good.'

The shabby little night office had one wall ranged with rows of time-clock card racks, the others covered with a tattered collection of official notices and pasted pin-ups. A greasy pack of playing cards scattered haphazardly across the table showed how the night men had been passing their watch when the shouts from above had interrupted them. The phone was on a wall-bracket. Straight away, Thane got through on it to Millside station and when he hung up two minutes later a police squad was already being organized to head for Hillman's.

Then he turned to Rose, standing impatiently beside the table, a venomous expression on his thin features.

'You seemed pretty surprised when I caught you on the fashion floor,' said Thane, sitting on the table-edge, 'and Joe, the commissionaire, seemed equally surprised to see you still in the store. What were you up to, Rose?'

The store 'tec replied stiffly, 'I was carrying out my duties. Investigating along certain lines of inquiry.'

'Snooping,' muttered Moss in scarcely audible tones as he produced another tea-biscuit from the seemingly inexhaustible supply in his jacket pocket.

'I heard that,' snapped Rose. 'Mind your manners, Inspector. I warn you both, the chief constable will hear about the way I've been treated. If you must know, Thane, I've been making some constructive progress in the matter of the store robberies which is more,' he sneered, 'than the police can claim so far.'

'So you were investigating,' purred Thane. 'Investigating

what . . . and why so late at night? All on your own, too, I suppose?'

'Of course I was on my own,' said Rose, conscious of Phil Moss sceptically rubbing the lump on the back of his head. 'I don't know anything about how your assistant came to be knocked out. I was busy elsewhere, I tell you. As for how I came to be in the store, that's simple. I never left it. I've been in my office or in other departments all evening. The night watchman saw me at his seven o'clock check.'

'You're in rather an awkward spot,' warned Thane, hitching his thumbs into the waistband of his trousers. 'Especially awkward when we'd been tipped off that something was going to happen tonight.' Still not raising his voice above conversational level, but with edged emphasis, he demanded, 'I'll ask you again, what were you doing?'

Rose licked his lips, then dived into his jacket pocket and pulled out a small, paper-wrapped parcel and a sheet of scribbling paper. 'Among other things, I was looking through Judith Marchand's desk,' he declared. 'Yes, going through the drawers. I've told you before I was convinced she was mixed up in it all. . . and now I've proved it. Look at these!'

The detectives took the parcel and opened it. Inside were three pairs of fish-net nylons. He glanced at Rose, laid down the parcel, and examined the sheet of scribbling paper. Dates . . . figures, small "doodled" remarks . . . and down the centre, a carefully tabulated column of dresses, costumes, underwear, women's clothing of different types.

'You see what it means,' said Rose eagerly, 'Judith Marchand is behind all these thefts. That list—it's a list of stolen goods, all stolen from her department. And the stockings—that clinches it. You know why? Because they are Bruce Brand. And even I know that we're the only firm in the city that stock them. I'll ask you a question now, Chief Inspector. Where is Judith Marchand? Off sick . . . ?' He snorted. 'You didn't find her at home this afternoon. I heard, never mind how. And let me tell you something else. I've been checking on articles bought by staff in the store— there's a record kept, and they get a percentage refund at the end of each quarter. Judith Marchand hasn't bought anything in the last six months. Why? Because she didn't need to. Anything she wanted, she just took.'

Inwardly Thane felt sick. If what the man before him said was true, Judith Marchand certainly seemed firmly tied to the ring. But it just didn't fit, somehow. Intangibly, slowly, a different idea altogether had been building in his mind, Idea? Hunch? Despite the signals, he might still be right, but, though he hated to admit it, the balance seemed gradually shifting against him.

'All right, Rose,' he decided. 'We'll take care of these, and we'll want a full statement from you about them. But remember . . . you came pretty close to laying yourself open to a charge of theft doing that. I'm not taking your word for your movements tonight. You said you knew Judith Marchand wasn't at home. How did you know that? Who told you—or maybe you had reasons for knowing yourself?'

Rose hesitated, his eyes narrowing. But he was saved from answering by the sound of voices out in the corridor. As they looked round, the small, dumpy figure of Henry Allen, the store's head buyer, bobbed through the office door.

'Good evening, good evening,' he greeted them. I didn't expect to find you here at this time of night, Mr. Thane . . . nor you, Mr. Rose.'

He beamed round at the commissionaire, standing just behind him. 'I was just saying to Joe, it's such a lovely night to have to come back to the store like this, but . . .' He left the sentence hanging in mid-air as he fumbled in his pocket and produced a rubber-banded note-book. 'It's our Summer Sale, you know. It starts on Saturday.' He fussed with the notebook and gave another, slightly sleepy smile . . . like the Dormouse in *Alice*, thought Thane, watching the podgy little man. Allen almost twittered as he went on, 'Mr. Farringdon's most insistent that we have our absolutely best lines displayed on the ground floor "taster" counters . . . terribly important, you know, to show our customers just how much we have to offer. I've been trying to plan out the best display we can manage. But it's so difficult . . .

73

and Mr. Farringdon's very exacting in his demands, you know.' He gave a tired sigh.

He'll roll up and go off to sleep in a minute, thought Thane, trying hard to refrain from smiling. He stuck his hands in his pockets, feeling for his cigarettes, and asked, 'What brings you back at this hour? More work?'

The little man nodded. 'Yes, I'd been at the cinema—silly on such a lovely night, I know—and just happened to be passing on my way to the bus. And a new idea struck me. I just thought I'd pop in and try to visualize it, on the actual floor, you know.'

This time Thane openly grinned. 'Work late often, Mr. Allen?'

'Quite a bit, I'm afraid, quite a bit. My wife doesn't like it, you know, but . . .' he sighed again. 'Can't be helped, can it, Joe?'

' 'Fraid not, Mr. Allen,' smiled the commissionaire. 'Though it's awkward if they don't understand.'

'Oh, I've no complaints there,' said Allen. 'Bella is an extremely understanding wife. Extremely understanding. But . . . why are you here, Mr. Thane? Is anything wrong? Can I help at all?'

Thane shook his head. 'Not just now, I'm afraid. And your plan will have to wait till the morning, Mr. Allen. I'm sorry, but I can't allow anyone in the building just now. Would you mind very much if I asked you to just go on home?'

'Why . . . yes, yes, if it's as important as all that,' said the little man nervously. 'It's just that I'm so terribly busy, you know. A problem can become so engrossing, and when I thought I had the solution . . .' he tailed off. 'I don't suppose I should ask what's happening—police secret and all that, eh? I'll hear about it in due course perhaps? It was just that seeing Mr. Rose helping you I thought . . .'

'That's fine then.' Thane led the store buyer towards the door, and out into the corridor. 'We'll see you in the morning, Mr. Allen.'

'I'll just get my hat and coat then,' agreed the little man. 'Oh, silly of me, I haven't got them with me. Such a fine day.

74

Well, good night, Mr. Thane.' The little man smiled again, gave a short, bobbing bow, and, Joe holding the street door open, walked out of the store into the street beyond.

'Nice bloke,' said the commissionaire. 'Conscientious too coming back like that.'

'Would it be asking too much to let me leave?' Rose, standing in the office doorway, was in an anything but pleasant mood.

Thane nodded. 'You might as well. But we'll want you in the morning, Rose, no matter what you think up for the Chief Constable.'

'You won't mind if I go to my office and collect my hat,' sneered the store detective with heavy sarcasm.

Thane shook his head. 'That's okay, as long as Inspector Moss goes up with you.' With a final snort, Rose left the night office, Moss trailing behind him. He came back down a few minutes later. Moss gave a broad wink to his chief as, his face like thunder, Rose marched out of the Hillman building, ignoring the commissionaire's formal farewell.

·   ·   ·   ·   ·

Minutes after Rose left, the Millside squad arrived, two night-duty C.I.D. cars and a patrol van filled with uniform men . . . twenty police in all, under a uniform inspector. Thane put two men on duty at the side door, another six to watch the building from the outside, then split the remaining twelve men into three parties of four each. He headed one group with Joe, the commissionaire, to act as guide, assigned a watchman to each of the other parties, Moss leading one, the uniform inspector the other.

'We'll take a floor at a time, and comb it to the last mouse-hole,' he ordered. 'Start at the basement . . . and stop when we've reached the roof.'

In the basement floor, an array of lights had to be snapped on to lift the windowless dark. 'Pretty easy here,' said Joe Deacon. 'The left section's nothing but main store-rooms, all double-locked each evening, and burglar-alarmed on a

75

time-switch, Just check the locks . . . there's a light above each door anyway that switches on if the alarm goes off.'

While Moss's squad fanned out towards the store-rooms, Thane continued to the right-hand section, the transport garage and despatch department.

'Bit messy here, sir,' warned Deacon. 'Watch your clothes.' The tramp of footsteps echoed from the hard concrete as the remaining two squads of police followed. The garage was like a vast subterranean cave, the scent of oil and exhaust gas mingling with a certain dampness. At one end a ramped drive-way led to street level. 'Place is riddled with rats,' commented their guide. 'There's a paper store in one corner . . . and rats just love paper.'

Parked neatly before the huge double doors, a dozen large vans, tailboards down, interiors loaded, occupied much of the garage area. But a couple of grey Humber saloons stood in one corner beside three five-hundredweight utilities. 'Delivery pool,' said Joe, as the police spread out and began their prodding search, looking under the vehicles, in their cabs, even scrambling into the bigger ones and checking the spaces between the loads. 'The two "privates" are for the bosses. The lads usually load up the vans last thing in the evening, ready for the road first thing in the morning . . . all but the ones that come in late, that is.'

Thane watched until the uniform inspector led his men back, shaking his head. 'First floor then,' he said, leading the way back to where Moss's party, also finished, were waiting. They trudged up to the ground floor, coming into its broad, still sun-lit area at the right-hand side, in the food section, where a strange, mixed odour of a hundred scents and smells met them.

'Gets a bit pongy at night, no through air and that,' said Joe. He picked an apple from a small mountain of the fruit piled nearby, wiped it on the sleeve of his tunic and took a bite. 'Help yourself,' he invited. 'Never miss another one.'

With a quizzical glance around, Thane selected a rosy-skinned apple, then waved, 'Spread out. Same routine.'

.   .   .   .   .

It was after midnight when they finished the search, checking the flat roof of the building by torchlight. Moss found the door to Farringdon's private office locked as they had left it. Just to make sure, however, he fished a small piece of hard Perspex from one pocket, tackled the simple cylinder lock with it, and quickly had the door open. But the penthouse, like the rest of the store, was "clean". Whoever had bashed him on the head—a small clotting of blood and a still throbbing bump were there as constant reminders of the attack—might as well have vanished into thin air for all the trace that could be found.

He went down to the sixth floor, directly beneath, to report, and found Thane and most of the others had gathered in the canteen. Joe Deacon had got one of the tea urns going, and had found some left-over milk.

Tea in one hand, cigarette in the other, Thane was busily quizzing the commissionaire.

Deacon was positive about several things. Officially and, as far as he knew, in actual fact, there had been no one but Rose in the building at the seven o'clock check. 'I didn't even know he was there,' he complained. 'The ruddy watchman didn't say a thing about it at the time. All the staff were clocked out by half-five, and about the last of the execs to leave was the boss himself.'

'Nobody working late, Joe?'

The man shook his head. 'Not tonight. Tomorrow, now, there'll be anything up to three hundred, getting ready for the sale. But there wasn't a single overtimer this evening.'

'And did anybody—anybody at all—look in during the evening?'

'Nope . . . unless you count the beat polis. He popped in for his usual cuppa about half-eight.'

Thane took in the two rows of ribbons on Deacon's tunic, noting the M.M. and Africa Star among them. 'How about your watchmen, Joe? They all right?'

'Square as they come, sir. Been here years, both of them.'

Thane nodded, and turned to Moss, waiting patiently beside him. 'We'll leave a sergeant and three men here for the rest of the night, just in case anything happens. Our bird's probably flown—don't ask me how. But if he knows his way around and has really gone to ground, well, it would take an army to find him. Pull the rest of the men out . . . we'll all away home now.'

'Home? To bed?' asked Moss hopefully.

'No. Home to the station. We've still got work to do.'

.　　　.　　　.　　　.　　　.

They got back to Millside at one a.m. The station had had a quiet night: a couple of "breach" arrests, a drunk, and a wife-beater, the latter more battered than his complaining spouse, were the sum total of the evening's arrests. Together they went upstairs to the C.I.D. section and into Thane's room. The window was still wide open, as it had been left in the afternoon, and a slight, cold breeze was fluttering the plain green cotton curtains. Thane closed the sash. 'Rain on the way,' he remarked. 'Place could do with it anyway. My garden's getting like the Texas dust-bowl.'

He lifted the phone and asked, 'Get me the Scientific Bureau at Headquarters, will you?' The connexion took only a matter of seconds, and a sleepy voice at the other end of the wire replied, 'Sergeant Larkins, Scientific.'

'Thane here. What luck with my notepaper?'

The sergeant's yawn came loud over the phone. 'Hang on a minute, sir. The man who did the check's out on a safe-blowing in the Northern Division at the moment, but I'll dig out his report.'

He returned to the wire in a couple of minutes. 'Ready, sir? We've compared the ink-written note labelled "A" with the writing pad labelled "B". Paper's the same all right, and when we "dusted" the notepad and checked it under a microscope there were faint impressions of the original note. Whoever wrote it used a ball-point pen—they always leave some sort of an impression for a few sheets down.'

'Fine,' declared Thane. 'How about prints?'

'Right again,' said the sergeant. 'There were no really

78

complete prints on the ink-written note, but one "dab" gave us about half a thumb-print. That drinking glass you gave us—label "C"—had the same print.'

'That clinches it,' said Thane. 'Now, I'll be sending over some more work right away.'

'Rush stuff, sir?' queried the sergeant, a slightly apprehensive note in his voice.

'No, a morning report will do. It's another sheet of paper. Let me have a photostat copy of it, sent back right away. Then check the original for "dabs". You'll find some of mine in one corner—that couldn't be helped. But I'm hoping for at least two other sets. There's another prints job—a plastic display arm—the kind they use in shops to show off gloves. Someone bashed Inspector Moss over the skull with it tonight.'

The sergeant whistled. 'Is Rumble-gu—— I mean, is the Inspector okay, sir?'

'He'll get by,' grinned Thane, looking over at Moss, who was yawning in a chair. 'Oh, one other item. Some nylon stockings. Just give them a general run-through. . . . I'm not expecting anything from them.'

'Fair enough, sir,' said the sergeant. 'We'll send you the usual written reports by the despatch car in the morning.'

'This is beginning to get interesting,' said Thane as he hung up. 'The boffins say that the tip-off note was written on the pad I "snatched" from Judith Marchand's house. They found prints—or a trace of them, anyway—that matched those on a glass I took from the kitchenette there, so it's pretty certain she wrote it. But why the hell tip off the police that something's going to happen, then disappear? And what was to have happened, apart from your getting bashed?'

'Maybe she fell out with the rest of the gang,' hazarded Moss. 'Maybe she got scared, or wasn't getting a big enough cut. Otherwise, why the stockings and the list in her desk—if they are genuine, that is.'

'I don't think Rose planted them in his pocket just to sell us the idea,' said Thane. 'He got the devil of a fright this evening. Yet not long afterwards he seemed all the more pleased to be able to pin our ears back in place with these.' He nodded to the parcel and the note lying on his desk. 'Let's have another look at them, anyway.'

The stockings were all Bruce Brand. Ordinary, never-used stockings, their price tags still intact. He pushed them aside, picked up the note by its edges.

'This could be a list of the stolen stuff, all right, or some of it. But'—his brow creased in puzzled lines—'what about those crosses? See . . . there's one cross opposite blouses on May 26, another opposite underskirts, here and . . . hell, another opposite nylons for June 2. It doesn't make sense. Look, Phil, say you had a clever, large-scale racket going, flogging stuff from Hillman's. Would you keep a neat little list of what you'd taken and leave it lying beside some samples in your desk? Of course you wouldn't.'

'Maybe the stockings were just that—manufacturers' samples, or stock she was examining,' suggested Moss. 'But the list . . . mind you, she could have kept that for business purposes. Or maybe she was on to something . . . and at that rate, someone may have knocked her off. Nasty thought, isn't it?'

Thane nodded slowly. 'Nasty . . . and it might be. Then what about the store tonight? What was to have happened? There's some work we can do, anyway, First thing in the morning we get a warrant to search Judith Marchand's flat. And we'll try to get the okay from Farringdon to go over her office. I'll put friend Rose on the grill good and proper. Then we'll have to make a major effort to locate a picture of the woman. And run a check on Deacon and his watchmen, though they seem square enough.' He lit a cigarette, and tossed the packet across the table. 'There's a man still keeping an eye on the Marchand woman's flat, just in case she does make a quick trip back.' He stifled a yawn. 'What's the time? Hey, it's nearly three a.m. Let's get what we can tied up, then shove off. Back here at nine, Phil?'

.   .   .   .   .

The darkness was already beginning to give way to the first faint greying light of dawn as Thane stepped out of the police car at his home in Southwood. He waved to the driver as the car slid quietly away, then, his mind sluggish with sleep, muscles heavy with fatigue, he turned and began to walk up the garden path to the house. From the big lilac bush in the far corner of the garden a bird began to chirp an enthusiastic welcome to the morning.

'Get back to bed, you stupid little devil,' grunted the policeman. 'Stop making such a ruddy racket.'

5

THEY found Judith Marchand at 9.24 a.m. on Thursday. She was hanging on a rack in the middle of a row of dresses stowed well to the back of the fashion department store-room. Two coat-hangers, tied together with string, had been placed under the shoulders of her buttoned white jacket, and then she had been neatly suspended by the hooks from the centre pole of the rack, the dresses on either side angled out to hide the slight bulk of her body. It did not need an expert to decide the cause of death. Her pale blue nylon scarf had been pulled through its ornamental silver toggle-ring with savage strength, cutting into the skin of her neck so deeply that bulging flesh almost obscured the wisp of fine but strong material. Her face was swollen and mottled, her staring hazel eyes wide in mute horror.

Neat white sandals swayed gently back and forward, a clear six inches off the floor.

Two shop assistants, helping in the weekly stores check, found her body as they were methodically ticking off items against their stock sheet. One screamed and stood quivering, hypnotized by the swaying body, the distorted, agonized face. The other, a fair-haired girl with a stomach strengthened by spare-time V.A.D. training, took a deep gulp of air then, white-faced, walked slowly and carefully to the stock-room door.

. . . . .

At 9.33 a.m. Jerry Watford telephoned Millside station. Three minutes later, Thane and Moss were in a radio car, screaming through the city streets towards the store, the first of three car-loads of police rushing from the station. Headquarters, telephoned the "murder" signal within three seconds of Thane hearing the news, were already despatching their emergency squad of crime technicians—photographers, finger-print experts, all the other members of the "boffin brigade". Even as their big, buff-coloured van, packed with the specialized tools of their trade, was fighting its way through the traffic, other phone messages were alerting the police surgeon, the city prosecutor, and, from his airy study at the university, Glasgow's top forensic medicine expert, Professor McMaster. One more vehicle would come later—the "shell" with its plain wooden coffin.

Watford was at the main door of the store as the three Millside cars, sirens wailing, cut through the Sauchiehall Street traffic and drew to a halt outside. Leaving one man at the store entrance, the procession of police shouldered their way through the rapidly gathering crowd, marched past the gaping customers inside the store, and went straight to the lift gates. Watford had a cage standing by, and, the eleven officers aboard, it swept up to the second floor.

The two-man crew of a traffic car, diverted to the building by a radio flash, were already guarding the store-room door. Rose, his staff of five shop detectives augmented by floor-walkers, had cleared the department of customers, and "closed" signs had been placed at each entrance. Farringdon, shocked and white-faced, was down from his penthouse eyrie and stood beside the store-room door, his voice for once hushed as he talked to Rose and to Allen, the head buyer. He moved his ponderous bulk as Thane approached, exchanged a quick, formal handshake, muttered, 'Dreadful . . . dreadful business. . . .' then moved to follow the detective into the death-room. Thane shook his head. 'Not yet. We'll have a look around on our own first. But I'd like you to wait.'

The store chief's state of mind could be gauged from his immediate acceptance of the Chief Inspector's decision. He stood back, joined by Watford, while Thane rapped orders. A detective sergeant and constable peeled off to interview the girls

83

who had found the body. Two men took up guard at the store-room door. Another two were despatched to search Judith Marchand's office, and a plain-clothes man was posted at the nearest phone, to establish a relay-point between Thane and Police Headquarters.

Only then did Thane open the store-room door. One of the traffic crew led him to the dress rack, then stood back. Gently, Thane removed the dresses on either side of the hanging body. The slight jerk sent the corpse swinging again in macabre fashion, and with a grunt of distaste he steadied the body with one hand.

Phil Moss gave a thin, surprised whistle as they saw the tightly-drawn scarf. 'If he'd pulled much harder, he'd have taken her ruddy head off,' he commented grimly. 'Well, we've found her, Colin. . . . How long ago was it, I wonder.'

Thane shook his head and, gripping one of the cold, dangling arms, attempted to flex it at the elbow joint. 'That's a job for the medics,' he declared. 'But her arm's stiff with rigor . . . my guess is that she may have been here since Tuesday afternoon.'

'It would fit in,' nodded Moss, 'and that would mean she was killed not long after she posted the note. It could have been lying in a post-box for a couple of hours before being collected and time-stamped.'

'Get a couple of the lads on to the job of finding out just how many of the staff were in the store after closing time on Tuesday,' said Thane. 'There shouldn't have been too many. They can get the details from the store time-cards, and by cross-checking with the departmental bosses. Oh, and send someone down to quiz Andy Richards, and any other doormen who would be on duty that day.'

'Will do, Colin,' said Moss, turning to leave. 'Oh, how about friend Rose?'

'If he was going to have done a bunk, he would have been far away by now,' replied Thane. 'He'll keep until we get cleared-up in here.'

Thane turned back to the woman's body, and peered closely

84

at her fingernails, with their light coating of pink varnish. It would need a medical man to decide whether there had been any real struggle. But the nails, well-kept, moderately long, appeared unbroken. He was conscious of the first, sickly-sweet odour of death beginning to come from the body—nearly two days in the dry summer heat of the store had accelerated the natural process. Slowly, he continued his examination. One waist seam of the dress was split and torn . . . the flesh-coloured nylon on her right leg was badly laddered. Pensively, he stood back from the pitiful figure.

Whatever the secret that Judith Marchand had guarded so carefully, it had almost definitely caused her death. Thane thought back to the mystery note he had received, and to the attack on Phil Moss the previous night. Supposing, just supposing, something had been planned for the Wednesday, and Judith Marchand had discovered it. She could have sent the note, then have tried to find out more . . . and paid the penalty. But would her killer—or killers—not then have called off their plan for the Wednesday night?

He took out a cigarette, lit it, and took a deep draw of the satisfying smoke—it helped to obscure the faint scent of death. That mystery note. If the killer had not known about it, then there must have been another reason for the murder. In its turn, that brought a fresh implication.

Maybe the Wednesday "job" had been cancelled, and in its place had been substituted the task of removing Judith Marchand's body from the store.

Slowly, the big man exhaled another lungful of smoke. Follow that possibility, and it led straight to the fact that the man—or woman, for that matter, he corrected himself—who knocked out Phil Moss the night before was almost definitely the strangler who had snuffed out Judith Marchand's life. And if Rose was also in on that job. . . .

It fitted. For if Judith Marchand's body had been got out of the way and safely hidden, she might well have remained the scapegoat in the eyes of the police. Rose's evidence would have helped in that direction. Rose and the other stranger could have

85

been preparing to remove the body when Thane had surprised them.

Colin Thane swore sharply, dropped the half-smoked cigarette to the floor, and ground it under the toe of his brown brogue. He was right back at the old mystery again. How could anyone get a body out of the Hillman building? How could anyone get large quantities of looted goods out of the department store unseen?

'Messing about as usual,' an amused voice cut in on his reverie. 'Come on, Colin, move over. We've got work to do.' Dan Laurence, the Scientific Bureau Superintendent, led his squad in, their arms laden with equipment. Laurence, navy-blue trousers and waistcoat topped by a worn, patched tweed sports jacket, his unkempt tangle of white hair looking as though it had never seen a comb in its long life, took in the situation at a glance. 'Interesting,' he murmured 'very interesting. Makes a change, anyway, from the usual Saturday night knife-in-the-back stuff.' With sardonic, almost brutal humour born of long years on the crime round he cracked, 'Who was she anyway? A dissatisfied customer?'

'A store executive. We were coming round to thinking she had scarpered rather than face a major theft charge.'

Laurence raised quizzical eyebrows. 'Didn't get far, did she? Was that the case you had us running the fingerprint tests on . . . the one that was tied up in the other stuff you sent in early this morning?'

Thane nodded.

'That's not so bad, then. You left a message saying you'd want a squad at Hillman's sometime today, and when the murder flash came in I wondered for a moment if you had second sight. Ah well, back to work, as the actress said to the bishop.' Laurence turned to his waiting squad. 'Mick, get the camera going. General view, then a plain shot for measurements. Move in close to get that hanger arrangement and the scarf round her throat. Bill . . . dust the lot—rails, hanger, her shoes, the door, walls, any ruddy thing you fancy. Take a set of her prints while you're at it. Got the Hoover, Johnny?' The detective

86

constable gave a thumbs-up sign, slid a small hand vacuum from its bag, and looked around for a power point to plug in the long flex.

'Fine,' said Laurence. 'Collect any dust or fibre samples you can in the place. You'll forgive Mr. Thane messing up the floor with his fag. No handbag on her, Colin?'

Thane shook his head. 'Not that I can find. Let's have a look in her pockets, though, Dan.' He slid a hand into the two side-pockets of the woman's jacket and extracted a miscellany of bus tickets and small change. 'That's the lot. Still . . .' He nodded to one of the Bureau men, who produced a small transparent plastic envelope. They placed the pathetic little collection into the envelope, and laid it aside for future labelling.

.   .   .   .   .

The boffin squad had been hard at work for some time when Professor McMaster, the university forensic expert, arrived, his tall, gloomy figure overshadowing his companion, Doc. Williams, the police surgeon. The professor gave a grunt of recognition to Thane, treated his horn-rimmed glasses to a quick polish, and went straight to work, poking and prodding the swaying corpse. Finally, with a soft hiss of satisfaction, he stood back, rubbing his hands.

'We take it she's dead,' said Laurence with poker-faced humour.

The forensic expert shot him a barbed look, then, almost grudgingly, declared, 'She is. I would say she had been for . . . oh, about two days, though the normal stages of rigor mortis and changes in skin tissue can vary in weather like this. Strangulation, of course . . . though, naturally, we'll investigate any other possible cause. Mphh. Very considerable strength used . . . right-handed man . . . note the manner in which the slip-ring on the scarf has been pulled to the left.'

'Any trace of a struggle?' asked Thane. 'I'm really hoping for some sign that she marked her attacker . . . you know the sort of thing, Professor, skin or blood under the nails, blood spots on her dress, anything like that.'

'Difficult, difficult to say,' mumbled McMaster. His beady eyes might already have been dissecting the corpse on the mortuary table, so abstract and intent was their stare. 'All depends on what you mean by a struggle. Have to wait for the post mortem results, really. There may have been another factor, perhaps a sudden secondary attack which would temporarily daze the subject.'

'A bang on the head?' queried Thane.

'That's what I said,' snapped the professor. 'Well, Dr. Williams and I can't really do very much here. I take it you'll be removing the rack and dresses for examination?'

Thane nodded. 'As soon as the lab. men are finished their preliminary work,' he declared.

'We'll be taking the door off its hinges too,' said Dan Laurence. 'The thing's lousy with prints, Colin. Probably nothing to them, but . . .' He shrugged. 'Hey doc, do you want to leave her hanging up there all day? Seems hardly decent.'

'Move her when you want,' said the police surgeon, examining the tightly-drawn scarf with keen professional interest. 'The professor and I can have an early lunch and then get down to work . . . there's really not much we can do here.'

'Mphh . . . good idea,' said McMaster. 'Incidentally, Thane, you appreciate that the deceased was probably ah . . . disposed of outside of this room? Note the faint dust staining the ah . . . seat of the dress. Probably concrete. And the back of the heels of the shoes are scuffed, the nylon stockings badly laddered. I would hazard the opinion—only an opinion, you understand—that the body was dragged by the shoulders some little distance.'

'And then slung up in this fashion,' finished Thane, marvelling for the hundredth time at the nimble-witted analytic ability of the gloomy figure before him. 'It couldn't have been very easy, though, professor, to have lifted her up on to the rail.'

'Problem in simple mechanics. Mphh. As you say, Thane, it would have been difficult with ah—if you'll forgive the pun—a dead weight.' A wintry smile flitted across the professor's face. 'However, it would have been a fairly easy task for two people.'

'Could a woman have strangled her?' pressed the policeman.

'My good man . . . how on earth can I say?' protested McMaster. 'However, looking back over my long years as an expert in the field, I would hazard a negative answer. It would require an exceptional woman to strangle our subject with such force, and an even more exceptional one, unless she had help, to elevate the body sufficiently to attach it to the rail. Now, if the superintendent is finished, perhaps we could ah . . . detach the cadaver from its present position?'

'I'll leave you to it,' said Thane, and thankfully departed from the store-room, to bump almost head-on into Phil Moss. The inspector gave an expressive grimace, and told him, 'Farringdon's climbing the walls. He says he must talk to you about Judith Marchand—and he's just finished giving Rose a bawling-out. I thought he'd clobber the little weasel at one stage.'

'I'll let him get it off his chest in a moment,' said Thane. 'How's the rest of the job going?'

'Pretty smooth,' said Moss. 'One thing, though. Your pal Richards, the doorman, hasn't turned up for work.'

'Any reason that anyone knows?' asked Thane, an uneasy thought suddenly creeping unbidden into his mind, his eyes narrowing.

Moss shook his head slowly. 'We'll need to find him, obviously, because of what he claimed to be on the brink of discovering. It wouldn't be any fun if he was lying around somewhere in the same state as the late Judith Marchand. I've dug up his address through the store records. He lives in "digs" out Maryhill way . . . seems he's separated from his wife.'

'Send a car over to see why he's not on duty,' said Thane. 'Has Sergeant MacLean got the statements from the girls who found the body?'

'Strictly routine,' replied Phil. 'They opened the door, began to count the dresses and there she was. While we're at it, the two men you put to going over her office have almost got through with the job. They've gathered together most of the junk she had lying about, and we can cart it back to the station if you want. I'll get the finger-print boys to concentrate on the desk, etc., once they've finished in the store-room. How'd it go in there, anyway?'

'Old McMaster's licking his lips and sharpening his dissecting knife,' said Thane. 'Still, there's no one to touch him at his job, that's certain. I'll give you the full gen later, Phil. Right now, Farringdon's coming this way under full sail.'

'I'll move,' said Moss. Then, in an afterthought, 'Oh, Headquarters called . . . no prints on the thing I was clattered with last night. But the list of dresses was covered in prints. I said they'd have a set from the body for comparison purposes. The lab. haven't got anything special on the nylons yet, but they say they'll report again later.'

.   .   .   .   .

Charles Farringdon's sixty years sat heavily on his overweight shoulders, and he seemed to have developed a sudden stoop. He blew his nose in a white silk handkerchief, stuffed the square back into his pocket, and asked almost meekly, 'Will you spare me a few minutes, Chief Inspector? Alone, I mean? It's . . . it's rather important.'

'Let's go over to the corner beside that perfume counter,' suggested Thane. They walked slowly across, both silent, both occupied with their thoughts.

Farringdon seemed reluctant to begin, Then, as Thane waited, refusing to make the opening move, the fat man placed both his thick, powerful hands on the counter edge. He stared ahead with unseeing eyes at a tinsel-and-gilt poster display for "Evening in Rome" perfume, and spoke in a slow, halting voice, startlingly different from his natural bellow. 'Rose, our store detective, tells me that you believe Judith was mixed up in the robberies. Is that the case?'

'I wouldn't go as far as that,' said Thane. 'She knew something. She may have been involved . . . but I'd go no further. Rose seems to have been jumping to conclusions.'

'He jumped too quickly,' said Farringdon grimly, gripping the counter edge until the whites of his knuckles showed clear through the skin of his hairy hands.

90

'He told me his version of last night's happenings. . . . I'd already had a full report from Joe Deacon, the night commissionaire . . . and then Rose went on to hint at some other things. I lost my temper—oh, I do that often enough, I know—but this time,' he swallowed, and for a moment Thane could have sworn that tears were close to forming in the store boss's eyes. 'This time, Thane, I could have killed him.'

Farringdon fell silent again. He picked up a lipstick container from the counter, and began to toy with it. Then, with obvious effort, still in that quiet tone, he went on, 'You know that Judith has—had I suppose it should be now—a son in Canada, and that she was saving up to go out and join him?'

'She told me,' agreed Thane.

'Maybe you thought that gave her a good motive, a need for money?' asked the store boss.

'It was something we had to consider,' replied the policeman.

Farringdon shook his heavy, greying head. 'You can forget it. This . . . this isn't easy to tell, Thane. I'm a pretty proud man, perhaps too proud. I dragged myself up by my own bootlaces from a twopenny clerk to be head of this place. If I want something, I usually get it. But I didn't get Judith.

'I loved her, Thane. Now'—he shrugged—'maybe I'm past that sort of thing, but I first became fond of her years ago, before she married. In those days, I was still clawing my way up the business ladder, and I couldn't afford the time to do anything about it. Then her husband was killed . . . drowned off Normandy in the early stages of the invasion. She was left with the baby. Well, I waited a decent interval, then asked her to marry me. She turned me down flat. That hurt, Thane, but I respected her for it, perhaps liked her more than ever. When the boy went out to Canada, I offered to loan her . . . give her, call it what you like . . . the money for her scheme. She wanted a shop of her own. When she wouldn't take the money, I tried to sell her the idea that I could be a silent partner. The offer was always open, she knew that. But . . . well, that's just the sort of woman she was. She wanted to do the whole thing on her own.'

He tossed the lipstick back on the counter. 'Judith didn't

need to rob to get the money, Thane. I'm a fairly rich man. She could have had anything she wanted, and no strings attached.' Tears were unashamedly trickling down his heavy cheeks as he finished.

Thane, suddenly moved by the emotion displayed by the man, laid a hand gently on Farringdon's arm. 'I never did believe it,' he said softly. Then, self-consciously jingling the change in his trouser pocket, he walked away.

.   .   .   .   .

Down at ground level, Hillman's Store faced a new crisis. Half of Glasgow seemed to be trying to press through its doors, eager, curious, sensation-seeking. Mingled with the rubber-necking crowds were reporters and photographers from a dozen different papers. Jock Dodds, crime reporter for the *Evening Hour*, led a press storming-party that reached the entrance to the fashion department, and the photographers managed to bang off a few plates on the general scene before the whole group were repulsed by the Hillman staff.

The pressmen retired a few feet along the landing, buzzing like a swarm of angry bees, then tried again. Voices on both sides raised in anger, and finally the shop's flustered publicity man appealed to Jerry Watford.

'What can I do?' he asked. 'Will I phone their editors, and ask them to keep the story out of print. I could remind them of our advertising contracts . . . think of the harm this will do. It's terrible, terrible.'

'There's not a snowball's chance of keeping this out,' replied Watford. Then, with a rare flash of cynicism, he asked, 'What are you worrying about, anyway? In all probability it'll be the best publicity handout you've ever had to tackle. Women will come flocking into Hillman's after this, just to say they bought their new dress "in the place where that poor soul was murdered". Some of your opposite numbers would give their right arms for a chance like this.'

'But what will I say?' pleaded the publicity man. 'This . . .

this is out of my depth. I've never had anything to do with this sort of thing before.'

Watford shrugged. 'Tell them the police will be making a statement soon, that the store will remain open for business . . . the sale must go on, and that sort of thing. Then let them use your office as headquarters, and lay on a supply of drinks. Now look, who's the publicity expert around here? Dig a couple of bottles out of the board-room stock. These boys can make or break us in a situation like this.' Then, seeing Thane coming out of the room that had been Judith Marchand's office, Watford walked quickly across. He told the policeman of the reporters' activities, and saw a smile flit across the big man's face.

'Someone on your payroll will be a good few quid the richer for the tip-off,' said Thane. 'There's not much you can do about it. These fellows can wriggle in and out of any situation . . . and they're pretty handy sometimes. I'll have a talk with them. They've got a job to do just as much as we have.'

. . . . .

Ten minutes later, Colin Thane held his impromptu press conference in the sixth-floor publicity room. Watford's instructions had been carried out, and the assembled reporters raised interested eyebrows as trays of tea, sandwiches, and, more discreetly, a neat row of glasses were laid out for their use.

'Home was never like this,' murmured Jock Dodds. 'Still, we can ring the changes, and charge a bit more on our expenses.'

'Maybe you can,' complained a colleague. 'Remember the "Barbara" sex-killing? I dropped a clanger that time. Three of us charged a couple of quid each for entertaining the chief suspect . . . all on the same night. Between us it looked as though we'd been recruiting for Alcoholics Anonymous . . . and now I can hardly get an exes sheet passed without a sworn affidavit.'

. . . . .

The conference dragged out. Thane gave a brief sketch of the finding of the body, but avoided all mention of the robberies, though he had only a slender hope that the newsmen wouldn't soon dig up that angle and link the two together. He admitted the difficulties of investigating a murder in a store with a thousand employees and a steady, twenty-thousand-a-day stream of customers.

And he made an appeal. 'We want anyone who saw Judith Marchand at any time after twelve noon on Tuesday, either in or out of the store, to come forward. She may have been at a local post-box at some time just about noon '

'Posting a letter?' queried a young reporter.

'People sometimes do,' blandly parried Thane, amid a low rumble of laughter. 'That's about all I can tell you just now, boys. Tell you what. I'll see you again at two-thirty this afternoon. Make it here again . . . that's in good time for your final editions.'

'Likely to have anything fresh then, Mr. Thane?' queried Jock. 'It's just so I can give the news desk an idea.'

'I'll keep my fingers crossed,' promised Thane, as the pressmen began to disperse. He heard a photographer give a low wolf-whistle, and turned to follow his gaze. Pat Miller was coming across the room, drawing the pressmen's eyes like magnets with her slim yet full figure, her long, chestnut hair brushing the collar of her close-fitting dress of purple silk.

But the girl's face was still flushed, her eyes a faint red that told of recent, quiet tears. She walked straight over to Thane, ignoring the interested, microscopically thorough inspection by the other men in the room. 'Inspector Moss wants to see you right away,' she said in little more than a whisper. 'I offered to find you.'

'I'll come now,' said Thane. 'I'll see you through this pack,' he offered, as the girl hesitated. They walked along the corridor to the lifts. 'What's up? Any idea?' asked Thane.

The girl shook her head. 'No, only that he said it was urgent. Mr. Thane . . .' She gazed earnestly at him. 'I—I just want to say that if there is anything, anything at all I can do to help

94

catch whoever did this, you've only to ask. It's so dreadful . . . I can hardly believe it yet.'

'I won't forget, Pat,' he promised. 'But for the moment, just keep doing your job, and keep your eyes open. Don't take that as a polite refusal. I've a feeling I may need your help before long. And don't worry. We'll get whoever it was, if it's humanly possible.'

Phil was still on the second floor, standing beside the fashion department store-room. 'Glad to see you,' he greeted. 'I've got news for you from the car that went out to Maryhill to locate Richards, the doorman. They've just phoned in. He's vanished. He didn't come home last night, and he hasn't been seen this morning.'

6

THE two detectives detailed to visit Richards' lodgings in Garscube Road made a thorough job of their mission. Richards' landlady, her straggling hair still in tight metal curlers, was as anxious as anybody to know more about the whereabouts of her lodger. 'The devil's two months behind wi' his rent,' she complained. 'If he's away, mister, the quicker you find him the better.' Richards was the only lodger in the three-room tenement house. 'My man and I sleep in the kitchen, and keep the best room,' she explained. 'We aye let the bedroom . . . though you'll no tell the Income Tax folk, will you?'

After a rapid assurance on that point she willingly showed them Richards' quarters . . . a small, untidy place, the walls covered in a faded Victorian paper, a dirty shirt ready for washing thrown carelessly on the shabby linoleum beside the bed, the empty fireplace speckled with burned-out cigarette ends. An enlarged snapshot of Richards, a pint tankard in his hand, was propped against the mantelpiece.

'All his stuff's here, mind you,' she declared, pulling open the doors of the wardrobe. 'First thing I thought was, Jeannie, make sure he's no done a moonlight flittin' wi' his things. But there's his suits an' his shoes.' She scuffed across the floor on worn slippers and pulled open the drawers of the small dressing-table. 'See, shirts, everything. If he doesnae come back, I can aye sell these at the Barrows, or at one of the second-hand shops. He was a polisman at one time, you know. Nothin' personal, mister, but you canna trust the polis like you used to. See here . . .' She pulled a bundle of letters from one corner of a drawer. 'Unpaid bills, the lot of them. I was havin' a look this mornin'. He owes money all over the place—specially to the bookies, Horses! You've never seen a man like him. Mind you, sometimes he got a winner but,' she shook her head, 'more often than not they went doon.'

'Where does his wife stay?' asked one of the detectives, thumbing rapidly through the bundle of bills.

'Och, the poor soul went away back home to her ma doon in London,' said the woman. 'Or at least, so he told me. He's behind in his maintenance payments tae her too. There's a lawyer's letter somewhere about it, but it didnae seem tae bother him much. If you ask me, he'd make a right scunner o' a husband.'

'And the last time you saw him was Wednesday morning?'

'Aye, he left the house as usual yesterday . . . that's one thing I'll say for him, he's aye punctual, except for payin' the rent.'

'How was he dressed?' pressed the policeman.

'Och, let me see . . . oh aye, he'd on his uniform trousers, a sports jacket and a soft hat. He always changed intae his fancy jacket and that skipped cap at the store. He always says he doesnae like travellin' around in his doorman rig-out.'

The detective snapped his note-book shut, quietly lifted the snapshot from the mantelpiece and, as they turned to leave, promised, 'We'll be back. If he does turn up, tell him to contact the police right away.'

'Ah'll tell him,' promised the woman, 'an' ah'll tell him a few other things, too, havin' the polis tramping in an' out of ma house like this.'

.   .   .   .   .

After the two men had telephoned their report to Hillman's and Moss had passed the news to Thane, the chief inspector was definitely worried. That worry considerably increased when a check at the commissionaire's box disclosed that Richards' sports jacket and soft hat were still hanging on their peg. Another of the doormen, in an identical scarlet-and-black uniform, could only tell them, 'He clocked out all right . . . I saw him do it myself, just at closing time last night.'

'Did you actually see him leave the building?'

'Yes, I did. He was standing outside when I left . . . he had an old raincoat over his uniform jacket, even though it was so warm. Andy didn't like going out in uniform . . . I thought it a wee bit queer at the time he hadn't slipped on his sports jacket. Look, sir, why don't you try the pub down the road . . . the Three Sons? He often looked in there.'

Thane glanced at his wrist-watch. 'They're open,' he nodded. 'We'll do that now.'

.   .   .   .   .

The Three Sons was the old-fashioned type of Glasgow pub: sawdust on the floor, a stout brass footrail showing the wear of generations of firmly planted boots, the woodwork everywhere a dark, uninspiringly dull brown oak. There were about a dozen customers round the bar quenching their early-morning thirst, including a trio of Teddy Boys, who perceptibly stiffened as the two detectives swung through the door. The charge-hand, sizing up the new arrivals at a glance, left the rest of the service to his two assistants and moved along to a vacant spot in the long counter.

'Trouble, gents?' he queried. 'This is a nice quiet house . . . can't think what brings you here.'

'Relax,' said Phil Moss. 'We want to ask about one of your "regulars" . . . just a few simple questions.' The Teddies, who had been straining their ears to catch the conversation, hurriedly emptied their glasses and left.

'Do you know a man called Richards?' Thane asked the charge-hand. 'He's a doorman at Hillman's Store.'

'The ex-cop,' said the charge-hand. 'I certainly do. He's in here most days . . . sometimes he has a credit "slate" running.' The genial expression left his face, his mouth went slack for a moment. 'Here . . . has this got to do with the murder up there?

The whole place has been buzzing about a body being found, but it didn't click with me when I saw you come in.'

'Maybe, maybe not,' said Thane. 'Right now, we're just asking questions. How's Richards' slate at the moment?'

'Oh, about fifteen bob or so,' replied the barman, wiping his hands on his grimy apron. 'He was in last night for a bit, and said he'd clear it as usual on Friday. He was expecting a bit of luck to come his way over some deal or other. But look, if he's landed in a jam, he's only a fellow that comes in for a drink as far as I'm concerned.'

'It's just a routine inquiry,' soothed Thane. 'Can you remember how long he was in for last night?'

'Let's see, he'd come in about half-five—just after Hillman's closes, you know—and he had a couple of beers. He left about six. I served him, and I remember him saying he'd need to keep an eye on the clock—he had some kind of a deal on, like I said. Not that I paid much heed. Richards is one of those blokes who, if he hasn't a cert of a horse or a dog lined up to win, is always on the brink of some fiddle or other. Mind you, he's a good enough sport when anything does turn up. Stands his hand with the best of them. Easy come, easy go, that's his way when he gets a break.'

Playing a sudden blind hunch, Thane pushed his hat further back on his head and asked, 'Can you remember whereabouts he was standing last night . . . when he wasn't bellied up to the bar, I mean?'

Moss flashed a quick, curious glance at his tall companion, but kept silent, waiting the charge-hand's answer. The barman frowned again, rubbing the bluing stubble on his chin with one hand, squinted reflectively, then said, 'Over there, I think . . . over by the window.'

'Looking out?'

'Maybe. It's a pretty busy time of the evening, so many blokes are trying to get a quick drink before they go home. I wasn't paying much attention. I just saw him leaving like I told you, round about six o'clock, and thought it was a bit early for him to leave. He'd often hang on till after seven.

'Is that about all, mister?' he asked, looking along the length of the bar. 'We're getting pretty busy now.'

Thane nodded his thanks, and, as the charge-hand got to work the two men strolled over to the window. 'Take a look, Phil,' Thane invited. 'From the window you can see right along Sauchiehall Street to the Hillman corner. Supposing Richards was watching the corner, waiting on someone. Then he spotted his man, and left in a hurry.'

Moss watched the stream of pedestrians constantly passing along the pavement outside the window. It was a first-class viewpoint. 'Okay,' he agreed. 'So now we can take it he was waiting for someone. And from there?'

Thane could only shrug his shoulders in puzzled silence.

.　　　.　　　.　　　.　　　.

They walked back along the busy street, towards the store. A slight, cool south-west breeze gusted along the gutter, scooping a cloud of dust and old tram-tickets along in its arms. The heat-wave was dying. 'Rain before night,' prophesied Thane again, then, as the white flash of news bills caught his eye, 'Let's see what sort of a press we've got . . . and hope for the best.'

The vendor, a wizened, bleary-eyed ex-burglar who had finally "gone straight" after rheumatism had reduced his agility to the almost ludicrous point where he had been unable to out-distance an old woman who caught him rifling her sideboard late one night, waved aside the proffered sixpence. 'Compliments of Willie,' he winked, handing over the first editions of the two evening papers. 'Having a busy time, Mr. Thane, eh?'

'How's the back, Willie?' asked Thane, who had a soft spot for the old lag. . . . Willie had been his first arrest as a C.I.D. officer, two days after he won promotion from the beat. He had been a much more agile Willie in those days . . . but then, mused the detective, Colin Thane had been a bit more streamlined himself.

'Not so bad, sir . . . the sunshine's the best medicine I can

100

get,' said the little newsvendor. 'But business is on the slide. Everybody watches TV now, nobody's got any time left to read papers. If it wasn't for the racing results, I'd be in a bad way, I can tell you!'

'Sell many papers across the way?' asked Thane casually, waving towards the vast, soaring bulk of the Hillman building. 'There's bound to be some of them keen on horses.'

'You're dead right,' chuckled the little man. 'Plenty of them have a flutter, and that goes for the bosses too.'

'Collect any of the lines, Willie?' asked Moss, following Thane's cue. 'Give us it straight, now—we're not interested in "lifting" you for being a bookie's runner, so don't worry.'

The little man hesitated, then somewhat reluctantly agreed, 'A few now and then—just a few, Mr. Moss, an obligement more than anything.'

'How about a bloke called Richards, an ex-cop who's one of the doormen?' fished Moss.

'Him?' Willie showed his opinion by spitting expertly on to the roadway. 'Throws his weight about, that b——. But the bookie's cramped his style. Cash on the nail, it is now, or no bet, till he pays what he owes.'

'Did you see him around last night, Willie?' broke in Thane. 'Think hard.'

The little man turned away to deal with a couple of approaching customers. When he had expertly slid them their papers from the huge bundle he clutched under one arm and had poured the correct change into their palms he faced the detectives again. 'Last night?' he queried. 'Aye, I saw the big basket.' He looked suddenly worried. 'Here, Mr. Thane, you're no askin' me to "grass" on him, are you? He can rot in the nearest sewer for a' I care, but ah canny "grass" on him. Ah've never been a polis stoolie yet, and ah'm no startin' now.'

'I'd hate to run you in, Willie,' said Thane in a soft, quiet voice. 'It can be pretty cold in the cells, even at this time of the year . . . maybe even damp. It wouldn't do your rheumatics any good.'

The little ex-con. gave him a reproachful look, saw the iron-

101

hard purpose in Thane's eyes, and gave a faint shrug. 'It's no your style, Mr. Thane. You must want him pretty bad. All right, ah'll tell you. It was about six, ah'd say. Ah'd just got ma last load of papers for the night, that's how ah mind. And this doorman bloke comes walkin' along as if he owned Sauchiehall Street, an' just about knocks me down; never a word of apology. He was busy bletherin' to someone.'

'Would you know the other man if you saw him again?' asked Thane. 'And can you remember how Richards was dressed?'

The little man shook his head. 'Honest, Chief Inspector, he was just another bloke to me. Ah've never seen him before. Richards now . . . och aye, he was in his doorman's rig-out, an' ah think he had a coat over his arm.'

'All right, Willie,' said Thane. 'And thanks. . . .'

'Mr. Thane . . .' the little man called him back. 'Would you really have jugged me if ah hadn't told you?'

'What do you think?' grinned the big detective.

'Aye, that's what ah guessed,' said Willie ruefully. 'But it's no the sort of chance ah like takin'.'

.   .   .   .   .

They stopped in the shade of a shop doorway to glance at the newspapers. Both "evenings" had splashed the Hillman murder, and the respective reporters had obviously vied with each other to get the most spine-chilling flow of descriptive copy into their stories. *The Hour* had wiped everything else off the front page for their account, and banner headlines led into a by-line piece by Jock Dodds, flanked by a four-column picture of the Hillman building and a single-column block of Thane, "Ace city detective in charge of investigations." Both pictures were obviously dragged from the *Hour* art library to meet the seconds-previous first-edition rush. Thane's photograph showed him in a heavy overcoat—a left-over shot from the villa murders case of the previous winter.

It was lunch-time in the sunbaked city, and Jerry Watford's

102

prophecy was already coming partly true. Hillman's was busier than ever on a basis of people in the actual building . . . but, for the moment, the store staff were finding little difference in actual takings. Most of the "customers" were office staff on their meal break, enticed by the weather and the news of the killing to abandon their normal eating habits in favour of a snack and a stroll down to the store. They seemed content to wander around in off-beat fashion, their primary aim a glimpse of anything resembling a policeman. A constant procession were taking the lifts to the third floor, then walking down the stairs again past the still-closed second floor, managing a quick peep over the shoulders of the police guard before trudging down to ground level again. There was little or nothing to see—but at least they could say they had been there.

For the second time in three days a meeting was in progress in Charles Farringdon's penthouse office. Ranged round his giant desk were the same group as before: Watford, Allen and Rose, Thane and Moss. This time, however, Farringdon was a silent, bitter figure, and it was left to Jerry Watford to answer most of Thane's crisp, fast-delivered questions. Sandwiches and coffee were before each man—except Moss, who had obtained a special dispensation of cold milk and lightly buttered brown bread in deference to his ulcer. The faint, gnawing pain coming from his rebellious stomach was reflected in his slightly drawn face. But when Phil Moss was on a case he would as soon have resigned as allow this mainly nervous reaction to interfere with his normal efficiency. There was no need for his note book, however, and he felt thankful to let it lie in his pocket. A police stenographer sat at a little table to one side, keeping a verbatim record of the conversation.

One corner of his mind keeping a grip of the question and answer exchange, Moss watched the men before him. . . . Farringdon, still obviously emotionally shaken, only the occasional growled interjection showing that the keen brain in his massive head was following the proceedings with rapt intent. Henry Allen, sitting forward on the edge of his chair, eager, nervous, yet his answers reflecting a prim exactitude of phrase

103

somehow different from the chubby little man's outward appearance of bewildered anxiety.

Rose . . . Rose had changed, too. Farringdon's searing rebuff of the morning, coming on top of the previous night's experiences, seemed to have undermined the man's acid, almost vindictive approach—or perhaps he knew he was close to fighting a more personal battle, with his liberty at stake? He was silent, watchful, his eyes flickering from one speaker to another, but always back to Thane—Thane who sat there, impassive, thorough, unnervingly calm, his normal friendly manner submerged, now a calculating, impersonal figure of robot-like efficiency.

And then there was Jerry Watford, cool, calm, completely in command of the situation, a quip always ready on his lips. A highly efficient young man. His girl friend was now head of the women's department: Farringdon had made the on-the-spot appointment that morning, while Judith Marchand's body was still lying in the nearby store-room. However much his personal life had been broken by the murder, Farringdon's long years of deliberate conditioning still kept the store uppermost in his mind.

Thane posed his next question: 'What's the result of this week's stock-check . . . does it show any drop in thefts?'

Farringdon, puffing yet another cigarette, shook his head. Watford, referring to a typed report before him, said, 'Anything but. Total losses are provisionally set at a thousand and fifty pounds—three hundred and fifty above the same week last year. And in that time we've caught only nine shoplifters, despite all the steps we've taken and the additional police you've drafted in. Our final loss figure is almost certainly higher. We can't complete the check in the fashion department until your men are finished in the store-room.'

The disappearing stock followed the same old familiar pattern—clothes, cigarettes, fancy goods, shoes—some light, some comparatively bulky, all far above the accepted shop-thefts level.

Some departments, however, like the Hillman circulating library with its normal sixty-a-week loss of filched novels, showed only the usual seasonal depredations.

'We've tightened up all round,' volunteered Watford. 'But short of searching every man, woman and child that goes in and out of the place, there's little more we can do.'

Allen, perching still further forward in his chair, asked, 'Have you any theory on that point, Mr. Thane? I mean'—he went a little red—'most of us who've talked about this terrible business feel that poor Miss Marchand's awful death is somehow connected with the losses. How can all this stock be getting out? Could there be some secret passage, do you think?'

Farringdon snorted like an angry bull. 'I've seen this place built from the ground floor up. There's damn-all secret tunnels here, Allen. Don't be a fool.'

The little man was profuse in his immediate apologies. 'It was just something that occurred to me, sir, just something I thought I should mention.'

'To be honest, it's as good a suggestion as any other I've heard,' said Thane. 'But it's time we faced up to a couple of what you'll probably find to be unpleasant truths . . . even if you've probably half-guessed them already. The first is that these goods are being stolen in an organized fashion, almost definitely by people working in the store. How do they get them out? Your guess is as good as mine, so far. And the other point is that, as most of you seem to realize, Judith Marchand's death was most definitely connected with these robberies.' He sat back, hands in his pockets, and delivered a final bombshell. 'And that's why, from tonight, there's going to be a police patrol inside and outside this building twenty-four hours a day. Starting tomorrow, every member of the staff from Mr. Farringdon downwards is going to be fingerprinted and interviewed, and will be asked to say exactly where he was on the Tuesday lunchtime and afternoon and last night. Your secret tunnel's out, Mr. Allen. We've already checked with the City Architect's Department, in case there might be an old sewer, a passageway, anything like that leading into the building. There's nothing that would fill your bill.

'Finally, there are certain other measures we're putting into operation. I'm not prepared to tell even you what they will be. The gang will probably lie low after Judith Marchand's death—

105

but just in case they don't I want the element of surprise to be complete.'

'That means you don't trust us, I suppose,' said Watford grimly. 'Do you think one of us in this room is connected with all that has happened?'

James Rose, white-faced, eyes wide and staring, jumped to his feet. 'I'll tell you what he means,' he almost shouted. 'He means that he thinks I did it . . . you all do,' the store 'tec accused the silent circle around him. In the corner, the police shorthand writer kept his pencil moving quickly over the pad.

'Well, I didn't, I didn't, do you hear?' Rose went on, the words tumbling faster and faster. 'I was in her office last night. I went through her desk . . .' His voice broke hysterically. 'I even looked in the fashion department store-room, where her body was, looked in there without knowing she was hanging on that rack.'

Rose stepped forward, bent close to Farringdon over the broad desk top. 'You were right, Farringdon. I didn't like her . . . I hated her, in fact. She was always out to score over me . . . that sweet, kind Miss Marchand that you all liked. This time I was going to score over her . . . and I found the evidence to do it, too.' He paused, drew a deep, rasping breath. The others were still, held amost hypnotized by the frenzy of the man's outburst. Rose turned towards Thane, swallowed hard, and in a more controlled tone declared, 'I did all these things, Thane. But believe me, before God, I didn't kill her . . . I didn't kill her, man . . . I didn't.'

The store detective suddenly spun on one well-polished heel and almost ran to the door. It slammed hard behind him as he left. 'Let him go,' said Thane quietly. 'He couldn't get far anyway. I've had a "tail" on him since he left home this morning.'

.　　.　　.　　.　　.

Leaving Phil Moss to handle the afternoon press conference and supervise the continued C.I.D. work at the store, the chief inspector went by car to Police Headquarters in St. Andrew's

Square. A steady stream of uniform men were leaving the tall grey building, just finished their midday meal in the police canteen and now going back on the beat.

He had to wait about fifteen minutes before Chief Superintendent "Buddha" Ilford, Glasgow's senior C.I.D. officer, was free. Ilford waved him to a big, leather-covered arm-chair in the dusty book-lined room, then slowly filled and lit his pipe while Thane sketched all that had happened. At the end, Ilford sat quietly for a moment, clouds of fragrant smoke rising from his pipe, his eyes fixed on the wall across the room in a blank, far-away stare—a stare that accounted for his city-wide nickname.

Finally, he took the pipe from his mouth to admit, 'It's a stiff one. We've handled all the various requests you made.' Briefly referring to a sheet of paper before him, he went on, 'She had exactly eleven hundred pounds in the bank . . . all in small savings, deposited over several years. Only one account, though of course there could easily be others in different names that we haven't been able to trace. We found the bank-book and some other stuff when we searched the flat. Just in case, we checked every tourist agency, airline office and steamship list, but we weren't able to find a trace of a passage to Canada being booked. As far as we know, she didn't even have a valid passport. The picture angle's a flop, so far . . . you might see if you can locate one, Colin, it would come in pretty handy. Just in case, I've told the lab. staff to take a couple from the body and try to touch them up so that they'll do at a pinch.' He turned over a second sheet of paper. 'This is the Scientific Bureau report . . . it came in just about half an hour ago. The prints taken from the body confirm that the "dabs" found on that warning note were hers. The same prints are plastered all over that list of stolen goods you took from what's-his-name, the shop detective. The Bureau had one of their gen-men examine the writing on that list and compare it with samples of her writing taken from her desk at Hillman's. She wrote the list all right.'

The Chief Superintendent tossed the report across and once more got down to lighting his pipe. Thane went through the typewritten memo slowly, digesting its contents, item by item.

107

'Nothing on that display arm that was used to cosh Phil Moss,' he commented.

'How is he feeling now, anyway?' queried the C.D.S., one broad thumb giving a final tamping to his glowing pipe.

'Bearing up,' said Thane, a twinkle in his eyes. 'Threatening to claim a week's sick leave when we're finished.' He read on down the report. 'Nylons. Slight trace of cellulose varnish dust and other dusts.' He glanced across the table at his superior.

'That could mean anything . . . or nothing,' said Ilford. 'These boffins put their subjects through every kind of test imaginable . . . you should see the equipment requisitions they try to get past the chief constable. It's enough to make your hair stand on end. Some of the stuff they want would make you think they were making H-bombs on the side. Cellulose varnish dust . . .' he shrugged. 'Well, it's there for the record, anyway. These nylons now, they came from her desk, didn't they?'

Thane nodded. 'That's where they probably got the varnish.'

Ilford puffed his pipe and asked, 'Isn't it possible, despite what the store says, that these stockings could have been bought somewhere else . . . or that they could have been samples of new stock she was keeping in her drawer? It seems a bit screwy to me to keep "hot" stuff handy if they were from the goods that were being stolen.'

Thane felt a sudden tingling sensation racing through him. He thumped the desk softly with his fist.

'Did I say something?' asked Ilford, raising a puzzled eyebrow.

'I think you have, sir, I think you have,' declared the younger man enthusiastically. 'We know she had some information about what was going on, Now suppose, just suppose, that these stockings had been bought somewhere else. She was the women's buyer at Hillman's. Maybe there was some marking on them that made her realize they had originally come from Hillman's. That would explain why they were in her desk. Remember the shop assistant whom we arrested when she tried to nobble a suit . . . and what she said about seeing her boss with those blouses? Supposing the same thing had happened again?'

'Corpses can't squeal,' said Ilford softly. 'If some of the gang caught on to her knowledge, well, the rest follows naturally for a desperate man.'

'That's the way I see it,' said Thane. 'I'll pass a teleprinter message to Birmingham and get the police there to have a bash at finding exactly who does get these stockings in this area. And I'll have another look over Judith Marchand's flat tonight . . . with some company.'

Ilford relaxed back in his swivel-chair. 'Glad to be of help,' he commented. 'That brings me to this other plan of yours. I've given the okay for the extra men needed to carry out this mass interviewing and fingerprinting at Hillman's. But I hope it's being emphasized that the whole matter is purely voluntary. Exactly what are you hoping to gain from it?'

'I've two reasons, sir. The first is practical, the second purely psychological. We've found a mass of fingerprints in that store-room and in her office. We want to know just where we stand with them all. And you never know what might turn up in the interviews. It's a big job, but I think it comes under the heading of inescapable routine under the circumstances. And secondly,' a slow grin came across his face. 'Secondly, it may put the killer, whoever he is, into a sweat. And when that happens, as you know, more often than not they make that little slip.'

'There's still no sign of this man Richards?'

'No, sir. Mind you, I don't think he's the man we're really after. But he may be tied in with the gang in some way . . . I got the feeling he was ready to "rat" if he could have seen some money coming.'

'Or he may have tried to put some "squeeze" on them and been put out of the way,' suggested Ilford. 'Put out an all-stations call for him—"wanted for questioning" will do, though we'd better not link it with the murder in any way yet. Then, as I said, see if you can get a picture of this Marchand woman. If we could get the papers to run it—and they'd grab the chance, I've had two art editors, a news editor and Lord alone knows how many others pleading for one—we might get a line from the public. Have a bash at the picture anyway, Colin. Keep in close touch . . . and the best of luck!'

'I'll need it,' said Thane ruefully, as he rose to leave.

.   .   .   .   .

He'd been right about one thing anyway—the weather—he told himself as the divisional car sped back along the road to Sauchiehall Street, and the department store. The first faint specks of rain dropping from the clouded sky built up rapidly on the windscreen. By the time the car drew up it was bucketing down, and he made a quick dash across the pavement to the shelter of the building. Thane gave a quick nod to the plain-clothes man standing patiently on duty at the main door, stopped to buy a packet of cigarettes at the tobacco kiosk, then threaded his way through the busy food counters to the lifts. He just managed to squeeze into the first "Up" cage. It stopped at the first floor, then swept past the second, to stop at the third— he'd momentarily forgotten his own suggestion that the second-floor gates should be locked. The third-floor lift doors opened out on the fringe of the shoe department. On an impulse, he went along to the counter where he'd noticed the display of boys' football boots during the previous night's search. The boots were still there . . . and appeared pretty good value for money.

When he continued his journey a couple of minutes later, he had a pair of size four boots in a brown paper parcel tucked under one arm . . . his young son was in for a pleasant surprise.

With a police guard at either end and the floor staff transferred to other departments, the fashion section was almost deserted. But the faint hum of voices was coming from the frosted-glass box that had been Judith Marchand's office. Aided by Pat Miller and a young plain-clothes man, Phil Moss sat surrounded by boxes of time-clock cards, flipping through them one by one. A large pile of rejects showed that the job had been in progress for a good many minutes.

'Found anything yet, Phil?' asked Thane.

The inspector shook his sandy head. 'Nothing desperate.

110

There's about twelve so far who punched out late on the Tuesday afternoon, another dozen or so who seem to have been working late last night for half an hour or so, and a few off sick. I'll put a couple of men to work checking on the absentees' homes when I'm finished, We've got Andy Richards' card, by the way, He punched out right on time last night.'

Pat Miller, seated beside Moss, laid down another bundle of the brown time-cards and asked, 'Are you really going to interview everybody in the store? Jerry was telling me, and Mr. Moss says you are . . . but surely it will be a tremendous size of a task?'

Thane shook his head. 'There's not much to it, really,' he declared. 'We can take a full set of fingerprints in two or three minutes. And a trained man with a short list of key questions can get through a considerable number of interviews per hour. There's a team of men coming tomorrow to start the job, as I told Jerry and the others. I'm planning on the whole business not taking more than three days.'

The girl did some rapid mental arithmetic. 'A thousand sets of fingerprints. Why, doing that could take a couple of days, easily, even working right round the clock.'

'We'll have six men taking prints,' explained Thane, 'and the same number interviewing, Nobody needs to worry about the fingerprinting business. You can tell anyone who complains that as soon as we've finished this case we'll destroy the lot.' He looked round the bare walls of the little office. 'Remember we couldn't find any picture of Judith at her flat, Pat? We're still very anxious to find one. Have you any idea where we could try?'

The girl shook her head slowly. 'No . . . I don't think so. Jerry had one, a group of us he took on a staff outing. But I had a look at it, and you can hardly make Judith out in it.' One hand played idly with her hair for a moment, then she said, 'Unless . . . maybe we could try Mrs. Allen. She might have one.'

'Henry Allen's wife?'

Pat nodded. 'That's right. She went to school with Judith, and they've always been quite friendly. Wait a minute, I'll look

111

up the telephone book and see . . . no, I can't. Your men took it away with all the other stuff.'

'We'll get another,' said Thane. He turned to the constable, still painstakingly ploughing through his bundle of time-cards. 'Scout up a phone-book, Jim, will you?'

The man returned with one in a few minutes, and Pat quickly found the address—Viaduct Road, in the well-to-do northerly suburb of Bearsden. Thane scribbled the address on the back of his cigarette packet. 'I'll take a run out there now,' he said. 'Will you be₀at home tonight, Pat? We'll want your help in a job I'm planning . . . I want to tidy up a few points.'

'I was going out with Jerry,' said the girl, 'but that was before . . . before they found Judith. I'll be at home.'

'Thanks,' said Thane. 'Oh, and Phil——'

'I know,' said Moss. 'Hold the fort till you get back. Before you go, Mary telephoned. She wondered if you'd be home for a meal this evening. I said we'd both be there at seven. Er . . . she just happened to say that it was a while since she had seen me, and, well, I said I'd just come along for a blether.'

'You were out seven days ago, and we had boiled fish in your honour,' said Thane sourly. 'What'll it be tonight? Milk pudding?'

.   .   .   .   .

Henry Allen's house was a large, comfortable, but rather old-fashioned stone villa set well off the main road. A magnificent display of tea-roses flanked the pathway up to the main door, bounding a patch of weed-free, gloriously green lawn. Thane thought of his own dried-up, daisy-sprinkled grass and envied the time and care that was obviously devoted to the house garden.

Gwynneth Allen was a fat, friendly woman in her late forties. A large, equally fat but not particularly friendly Persian cat slid unwillingly from its comfortable place on one of the two arm-chairs as the woman ushered Thane into the lounge. 'Would you like some tea?' she asked as Thane sat down on the chair, watched by the frankly insolent cat. 'I'll just slip the kettle on . . .'

'No, thanks, Mrs. Allen,' smiled Thane. 'I'll only take up your

112

time for a minute or two. You know what's happened at the store, of course?'

'Oh yes, it's . . . it's terribly shocking.' The smile had left her face, her bright blue eyes were already clouding. 'Henry telephoned me with the awful news and then the gardener showed me an early paper with the story in it—he always buys the paper, to watch his stocks and shares or something.'

'The gardener?' queried Thane.

'He comes twice a week,' explained Mrs. Allen. 'Poor Henry has to work late so often, sometimes two or three nights a week. Tell me, Mr. Thane, don't you think that man Farringdon is an absolute slave-driver . . . my Henry never seems to get a moment's peace any more, always having to work late or go to this meeting or another.'

'He sets a pretty stiff pace, from all I hear,' agreed Thane.

'A stiff pace,' echoed the woman. 'My poor Henry comes home exhausted after a day there. Mind you,' she fluttered her eyelashes in a way that might have been coy when she was some twenty-five years younger, 'I'm sure you wouldn't say a thing about what I've told you. It might reach Mr. Farringdon, and then my Henry would get into trouble.'

'Rely on me,' assured Thane hastily. 'You were a pretty close friend of Judith, weren't you.'

'Yes, the poor dear. Who could do such a thing, Superintendent? She was such a sweet woman.'

'You went to school together?' persisted Thane.

Gwynneth Allen agreed. 'We went to Rowan Bank. We were in the same class, actually. I was just saying to Sam, the gardener, I couldn't imagine anyone less likely to be murd——'

'I understand,' Thane interrupted desperately. 'Do you have a picture of her, Mrs. Allen? A recent one, I mean.'

'Oh. A picture. Yes, I should have some. She stayed here, you know, just after her husband was drowned. She had no relatives of her own in this country, and with the baby coming . . . well, it was the least Henry and I could do for a friend. She was here for several months. Then she insisted on putting the baby into a day nursery, and going back to work at Hillman's.

And, of course, we've seen a lot of each other since.' She dabbed delicately at her eyes with a wisp of handkerchief. 'A picture . . . now I wonder . . .' She opened the flush-surfaced door of a wall cupboard and rummaged about in its shelves, while the cat and Thane exchanged wary glances.

'Ah, here we are.' The woman swung round, the cupboard door bounding back as it received a blow from one well-padded hip. She came across the room with a large album in her hands. 'Now, let me see. Henry and I at Largs. Henry and I at Loch Lomond. Oh, and the cat show. There's Ladyfair . . . isn't it a lovely picture of her, Superintendent?'

The cat looked no better in the black-and-white print than in its real, sharp-clawed life, decided Thane, But the woman, ignoring his pointed silence, kept turning the pages and giving a running commentary on the carefully mounted photographs.

'Here we are,' she finally declared. 'I knew we had some recent pictures of Judith. Look, Henry took these in the garden last summer. She looks so happy, the poor dear.' Her eyes blinked as tears began to swell up in them again. 'I . . . oh dear, Superintendent, whatever will you think of me being so silly. But my poor Judith . . .' She dabbed vigorously again with the handkerchief.

'Do you mind if I borrow these two?' asked Thane, pointing to a pair of snaps of the dead woman, standing beside a cluster of rose bushes.

'You're very welcome to them,' said Mrs. Allen. 'But you will let me have them back, won't you . . . ? I want a reminder of her, always.'

Thane collected his hat, resisted the temptation to wipe the supercilious smirk off the cat's face by giving it the toe of his boot as he went past and, feeling limp, finally escaped after a final good-bye at the front door. 'Poor dear Henry,' he muttered as he walked back down the pathway. 'Strewth, that woman would drive me round the bend in a week, heart of gold or not.' He took another envious look at the well-kept grass. 'Bringing in a gardener . . . huh, cheating.'

The quietly humming police car radio was just finishing a

114

special search message concerning a stolen car as he climbed back aboard the Jaguar. 'Hillman's again,' he ordered, and settled back in comfort as the saloon purred to life and slid away from the kerb. The sun had come out from behind the short-lived rainclouds, and the pavements were drying fast, sucking any moisture they could into their bone-dry depths before the warm rays vapourized it completely.

Those few hours of sleep he had had were beginning to tell on him, he realized, yawning. Still . . . he shook his head, blinked, and concentrated firmly, racking his brain over the many facets of investigation already under way, trying to think of any possible angles as yet uncovered.

The bark of the police radio cut in on his thoughts. 'Car 23 . . . come in 23.'

'That's us, sir,' said the driver.

'Okay.' Thane picked up the hand-microphone, pressed its sending button, and replied, 'Hello control. Thane here in 23. Pass your message. Over.'

'Hello 23. Return to Millside immediately please. Message from Detective Inspector Moss. Over.'

'Roger, over and out,' replied Thane, automatically. He tossed the hand-mike back on to its shelf, and met the driver's questioning gaze. 'You heard,' said Thane. 'Put your boot down . . . hard. That sounds like trouble to me.'

. . . . .

Two irate bus drivers, an annoyed old lady and a half-dozen amber traffic signals later, the Jaguar swept into the courtyard of Millside police station. Thane was out of it and sprinting into the station building almost before the police driver had switched off his engine.

The duty officer at the bar glanced up as the swing door flew open and called, 'Mr. Moss is upstairs, sir . . .' then gave an appreciative, somewhat envious grin as the chief inspector sped on his way. He turned back to his ledger with a sigh. Totting up lost property might be a peaceful change from the beat, and have

115

regular hours, but these C.I.D. glamour boys certainly had all the fun in life.

Phil Moss was out in the main C.I.D. room, busily telephoning, as were two other detectives. Thane listened to the monotonously one-sided end of the conversation. 'Yes . . . yes . . . no. I've got that . . . are you sure? Two miles past? Okay. Right . . . you've got the man that found it standing by still? Right . . . we'll be down soon.' Moss gave a final "cheerio" and hung up.

He looked up at Thane, a curious mixture of humour, dismay and eagerness on his face. 'It's getting monotonous, I know,' he declared, 'but we've got another body on our hands. That was Lanarkshire police. I got the first call at the store, and came straight back to do the rest from here, after asking the radio boys to call you in. A coalman was taking a short-cut home along the railway near Bishopbriggs, and found that someone had laid his neck down on the rails . . . very neat, the train wheels took his head off clean as a whistle. The body was in a black and scarlet uniform, and there were letters in the tunic pocket addressed to Andrew Richards.'

7

GENERALLY speaking, the suburb of Bishopbriggs is synonymous with peace and quiet . . . a village to the north-east of Glasgow long since swallowed up by its mighty neighbour city, and now linked by an unbroken line of building. But its inhabitants, city business men and office workers for the most part, still like the fact that their postal address is "county" as distinct from Glasgow . . . even if the nearby Lanarkshire boundary line means they pay higher rates for the privilege.

Snaking through the suburb, carried by a shallow cutting most of the way, then suddenly rearing up on to an embankment, the sweeping path of the railway drives its parallel ribbons of shining steel rail through grass- and weed-lined verges, tunnelling under the main road for a moment as it holds its course out towards the open country.

Close to the bridge, only a few hundred yards inside the Lanarkshire county boundary on the one side and from "the 'Briggs" police station on the other, sufficient strange activity was in progress to tempt many a local housewife to peep from her window, or suddenly decide on a message which would take her past the three cars parked just off the main road . . . two police Pathfinders and a shabby little Morris saloon with a "Doctor" sticker on its windshield.

Thane's Humber pulled in behind the other vehicles, and a uniformed Lanarkshire constable, the proud eagle badge of the county force shining bright on his cap, saluted as the two men walked towards him.

'Down the side of the cutting there, sir,' he said, waving

towards the nearby line. 'Then head along the track about forty yards to the right. Superintendent Bryanston is down there now with the C.I.D. . . . it's just at the tunnel mouth.'

Thane and Moss scrambled down the grass slope, stepped over the signal wire on to the ballast track, and saw a small group of men gathered at the side of the line a little way along the rails. A stout, burly man in a grey pin-stripe suit and brown Homburg hat came to meet them as they walked down the line.

'Afternoon,' he greeted. 'Chief Inspector Thane? I'm Bryanston . . . local Super., for my sins. You made good time coming out.' They exchanged a quick handshake.

'This is Inspector Moss . . . you spoke to him earlier,' said Thane. 'You've probably gathered we're very interested in this body you've landed.'

'You're welcome to it,' grunted Bryanston. 'I've got a ruddy load of work on my hands without Glasgow starting to dump surplus cases in my parish. I was tempted to have the lads drag it down the line over to your side of the county boundary when I heard about it. Come and have a look,' he invited.

The headless corpse had been left exactly as found. Lying about twelve feet inside the mouth of a short tunnel, the body had been jerked a good couple of feet away from the side of the rails by the sheer impact of the engine wheels, which had severed the neck with all the neat force of a guillotine. Richards had been lying with his body hunched in the space between the outer rail and the tunnel wall. His severed head had rolled and bounced like a grotesque football down the sleepered track, hitting the underside of the fast-moving train more than once, to judge from its battered, torn flesh. It now lay to one side of the line, a chalked cross on the permanent way marking where it had been found. The task was not easy, but the smashed features were just discernible as those of Andy Richards.

Thane felt his stomach give an involuntary heave at the sight. 'That's enough to get on with,' he said, turning away. 'Any idea what happened.'

'There's a note addressed to you . . . found it in one of his pockets,' said the Lanarkshire man. He turned to an aide, who

118

handed over a small white envelope, still sealed. Thane tore it open, and pulled out the single sheet of paper it contained. He whistled softly as he read the letter.

'Listen,' he invited:

'DEAR MR. THANE, I'M TAKING THIS WAY OUT BECAUSE IT WON'T BE VERY LONG BEFORE YOU FIND THAT I DID FOR JUDITH MARCHAND. I KNEW SHE WAS IN ON THE STORE THEFTS, AND TOLD HER SO JUST AFTER THE STORE CLOSED. SHE WAS SHAKEN, AND THEN LIKE A FOOL I MADE A PASS AT HER. SHE STARTED TO SCREAM, AND I HAD TO SHUT HER UP. THEN I JUST LOST MY HEAD, AND THE NEXT THING I KNEW SHE WAS DEAD. THIS WAY EVERYTHING'S SQUARED UP.

Andrew Richards.'

'Let's see,' asked Moss.

Thane handed over the letter. 'Printed in block letters except for the signature,' he said. 'Anything else on him?'

'Usual papers,' said Bryanston. 'Wait a minute . . . might be something to compare the writing.' He thumbed through a small bundle of envelopes, enclosed in an old leather wallet. 'Old identity card,' he grunted. 'There's a signature on it.'

Thane compared the two. 'Identical,' he admitted.

'If the signature's anything to go by, he probably printed the rest to make it more legible,' said Moss.

'When was he found, Superintendent?' asked Thane.

'There's umpteen trains a day pass on this line,' said the Lanarkshire man. 'The body was found at two this afternoon. But it could have been lying for long enough. Anything lying here is out of sight of the main road, and your pal was too close to the track to be seen by any train passenger. As for engine crews . . . I don't give a darn what British Railways say, there's precious few train drivers who have time to watch the scenery they pass on the way. They're too busy with signals and such-like. And as for a body in a tunnel . . .' He shrugged.

A young, fair-haired man, dressed in blazer and flannels and sporting a Glasgow University tie, was standing near, talking to another man, whose blackened face, dirty clothing and muscular build made his job in life an easy matter to guess.

'Doctor McGuinness,' introduced Bryanson, 'and this lad is Joe Merrol . . . he found the body.'

The young medico could add little. 'He's been lying here for a good few hours, I'd say, judging by the body temperature and the congealed state of the blood that's spattered around. That's a job for the experts . . . maternity cases are more in my line.' He sighed. 'These suicides always amaze me. . . . There's so many simple, quiet ways of slipping away from life, and they keep choosing the worst they can find.'

'There's plenty in what you say, if it was suicide,' nodded Thane.

The young doctor flushed. 'Well, why not suicide?' he asked. 'Is there any reason to think that it's anything else?'

'There's a note,' agreed Thane. 'But he could have been bumped on the head and dragged down.'

The doctor rubbed his downy chin. 'Why write the note, then?' he asked. 'You're suggesting murder . . . but it would be one devil of a job to prove, even if it was the case. His head's not a pretty sight, to put it mildly. And it's got more fractures in the skull than I've got National Health patients.'

Joe Merrol, beads of sweat washing narrow channels down the coal-dust on his face, a piece-tin clutched in one massive hand, shuffled his heavy boots awkwardly. 'There was a goods train went past just before ah got here,' he volunteered.

'You found him about two o'clock, didn't you, Joe?' asked Thane.

'Aye, that's right, sir,' said Merrol. 'Ah was goin' home to Springburn for a bit of food, an', well, this is trespassin' fair enough, but it saves me a helluva long walk round to the tram stop. It fair shook me, mister, ah can tell you, seein' him just lyin' there. Ah ran up to the nearest house, and phoned the polis from there.'

'Did you come down this way in the morning, Joe?'

'No. A pal gave me a lift on his motor-bike,' replied the coalman.

120

'But wouldn't other fellows maybe use the same short-cut?'

The coalman grinned awkwardly. 'Better ask the polis,' he suggested.

Bryanston nodded. 'The railway company have been complaining about trespassers quite a bit lately. We had a couple of men pretty busy here all last week, and nailed quite a few. We'd probably have booked Joe too . . . but we'll forget about it under the circumstances.'

Thane turned back into the gloom of the tunnel, and, ignoring the rust-red splashes of dried blood coating the sleepers and ballast and the lower parts of the rail, took a closer look at the headless corpse. Richards' uniform jacket—by a freak, the collar, though saturated in blood, was uncut—had been opened by the police, and a small collection of change, a penknife, a cheap ballpoint and a bundle of keys lay nearby.

'Nothing else apart from the wallet?' he asked.

The Lanarkshire superintendent shook his head. 'Not a sausage. And we were pretty thorough, especially when I checked with headquarters at Hamilton and found that Glasgow were on a pretty special look-out for this fellow. The note ruled out a lot of worry, however . . . though it's a bit odd it being printed, isn't it?'

'Aye, it is strange,' mused Thane. He picked the pen from the little pile of belongings, and flicked the point down with his thumb. 'Well . . . look at this!' He ran the ball-point over the palm of his hand. 'Red ink. Let's have another look at that suicide note,' he brought the envelope out of a pocket as Bryanston came closer, puzzled. 'See what I mean? The note was written with a blue ball-point. Yet Richards only has a red ink pen in his pockets. Why the different colour? And where has the other pen disappeared to?'

'Maybe he wrote the note at work, or at his lodgings, and left the other pen there,' said Bryanston slowly. 'That's just a suggestion, though. The more you think of it, there's something wrong.'

'Look at the signature again,' said Thane. 'It's a job for an expert, of course . . . but compare it with the signature on that identity card. It's too alike in exact length. The card's years old, yet the signature matches perfectly. Most people find their signature changes slightly with the years.'

'A copy?' suggested Phil Moss, who had been listening intently. 'Is that what you're hinting at, Colin?'

Thane nodded. 'A phoney note. It may be hard to prove it actually is a phoney, though the lab. boys can "blow up" both signatures and look for flaws. But it seems phoney enough to me to make me rule out suicide. Anyway, leave that for the moment. Any ideas about how he got here, either walking or being carried?'

'Not the slightest,' said Bryanston. 'We hadn't got round to thinking much about that. But if being carried is in your mind, there's a quiet patch of waste ground about sixty yards away, where a car could have been driven in off the road.'

'Let's follow it along,' suggested Thane. 'Can you bring a couple of men with you?'

'Easy enough,' said the superintendent. 'They're standing around like so many sheep at the moment, and if they're like me, they're getting a bit sick of watching the flies gathering around that body. Macdonald . . . Gibson, come and lend a hand.'

Two shirt-sleeved policemen followed Thane, Moss and the superintendent back along the line. Why was it, thought Moss as he stalked along, that railway sleepers are always laid just that few inches short of anybody's normal stride? Behind him, one of the local men stubbed his toe and gave a muffled curse.

Bryanston held up his hand suddenly. They stopped, and next moment he waved them clear of the line. 'Train coming,' he declared. The faint vibrating whine drew louder and then, with a rush and a roar, an express came thundering through the nearby tunnel towards them, passing in a hissing, rumbling clatter of wheels and sun-glinting carriage windows. The very ground seemed to shake at its passing.

'You know, if it was suicide, it would take a bit of nerve just to lie on that rail and wait for a train coming,' remarked Bryanston. 'You'd feel the vibration in your throat for a good half-minute before, then . . . clonk!' He stared back down the

122

line in open, morbid fascination, then shrugged and said, 'Another few yards yet.'

They had to scramble up the side of the cutting again, seizing long tufts of the wild grass and weeds to aid their progress. Then they were standing on the waste patch.

'Your show, Thane,' said the Lanarkshire man. 'Want us to spread out and search, I suppose?'

'That's the idea, Superintendent,' agreed Thane. 'You and I can take the centre, while the rest check the edges.'

'Fair enough,' nodded Bryanston. 'Let's get started.'

Slowly, they began to pace through the patchy grass, eyes fixed on the ground. 'Reminds me of looking for a ball in the rough,' remarked the super. 'Play much golf, Thane?'

'When I get the time,' replied Colin, stooping to take a closer look at a glinting object . . . just the edge of a smooth, sharp stone projecting from the soil. 'But that ruddy garden of mine keeps me busy. Plays the devil with my swing on a drive, too . . . uses all the wrong muscles.'

'Got a nice stretch of jungle at home myself,' said his companion. 'But my two boys keep it reasonable . . . they've got to, or their pocket money is docked . . . oy, oy, what's this?' He bent down, parting the grass gently. A small vest pocket comb lay there, clip end down. Kneeling beside him, Thane read the printed lettering on its side: "James Baillie, commission agent. Safe bets."

'His?' queried the superintendent.

'Probably,' nodded Thane, slipping the comb into a small plastic envelope. 'He was a betting man . . . we can pretty easily check if he had one like it. And it certainly points to his having come this way.'

'If he was carried over someone's shoulder, and the comb slipped from his pocket, that would account for it being here,' mused the superintendent. 'Pity the ground's like rock. Not a hope of finding car tracks. And the grass isn't thick enough or high enough to show a clear trail.'

For twenty minutes they searched the area without further reward. Then, temporarily, they gave up. Leaving arrangements for the body's removal to the Lanarkshire police—Bryanston willingly agreed to Thane's request for a full-scale P.M., and that the Glasgow force's scientific bureau, often used by the County, should have a free hand—Thane and Moss returned to the oven-like interior of the Humber, which had been lying baking in the sun.

'I'll have men interviewing round the area on a saturation scale,' promised the Lanarkshire man as they stepped into the car. 'If anyone saw or heard anything out of the usual, we'll find him. On the surface, I'd written it off at first as a rather complicated suicide . . . but with the background you've got to him, well, I think the odds are you're right, and it's murder.'

.   .   .   .   .

Murder . . . or suicide? A cleverly, in fact diabolically, planned killing was on the cards, thought Thane as the Humber purred in through Springburn towards the city, every window open. But assumptions don't stand up in police reports, or in court hearings. On the face of it, unless the suicide note could be proved a fake, Andy Richards could have gone into the cutting and could willingly have laid his neck down on the bright metal of the line, to die in one blood-red revolution of an engine wheel. The handwriting experts, the forensic medicine specialists, might between them gather a different story from the information before them. They held the key.

Murder, or suicide? The more definite answer lay in the scattered, still uneven jigsaw pieces of Andy Richards' movements on the Wednesday night from the item the little newsvendor has seen him walk away with the stranger.

Richards' death had to tie in with Judith Marchand's murder. Both, somehow, were connected with the Hillman robberies. Crack the mystery of any one, and the other two should become solvable equations.

'Muttering away to yourself won't help,' said Phil Moss. The wiry little inspector had finished his notes, and was leaning back against the window, a gloomy expression on his sun-

124

reddened face. 'Want me to start a probe into Richards' background?'

'You'd better,' nodded Thane. 'And have a couple of men trying to trace him from the time he was seen by Willie the newsvendor.'

'Going to bring the papers into it?'

Thane pursed his lips, obviously undecided. 'They'll have a Roman holiday with the story. They're bound to hear of it eventually . . . though we could sit on it for as long as possible. No, I've got it . . . we'll ask Lanarkshire just to list it in their book in a straightforward fashion: "Andrew Richards, retired policeman, found dead on the line." Blast, that won't do either. We'll have to come more or less into the open. Tell them that the Hillman doorkeeper has been found dead, but say that it looks like suicide. There's no lie in that . . . on the surface, anyway, whatever we believe. When's the next press conference fixed for, anyway?'

'Nine-thirty tonight, at Millside,' said Moss.

'They'll be lucky. There's a fair amount of work to be gone through before then,' declared Thane. 'First, though, we'll head out to Southwood, and have a break at my place for that meal. It's early yet, but Mary'll be able to cope—and I don't want to let her down two nights running.'

Minutes after eight that evening, two police cars drew up outside the Hillhead tenement that had been Judith Marchand's home. From the first came Thane, Moss and Pat Miller. They had picked up Pat at her mother's house in Shawlands while on their way back into the city from Southwood. Two figures stepped from the second car . . . first came a uniformed policewoman, then, reluctantly, out climbed Jenny Rey, the young shopgirl still awaiting sentence. The policewoman held her by one arm in a light but sure grip.

Up the cool, shadowed stairway they went to the first floor. A rough piece of boarding had been fitted in place of the smashed glass in the door. Thane rang the bell, and in immediate response a C.I.D. man, one of a team who had been maintaining a day-and-night duty in the flat, opened the door. He stepped back to let them enter.

'All quiet,' the detective reported laconically. 'Just the mail—a couple of soap coupons and this . . .' He handed over a blue air-mail letter form. 'It came with the afternoon post.'

'Canada,' said Thane. He turned the envelope over, and read the sender's address on the back: ' "From William Marchand, c/o Box 8, Lakeview Highway, Toronto . . ." That'll be her son, poor little devil.' He opened the letter and skimmed through its contents while the others waited. When he finished, there was a suspicion of a misting in his eyes. 'Just a kid's letter home,' he commented. 'I sent off a cable to the Toronto police this morning. He's probably been told by now.' He hoped the Toronto cops had been kind . . . the Marchand boy was only a few years older than his own boy.

'I'd like to write to him myself,' said Pat. 'But somehow . . .' she raised her hands in an expressive little gesture of helplessness. . . . 'somehow, I just don't know what to say.'

'Writing that kind of letter's one of the most difficult things anyone can tackle,' he agreed. 'Well, let's get down to business.' They trooped after him into the lounge of the flat, its comfortable furnishings somehow lifeless and empty, waiting without purpose.

'Sit down,' he invited. 'I want to explain why we're here.' Thane waited until they were settled . . . Moss and Pat in facing armchairs, Jenny and her policewoman escort side by side on the couch.

'Jenny, you told me that you'd seen a couple of blouses lying on Miss Marchand's desk one night. That was the time you went back just after the store had closed. You also said you could recognize them anywhere.' He gazed inquiringly at the quiet shopgirl, her face scrubbed bare of makeup, her eyes swollen from repeated weeping.

She licked her lips, and agreed, 'I did, and I can, mister. I wanted one myself, that's why I'm so certain.'

'All right. You'll stay here with the policewoman, and we'll

126

try and find these blouses . . . they weren't in Miss Marchand's office.' He turned to Pat Miller. 'You and I and Inspector Moss are going to rake through Judith's clothing.' The girl's face whitened a little, but he went on, 'Maybe it isn't the happiest of jobs to ask you to do, but it's got to be done. You said you wanted to help . . . now's your chance. And while you're at it, I want you to keep your eyes open for any other stuff that might . . . I said might . . . have come from Hillman's.'

Leaving Jenny and her escort, they walked through the hall to the tiny bedroom, with its gay, cherry-coloured woodwork and bright feminine fittings. Methodically, they got to work, Thane taking the wall cupboard, Moss the dressing-table, and Pat slowly, almost unwillingly, beginning to inspect the closely packed contents of the wardrobe.

The girl's hands moved slowly through the clothes . . . coats and costumes, that new summer dress that Judith had bought and would now never wear, the bottle-green evening dress she had on at the last store dance . . . she felt a sudden flood of emotion sweep over her as the faint, wafting scent of the dead woman's favourite perfume, a light but lingering French concoction, reached her nostrils. Half a dozen blouses were hanging together in the right-hand corner of the wardrobe. She lifted them out bodily, hangers and all, made another, final check through the rest of the clothing, and turned to Thane.

'These?' she asked dully.

Thane came across, and took the blouses. 'We'll try them,' he declared. 'You keep on, Phil.' He went back into the lounge, and threw the blouses down on the couch. 'Are they there?' he demanded.

Jenny flipped through the six, and shook her head. 'Nothing like them,' she declared.

'You're sure?'

'Honest, Mr. Thane,' she assured him. 'But I did see them, just like I said, lying on her desk in that office.'

'The dressing-table's "clean", Colin,' reported Moss, re-entering the room. 'Here, girl, are you sure these blouses ever existed?'

127

'Try this room,' said Thane. They spread out, searched cupboards and drawers . . . and drew another blank.

'But I did see them at the office,' protested Jenny, rising from her seat, one arm still held by the alert policewoman. 'Maybe they aren't here, Mr. Thane, but I did see them, honest.'

'I'll try the kitchen,' offered Pat. 'Oh . . . I've just thought of something. I didn't look at the foot of the wardrobe. That's where I often throw stuff at home.'

Thane followed her back into the bedroom, and propped his burly figure against the door-frame. 'Where's Jerry tonight?' he asked, as she opened the double doors of the wardrobe again and knelt on the carpet beside it.

'I'm not sure,' she replied, in a tone so patently disinterested that it defeated its own ends. 'He said he was going out on his own, but I didn't bother to ask . . . there's quite a few things down here, Mr. Thane. . . .'

'Been having words with him?' asked Thane, trying hard to smother his amusement. '. . . just have a look through them all, Pat.'

'I don't know how you got that idea,' she said stiffly, half-turning towards him. The sudden movement caught her dress by surprise, and swept a long length of smooth, slim leg into view. Unconcerned, she smoothed her skirt and, head turned to the wardrobe once more, told him, 'Jerry just didn't seem to understand that I couldn't come out tonight . . . he'd made a special arrangement for us to meet some out-of-town friends of his.' She began rummaging again.

Tiredness was stealing up on Thane again. With any luck, he thought, I'll manage home before midnight . . . unless something turns up concerning Andy Richards. If it did, he almost hoped it wouldn't happen until morning. Sure, it was a double murder he had on his hands . . . but things were at a slow, ticking-over stage. . . .

The girl gave a little cry of surprise . . . and then hard on its heels gave a soft gasp of pain.

'What's up?' he asked, moving quickly across the room to her side.

128

'This parcel . . . there are blouses in it,' winced the girl. 'But I've run a splinter of wood right into my finger, just under the nail . . . I got it from the floor of the wardrobe. Here . . . take the parcel.' She turned towards him, holding up a half-opened brown paper bundle, the shop tape still lying loose around it.

Hungrily, he tore the paper back. There were the blouses . . . "a queer yellow colour, with red embroidery . . ." just as Jenny Rey had described them.

'They're . . . !' Pat hesitated, her question unasked, her eyes deep, troubled pools.

Thane nodded. 'I think so. Come on, we'll ask the girl.' He led the way back to the lounge, and as Jenny glanced up from the couch, pulled one of the blouses from its wrapping and held it towards her. The girl's sullen, drooping mouth opened wide, then she gasped, 'That's it, mister . . . that's one of them.'

Silently, Thane showed her the second blouse, and again the girl's forthright indentification removed any shadow of doubt.

'You'll swear to it, Jenny?' he asked.

'Anywhere, mister.' Then, a cunning look came into her reddened eyes. 'Here, will this do me some good tomorrow? I've to come up before the court again . . . couldn't you get me off, now that I've helped you?'

Slowly, Thane shook his head. ' 'Fraid not, Jenny . . . but 'twill make things a lot easier for you. We'll make sure the court knows you've helped the police. If you're lucky, you'll get off with a fine.'

Jenny Rey's shoulders sagged. Then, in faint bravado, she sneered, 'Well, she may be dead, but I don't care . . . at least I've shown you I wasn't the only one at it.'

'That's enough, Jenny,' snapped Thane. 'Take her back to the station now,' he told the policewoman. 'Her part's finished.'

.   .   .   .   .

Pat Miller waited until the shopgirl had been led from the room, then sank into one of the armchairs with a sigh of something like despair. 'I don't understand it,' she protested. 'I thought you were sure that Judith hadn't been taking the goods that were being stolen . . . I thought you were as sure as I was. And now we've found the blouses, I don't know what to believe. I remember these blouses myself . . . I thought they were pretty ghastly at the time we bought them in, though Judith didn't often make a mistake when it came to judging the market. And now they're here, although they were definitely reported stolen. These are "Maxine" models . . . and we take almost all their output. They must be the same ones. What does it mean, Mr. Thane?'

Colin Thane did the thing she had least expected. He gave a broad grin. 'It means we've got our first hard lead,' he told her. 'Look . . . never mind the blouses a moment. See the tape round the parcel . . . see what's printed on it? "Greenmantle, Napier Street, Dennistoun, ladies and gents outfitters." Do you know what that suggests, Pat? She bought the blouses outside of the store.'

The girl came over, her eyes suddenly bright, and examined the shop tape. Then she looked puzzled again. 'But how far does that help find who murdered Judith?'

'It will,' promised Thane. 'Phil, go through every scrap of paper in that desk in the corner . . . the boys have been through it before, but not for this. See if you can find a receipt by a firm called "Greenmantle".'

'Okay,' said Moss, opening the desk front. 'You think she saw the blouses in the shop, knew they had been stolen from Hillman's, and went in and bought them to make sure? And that someone found out later that she was on the trail?'

'That's the score,' agreed Thane.

'Here's something,' interjected the girl. 'Look at the blouses again, Mr. Thane. They're the wrong sizes. This one is a thirty-eight, the other one is a forty bust. Yet Judith took a thirty-four bust . . . see for yourself.' She picked up one of the half-dozen blouses she had found hanging in the wardrobe, and showed the size tag on its inside neck. 'She didn't buy those two to wear.'

130

'And here's your receipt,' said Moss from the desk, excitement creeping into his voice. 'Greenmantle . . . to goods, three pounds.'

Thane almost snatched the tiny slip of paper from him. 'We're on to it,' he said. 'This is what we've been needing. The way I see it, she bought the blouses because she recognized them as stolen . . . we'll need to check with the makers, of course, but it's an automatic conclusion.'

'They're Hillman stock, definitely,' declared the girl. 'Just like the stockings that Rose the store detective found.' A sudden thought struck her. 'What size were the stockings, Mr. Thane?'

'Size? I'm darned if I know, Pat . . . wait, I see what you mean. Were they the size that she wore?'

'Just a minute,' said the girl, a quaver of almost hysterical tension in her voice. She ran back into the bedroom, and the two men could hear drawers being pulled open. In a few moments she was back, her face flushed, her eyes bright. 'Eight and a half,' she said. 'Judith wore an eight and a half.'

'We'll check,' said Thane. 'And then we'll move in on "Greenmantle". . . . They'll need a darned good story to get out of this. Get your handbag, lass, and we'll run you back home. You've done a good night's work.'

'It's a pleasure,' laughed the girl. 'You don't know how much this means to me.' She grew serious again. 'All I want is to see you catch this killer. Oh . . . do something for me before we go, will you? Could you get this splinter out of my finger? I'd almost forgotten it.'

'Here, Phil, you do it,' suggested Thane. 'You're the bachelor around here. I'd get heck from Mary if I started holding pretty girls' hands at my age.'

'It's a pleasure,' said Moss with awkward gallantry. 'Here, Miss, let's see . . . you'll need to excuse my dirty fingernails, though.'

.   .   .   .   .

It was nine-fifteen when the police Humber stopped outside Pat's home in Shawlands. 'Thanks again,' said Thane, as the police driver opened the rear door for the girl. 'Mum's the word about it all, though . . . and incidentally, there's a rather miserable young man looking in a shop window a few yards down the street. I think you know him.'

Pat glanced quickly along the road, surprised, then her eyes softened. She smiled, gave her hair a quick pat to make sure it was in place, then began to walk slowly, casually, along the pavement towards Jerry Watford.

'Where now, Dad Cupid?' asked Moss sardonically. 'And why didn't you tell her about Richards being dead?'

'I didn't want to spoil her evening any more than we had already, I suppose,' said Thane. 'Stop peeping at them, Phil . . . don't be jealous.' He ducked the mock punch aimed at him.

.   .   .   .   .

The nine-thirty press conference at Millside started at ten p.m. But that, most of the newspapermen present would have agreed, was abnormally punctual. When a police conference was fixed, they could usually count on it being at least an hour later than the stated time . . . and in some cases, particularly in a certain notorious neighbouring county, reporters could wait around till the early hours of the morning then find that the officer concerned was home and snug in bed, having forgotten all about them.

It was a long drawn-out affair. Two of the "morning" men had already heard about Richards' death through "contacts" . . . just who these contacts were, Thane would dearly have liked to know . . . he would have suspended them on the spot. The story put the two reporters in an awkward position. They could have kept quiet, and been unable to get any police confirmation. Or they could speak, and let the other pressmen "in", ruining a possible exclusive. But their information was too thin to take chances. Finally, they broke, and asked.

'Lanarkshire police have found the body of a man, Andrew Richards, who was a Hillman doorman,' Thane agreed. 'But for all we know, he may have been knocked down by a train while crossing the line. That's all I can tell you, except, off the record,

132

it looks more like suicide. Honestly, boys, there's nothing to link the pair.' But you'll have a darned good try, he added humourlessly to himself, watching the semi-circle of sharp-eyed poker-faced newsmen.

'We've got a picture of Judith Marchand to distribute,' he told them. 'Get in a queue and I'll lash them out. Do me a favour . . . run another appeal with them, on the same lines as the evening papers did. Ask anyone who saw her from noon on Tuesday onwards to come forward.' He gave out the photographs, copies of the snapshots he had borrowed from Mrs. Allen that afternoon, then quickly faded before any more awkward questions were asked about Andy Richards.

.   .   .   .   .

Phil had two mugs of tea waiting back in Thane's office. 'I'm out of cigarettes,' he volunteered, as Thane settled back in his chair with a sigh and put his feet up carelessly on the paper-covered desk.

'Hard luck, mate . . . I'm all right,' said Thane, lighting one for himself. Then, relenting, 'here, catch,' he tossed another cigarette across the desk top. 'Food, fags . . . why don't you ask my wife to do your laundry while you're at it?'

'Do you think she'd mind?' parried Moss, then, taking a gulp of the scalding-hot tea, reported, 'nothing further on Andy Richards yet, Colin. Lanarkshire police have drawn a blank locally. No one saw or heard anything overnight or in the morning. Professor McMaster's finishing the post mortem on Judith Marchand tonight, and he'll give us the report first thing tomorrow . . . then he's tackling Richards' body.'

'Shove over the phone, will you, and I'll get the sizes of those stockings from the lab. That report from Birmingham should be on your desk somewhere . . . you know, the one the local police were getting from the manufacturer.'

'Let's see. . . .' Thane took his feet off the desk and wriggled into an upright position, searching through the papers, while Moss got busy on the telephone.

'I've got it,' he mouthed silently as his companion finally got through to Headquarters and asked for the Scientific Bureau. He began reading the long teleprinter message, while Moss asked a puzzled police lab. technician to find the stocking sizes. 'Two nine and a half, one ten,' back-checked Moss over the phone. 'Right, mate . . . oh, send them back round here if you're finished, will you?' He hung up. 'She bought the wrong sizes again, Colin. We're on to them, all right.'

'It's not quite so simple,' said Thane slowly, wrinkling his forehead. 'If she bought them from this Greenmantle shop . . . and we haven't even got a receipt to prove that . . . there's no reason why it couldn't have been above board. Listen to this . . .' he began reading the teleprinter message.

'Bruce Brand, nylon makers, say main supply goes to Hillman's store as per your message. But also supply small excess quantities to number of small firms in different cities including . . . oh heck, never mind the full list. There's eleven shops altogether, and Greenmantle is the only Glasgow concern.'

'So maybe they got the blouses on the legit. too?' said Moss ruefully. 'Though it's a hell of a long coincidence. I'm going to have a plough through that bundle of papers we brought to the station from her office at Hillman's. They're lying in the main office . . . maybe there's another Greenmantle receipt among them,' he added hopefully.

He came back into Thane's room a few minutes later. The chief inspector was sitting hunched over his desk, chin resting on his hands, gloom written broadly over his face. 'No receipt?' he asked, without looking up.

'Nope.' Moss slumped back down in the chair beside him. 'Strewth, this heat's getting me down . . . eleven at night, and it seems warmer than ever.' He drew one hand across his perspiring forehead, then sat idly scraping his thumb nail across the desk top.

'Don't do that, Phil,' pleaded Thane. 'You'll scrape what's left of the varnish off it and . . .' his voice faded. He suddenly stared hard at the desk. Then one hand shot out and gripped Phil tight by the shoulder. 'Do you get it!' he shouted excitedly.

'Fair enough, fair enough,' said Moss. 'Take it easy, Colin, I'll stop.'

'Not that, you clot. The varnish. Remember what I told you about the lab. report on these nylons? Here, I'll read it again. Where the hell is it?' He threw the papers on his desk around in a reckless fury of energy, found the memo sheet he wanted.

'Listen . . . the nylon stockings showed traces of cellulose varnish dust. But Judith Marchand's office desk is a metal one. Don't you see?'

'See what?' Phil Moss was completely puzzled.

'Where would the stockings get that dust?'

'Oh, in her wardrobe, maybe,' said Phil. 'Or on the shop shelves.'

'Even if she ever had the stockings home, the inside of that bedroom suite was plain wood,' said Thane impatiently. 'I noticed that when I was there tonight. And remember that splinter you took out for Pat? Plain white wood. I thought it was a bit unusual . . . most modern suites are painted inside as well as out . . . well, not painted, but paint-sprayed. Now do you see? What goes out of Hillman's store at regular intervals that's paint-sprayed with cellulose varnish, and could hold stolen stuff . . . plenty of it . . . without anyone thinking to open it. What's a perfectly natural thing to leave the store at regular intervals, and might easily have varnish dust lying around it? Furniture, of course. They ship out furniture by van . . . and the vans are loaded up the night before. What's to stop anybody hiding in the store until after it's closed, then loading up some of the drawer space, or even the inside of a wardrobe with clothes, or any other goods?'

'They could still have got that dust on a shelf,' persisted Moss.

'And my grannie could be Queen of the May,' said Thane rudely. 'Look, Phil, it's a natural. And if the driver and his mate were both in on what was going on, they could unload the stuff before delivering the furniture to whoever had ordered it. Oh, bless these lovely long-haired geniuses over in that ruddy lab!' He pressed the buzzer button at the side of his desk, and when the orderly knocked and entered the room, ordered, 'Take these two blouses over by car right away to the crime lab. Tell them to run tests on them with all they've got, trying to find cellulose varnish dust on them. And tell whoever's on duty I want a report as fast as they can give me it.' He rubbed his hands together as the orderly departed. 'Next . . . find out more about Mr. Ruddy Greenmantle. Who's on the fraud squad these days?'

'Big Joe Lindsay, I think,' said Moss. 'But look, Colin, aren't you going off a bit half-cocked on this? I admit it sounds good, but . . .'

'Maybe I am,' said Thane. 'But I don't think so.' He snatched up the phone. 'Get me Inspector Lindsay at Headquarters,' he instructed the operator. 'If he isn't there, dig him out at home.' He bashed the receiver down again. 'I'm playing a hunch, Phil. I still haven't a clue who's behind this in the store . . . or,' his eyes narrowed a trifle . . . 'maybe I'm just beginning to have an idea about that too. Tell you what. First thing in the morning, get on to those blouse makers . . . Maxine or whatever they're called. Find out if they supply Greenmantle with them. You'll probably find they do . . . and it doesn't matter! In fact, it makes me all the more certain I know what's going on. Then double-check with the nylon makers, I want to know everything about these stockings down to the day they were made!'

'I don't pretend to be following your mental acrobatics,' said Moss, taking a small pill-box from his pocket. 'But if we're going on like this . . .' he popped a couple of pellets into his mouth, and swallowed. 'Tranquilizers,' he explained. 'Soothes the nerves, keeps the stomach under control. Like one?' Thane shook his head.

Phil Moss drew his chair closer. 'If you are right . . . and I said if, remember . . . then I think I know how they could have got Judith Marchand's body out of the store that night,' he declared. 'Remember what Jerry Watford told us about the man who had hid in a wardrobe? What's to stop them hiding a body in a wardrobe, if it comes to that, and driving it out of the store the next morning. And maybe, when we scared them, one

136

of them hid in the wardrobe instead . . . we never looked inside
the furniture that was loaded in the basement garage.'

'It could be,' said Thane softly. 'It could be at that. They
would have moved it . . . if we hadn't butted in.'

The phone at his side gave a tinkle. 'Your call to Inspector
Lindsay, sir,' said the night operator.

'Joe? Where are you?' asked Thane. 'Still at Headquarters?
Good. Look, be a pal and look up your company lists for me,
will you? I want to know who is the boss of a dress shop called
Greenmantle. Aye, all right, I know you were just going home.
But it'll only keep you a couple of minutes, and it's hellish
important.'

Joe Lindsay grumbled and growled. But he was back on the
telephone within a couple of minutes.

'Greenmantle. Registered about six months ago. Carry out
business as outfitters and general dealers, with three shops in
Glasgow . . . all small . . . at Napier Street, Henderson Road
and Harrison Street. Registered capital one thousand pounds.
Perfectly legit. as far as we know . . . never any complaint.
Director . . . huh, this'll give you a laugh . . . John Buchan,
86 Camelon Crescent, Partick. That all you want?'

'More than enough,' said Thane. 'Thanks, Joe . . .' He hung
up, and rapidly read over the message. 'Partick . . . that's the
Marine Division.' He beamed enthusiastically. 'Come on,
Phil, another trip. We're going to see the bobby on the beat at
Camelon Crescent.'

.   .   .   .   .

The constable was a veteran . . . one of the old school who
had, in his young days, batonned his way through the Billy
Boys, the San Toy, the Cheeky Forty, and all the other multitude
of Glasgow razor gangs with a cheerful impartiality.

Now, he readily admitted as he talked to Thane in the dark,
deserted avenue with its widely spaced, old-fashioned street
lamps, he was "out to grass" on a nice, comparatively quiet
beat. 'I've been two years here,' he said, in a soft voice that still

137

betrayed its Hebridean origin despite nearly forty years in the big city. 'I've only another six months to be doing, and then I can be going back up to the Islands again, with my pension, and a nice wee croft waiting ready for me.'

Yes, he knew most of the people on his beat. 'They're friendly folk,' he declared. 'I've nothing much else to do but have a bit of blether to pass the time, and so I know most of them, very well indeed, sir.'

'How about a man called Buchan, John Buchan?' asked Thane.

'Och, Mr. Buchan . . . yes indeed, the gentleman who has the garage,' said the old policeman. 'He is not perhaps the friendliest of people . . . but that might be because I haff had to serve him with summonses for breaking the Road Traffic Act. In fact,' he scratched the back of his neck with the tip of his baton, 'he was very rude the last time. And I haff heard that that isn't the only kind of trouble he hass been in in his time . . . Mr. Buchan hass been around.'

'He runs a garage?' asked Thane. 'Are you sure? Doesn't he have some dress shops?'

'Och, yes, I believe he hass now, but he runs this wee garage up in Rook Road. He hass had it four years, that one.'

'He may have a record,' mused Thane. 'And he's got a garage business as well . . . it all fits in.'

'Iss the gentleman in trouble again?' asked the Highlander. 'I won't be asking what, but if he should be putting up a struggle, would you be kind enough to give him a good kick in the teeth for me?'

'I'll remember if the opportunity arises,' promised Thane. 'But we'll postpone that pleasure until the morning.'

8

In bed at one a.m., Colin Thane wakened again at six thirty. He silenced the whirring alarm clock, fought against the almost overwhelming temptation to roll over and go back to sleep, and sat up. Beside him, his wife yawned sleepily and raised herself on one elbow. 'I'll get breakfast,' she volunteered half-heartedly.

'I'll fix it . . . away back to sleep,' said Thane, stripping off his pyjama jacket and groping for his shirt on the chair beside the bed.

'You don't mind?' murmured Mary, giving another yawn.

'Uh, uh,' Colin bent over, gave her a quick kiss, and she burrowed happily under the bedclothes again.

.   .   .   .   .

The green, canvas-topped Post Office van pulled up at the road's edge, just before eight a.m. Two overalled telephone linesmen, whistling as they worked, put up a small shelter round the square metal manhole cover at the roadside, pulled off the cover to expose the solder-covered cable core beneath, and began to lay out an assortment of tools and blow-lamps. Not long afterwards, one of the men sauntered across the road to the garage opposite, kettle in hand. An elderly attendant was just unlocking the garage petrol pumps, ready to start the day's trade.

'Any chance of some water, mate?' asked the linesman. 'It's our time for a brew-up.'

'A brew-up? Jings, you blokes like your comfort. Aye, sure,

give us the kettle,' said the garage man. He filled the kettle from a tap beside the pump, and handed it back.

'Fag?' offered the linesman, holding out a battered pack.

'Ta.' The attendant shared a match, took a deep draw, then looked inquiringly at the van across the road. 'Something up with the phones again?'

'Aye. We've a bit of testing to do that'll probably take us a few days. Still, as long as the weather holds fair, it won't be too bad. How's business?'

'Pretty quiet. But we'll get busy enough after dinner-time. Most blokes seem to run their cars almost dry on a Friday morning, then fill up as soon as they've drawn their pay.'

'Are you on your own at the pumps, mate?' asked the linesman.

'Aye. Catch the boss giving me any help. There's me out here, an' him and a couple of mechanics in the yard doing repairs . . . that's the lot. We're kept hard at it, believe me.'

'Still, you'll have the five-day week,' consoled the linesman.

'Huh . . .' the attendant screwed up his face. 'You know his latest idea? We work all day Saturday, and get Thursday off instead. The basket says Thursday's a "dead" day. The two mechanics he used to have moaned when he started it.' He shrugged his narrow shoulders. 'They said they wanted overtime for Saturday work so he gave them the heave and brought in a pair of non-union men.'

'So the place just closes down completely on Thursdays?'

'Not likely. Catch him missin' anything. He comes in himself to work the pumps. A ruddy miser, so he is.'

'That's the way of it,' the linesman sympathized. 'Well, thanks for the kettle, mate. Be seeing you.' He gave a wave, and, cigarette dangling between his lips, strolled back across the road to the van. He placed the kettle on a small metal stand, and set a blow-lamp's flame playing under it. Tea was on the way.

Legs dangling over the hatch, the second linesman had already spliced a headphone set into the cable. He nodded to his companion. The first linesman took his place, fitted the set on his head, and asked the operator at the other end of the wire

140

for a number. The connexion came swiftly. The linesman looked cautiously around, then said, 'That you, sir? Sergeant MacLeod here. We're in position, and the natives are friendly. Found out something that may help. The garage staff are off every Thursday. Only the boss remains on duty, to look after the pumps.'

'That's interesting,' mused Thane, speaking from his office. 'Well, you know your orders. How about the camera?'

'The telephoto's focusing easily from inside the van. Jenkins is hidden inside with it. He says we'll get a clear shot without trouble . . . and there's no sign of the lens from outside the van.'

'Keep a good look-out,' warned Thane. 'Never mind the casual customers, but let me know if anything unusual happens, or if anyone stays to talk. You'll get me at Hillman's from nine a.m. if it's desperate.'

The "linesman" laid down the headphones and looked towards the kettle. Steam was starting to issue from its spout. 'Tea up,' he called.

.   .   .   .   .

By the time Sergeant MacLeod reported that the observation van was in position, the Millside chief had already been at work for over an hour. His plans were finalized for the mass interviews due to begin at Hillman's. Police interview teams would move in at nine-thirty. They had been fully briefed in their role the previous night. Thane rose from his chair, stretched, and went into the little washroom set off his office. He splashed the last remnants of sleep from his eyes with cold water, dried his face with the coarse police-issue towel. Now a shave. The electric razor felt cool and satisfying as it purred through the stubble on his chin. Slipping on his jacket again, Thane strode briskly back to his desk and coughed and spluttered his way through the first cigarette of the day as he once more read the overnight reports on his desk.

Scottish Criminal Records Office. "John Buchan, aged 46,

company director. Two convictions for fraud, the last in 1948, one year's imprisonment. An assault charge back in 1937 . . . four months." The attached photograph, taken at the 1948 conviction, showed a swarthy little man with a heavy dark moustache and thick, dark hair. Mr. Buchan was obviously not on the side of the angels.

Lanarkshire C.I.D. "Interviews in the Bishopbriggs area have produced no evidence of a strange car or persons being noticed in the area of the railway line prior to Richards' body being found." The post-mortem was to take place that morning, Thane knew . . . Professor McMaster, who had visited the spot, felt that Richards had been alive when the train had decapitated him, basing his theory on the area over which blood had been spattered. 'The heart muscle had still been beating, it would appear, otherwise blood would not have been so widely present,' said the county message.

Routine report, D.C.s Strong and Charles. "James Rose . . . shadowing detail. Movements apparently normal. But subject spent one hour in the evening drinking heavily in an Argyle Street bar. Then returned home, where remained. Watch continues."

Then, the last, but perhaps most important, the Scientific Bureau report. "Suicide note taken from possessions of man Richards and checked beside enlargement of signature on personal documents shows strong possibility of being forgery. Style of writing dis-similar from style used in printing. Examination continues, but almost definite that Richards did not write note. Other items: No trace of cellulose varnish dust on the two blouses taken from Judith Marchand's flat. Blouses show no trace of having been worn. Fourteen sets of fingerprints, including the dead woman's, so far located in articles taken from the store-room in which her body was found and on furnishings in her office. All awaiting fingerprint check at store for final classification."

The report cleared any remaining doubt from the big man's mind. Richards had been murdered . . . murdered because he had discovered too much, the same reason which had caused

142

Judith Marchand's death. Perhaps the post-mortem on Richards would disclose more detail of the way he had died.

He hesitated about phoning Professor McMaster at his home. The P.M. report on Judith should have been finished by now . . . McMaster and Doc. Williams had been working on the corpse at the City Mortuary until after midnight. Och, no, it wasn't worth it . . . McMaster in his usual methodical manner would be around soon enough with a full copy of his report . . . and a verbal boil-down fit for human consumption. The professor's reports were masterpieces of medical jurisprudence, but incomprehensible jargon to the layman.

As he turned back to the other items, the door opened, and Phil Moss, hat on the back of his head, walked in, a bundle of newspapers under one arm, his new tie, already egg-stained, flopping outside his jacket. 'The press boys have been enjoying themselves,' he declared, tossing the bundle on the desk.

Thane picked up one, shuddered, laid it down, chose another . . . another . . . the same black headlines in them all. Second Hillman Store Death. Man dead on line . . . police deny link. Columns of copy . . . interviews with Judith's friends . . . Richards' landlady . . . one paper even had a picture-story with the doorman's wife, dug up by it's London staff. He swept the bundle into one corner of his desk. 'The Chief Constable's going to love this,' he grimaced. 'Still, there's not much we can do about it. And we can give them the mass interview story today . . . that'll keep the ratepayers happy, and sure they're getting their money's worth.'

Phil finished thumbing his way through the overnight reports. 'When are we leaving for Hillman's ?' he asked.

'I'll go on my own, Phil,' replied Thane. 'You'd better stay here, and make those queries about the blouses and nylons direct by phone to the makers. They're lying in my top drawer. Once that's done, take a drive round to this Greenmantle shop, and size up the place. See if any of the assistants can remember Judith Marchand coming in . . . and leave a man to watch the shop. You could take a look at the other two shops this character Buchan owns while you're at it . . . buy a pair of shoelaces or

143

something, and see what the set-up is.' He glanced at his watch. 'Eight fifteen. That Chinese restaurant down the road should be open . . . want to join me in a quick breakfast?'

Hillman's seven floors were just stirring to life, the first few customers drifting in the doors, assistants having a brief gossip in corners, delivery trucks bringing fresh supplies of goods to depleted counters. There was a new doorman on duty at the main entrance, standing self-consciously in his freshly-pressed uniform. Thane climbed the stairs to the second floor. A uniform man was still on duty at the stock-room, standing beside the door-frame . . . the actual door was now in Police Headquarters. The chief inspector gave the man a friendly nod, and walked on down the long department floor and into the little glass-walled office. Pat Miller, cool and fresh in a crisp white blouse and flared blue linen skirt, glanced up from a pile of advertisement proofs as he entered.

'I was just going to phone you,' she said. 'Can we let customers into the department now, Mr. Thane? I was asking the policeman outside, but he said we'd have to see you about it.'

'There's no reason why you shouldn't, as far as I'm concerned,' said Thane. 'But you can't use the stock-room, I'm afraid, and we'll need to keep a guard on the door for a few days yet. If it helps, I'll have a plain-clothes man instead of a uniform constable.'

The girl looked relieved. 'Mr. Farringdon was speaking to me about it first thing this morning . . . with the sale starting tomorrow, this department being closed would amount to a financial disaster. These are the advertisements . . . I'm just correcting the proofs before they go in this afternoon's papers. It's just as well too,' a laugh bubbled on her lips. 'Look at this. "Women's cocktail dresses, 64 hips." ' She crossed out the figure and substituted a more moderate "36". Then, laying down the pencil, she asked, 'have you tracked down the stockings, yet, Mr. Thane?'

'Inspector Moss is working on it now,' said Thane. 'I should know within the next hour. I can tell you this, though. They weren't her size.'

144

'Then you're right,' exclaimed the girl. 'Judith was investigating the robberies. She wasn't mixed up in them at all. If only she'd told somebody or gone to the police . . .'

'But she didn't,' finished Thane. 'And that's an important pointer, Pat. Why didn't she? She wasn't the kind of woman who'd play detective for the thrill of it. There must have been some strong reason.' He whistled softly, tunelessly, to himself for a long minute. 'It shouldn't be long now,' he promised. 'Well, I've got to go and see Jerry Watford now, and arrange the start of the interviewing. Just so as I know, are you two on friendly terms again?'

The sparkle in her eyes was answer enough.

.   .   .   .   .

Charles Farringdon was the first of the Hillman thousand to be fingerprinted and interviewed. The store's managing director made a point of it. Back to his normal brusque, forceful self, he came down from his penthouse office to the typists' room, cleared of its normal occupants for the massive process, and asked a flow of questions as a C.I.D. man took his broad, hairy hands in a firm grasp, rolled each individual fingertip on an ink pad, then carefully, one finger at a time, registered the ten prints on a form. As the fingerprint man finished, the other officer seated at the desk took over. The set questions were quick and simple. Name, age, address . . . when did you leave the store on Tuesday . . . when did you leave Wednesday . . . did you clock out . . . when did you last see Judith Marchand . . . who was she with . . . have you noticed anything irregular happening in the store that might have a bearing on our inquiries?

It was swift, outwardly cursory. But the questions were enough on their own to give a skilled interviewer a lead to a hesitant witness, or to give some gossip the chance to tell a tale which might well contain a valuable crumb of information. Twelve C.I.D. men, divided into six fingerprint-interview teams, were ready at the desks. Behind them, a sergeant would take over any leads that might be found.

'Nice job of organizing, Thane,' rumbled Farringdon, as he finished being "processed". 'Good production-line stuff. Five minutes dead. You won't mess us up too much, I hope . . . you know I'll co-operate to the limit, but at the same time, we've got to keep the store running. Can't have the whole staff standing in a queue.'

'You'll hardly notice it,' promised Thane. 'I've arranged with Mr. Watford that we'll get a batch of six from each floor every hour on the hour. The transport department may be a bit more difficult, with their comings and goings . . . we're going to start with as many of them as we can, then do the others whenever they become available.' And he added mentally, if we get what we're looking for from there, the rest of the staff won't matter so much.

'I'll leave you to it, then,' agreed Farringdon. 'Don't forget . . . if I can help, just come right up. I'll be at my desk throughout the day . . . with the summer sale starting tomorrow and all the other fuss and publicity, well, you know my personal feelings, but business comes first . . . and I think we're going to be swamped. I'm bringing in a hundred extra staff as an absolute minimum . . . if the Labour Exchange can find them for me in time.'

Thane whistled. 'Sounds like you're expecting an army.'

'The more the merrier. With luck, they'll start queuing the night before, and give us a free "puff" story in the morning papers. We always serve tea and buns to the first arrivals at about 6 a.m. . . . they deserve it after a wait like that.' The big man smiled. 'I've been busy on something else. It took quite a few cables and a devil of a long transatlantic phone call last night . . . but I've managed it. Young Billy Marchand's Canadian relatives have agreed to let him come over in about a month, to have a holiday with me. I'll let him see his way around here, and, well, I'm hoping he'll stay. There's a job waiting for him soon as he finishes school, if he wants it . . . and if he shapes the way I hope, well, all I can say is he'll get every chance.' The affectionate glint in the store chief's eyes was the lad's promise for the future.

.　.　.　.　.

146

Looking back, it was the calm before the storm . . . a time sequence that somehow emerges in the pattern of almost every investigation, when, like on a photographic plate, the final image is chemically trapped, invisible to the eye, but still awaiting emergence. Thane's work was nearing its climax. How soon, it was impossible to gauge. An hour, a day, even a week. . . but he felt that sudden lightening of spirit and increase of tension that he knew full well. There was plenty of work ahead. But somehow he knew that the mystery was about to be cracked open.

He stood in the interviewing room for a while, watching the first batches of staff arriving, some giggling, some serious, others nervous. They were mainly black-and-red overalled assistants, but a small knot of dungaree-clad men from the transport department were grouped in one corner waiting their turn to be called. The faint hum of voices and the rustle of paper filled the air. Colin Thane caught the eye of a uniform man, one of several helping organize the queuing workers. 'Find out the address of the night commissionaire, a man called Deacon. Then get a car to go round to his home, and ask him to come straight to the store . . . tell him it's important. He'll probably be sleeping, but that's just too bad.'

The murmur of voices continued. 'But I'm always on time . . .' 'So I said to my friend Molly, I'll just tell . . .' 'Me late, mister? Not with that hatchet-faced supervisor . . .' 'She was such a nice woman . . .' 'Punch the clock? Aye, we've some characters here, but . . .' 'An' I just told her to climb back on her broomstick . . .' Press each finger on the pad, then on the card. Name, address, age. 'No, the ink won't stain, madam. Just give your fingers a rub with some soap and water.'

He picked up interest as a middle-aged woman was led from the interviewing desk to the waiting sergeant inquisitor. But the sergeant, after a few questions, looked across the room and slowly shook his head. Twenty, thirty, forty minutes ticked by.

The telephone buzzed, and a D.C. answered. He spoke for a moment, then gestured to Thane. Colin moved between the desks, and took the receiver.

'Constable Laurence, Car 37, sir. We've been at the home of this man Deacon. He's not there, I'm afraid. His wife says he's gone into town to do some private business.'

'Does she know where he'll be?'

'I asked, sir. Any one of half a dozen places. She doesn't expect him back before noon.'

'Leave it just now,' ordered Thane. 'But tell her we'll be back, and that we want her husband to stay home till we collect him.'

He hung up, and turned to head back through the desks, stopping beside the detective sergeant. 'What's the score, Sarge?' he asked.

The detective sergeant shook his head. 'One old wife who says she heard someone say that Judith Marchand was staying late in the store on the Tuesday . . . but can't remember who said it. A couple of gossips with theories. Six . . . no, seven who were late in the store on the Tuesday for some unofficial reason or other. But there's nobody who saw her after closing time that day.'

'Phone again, sir,' called the detective constable. 'Another outside call.'

The voice was low, cautious. 'Mr. Thane? Sergeant MacLeod at the observation van. It arrived, as you said it would. Hillman furniture van, registration number HAG 327. Drove into the yard of the garage about fifteen minutes ago, then the driver and his mate got out and went into the garage office. They're still inside.'

'Did you get the camera on them?'

'Part of the way, sir. We can't get a shot of the men going in, because of the angle. But we've got the van okay.'

'Wait till it leaves, then see what you can get out of the pump attendant,' instructed Thane. 'Call me back.'

The first batch of interviews were over. The second group of employees were beginning to trickle in. Jerry Watford was there, talking in animated fashion to Pat. The girl shook her head. Jerry began again, and finally the girl seemed to agree. They walked across together.

'We want to tell you about something . . . it concerns Richards,

148

the doorman,' said Watford. 'But . . .' he looked a trifle sheepish, 'it's rather awkward.'

Thane turned to the girl, inquiringly. She dimpled, dropped her eyes.

'It was on Wednesday afternoon,' said Watford. 'We . . . Pat and I, that is . . . well, we were alone in the invoice file room, down in the basement.'

'Working?' asked Thane, his lips puckering.

'Well, yes and no . . . that is . . . we were having a private chat,' stumbled Watford. 'And we heard voices outside. The door was shut, and we couldn't really make out anything that was being said. We just knew that two men were talking. Then they seemed to part. But one of them shouted something to the other just outside the door. We recognized the voice then. It was Richards.'

The dry amusement had gone from Thane's voice, replaced by interest rather than excitement. 'You're sure it was Richards?'

They both nodded.

'What did he shout?'

'We're not quite sure,' said Pat. 'That was what we were discussing before we came over. But as near as I can remember, it was something like "Don't forget . . . I want it settled. No empty promises." '

'I just thought it was some private business he was up to,' said Watford. 'But, well, since we found out this morning that he'd been found dead, I told Pat we'd better report it.'

'And you haven't any idea who the other man was?' asked Thane.

'No . . . we stayed in the invoice room for a few minutes more. There was no one there when we left,' said Watford. Thane rubbed his chin. 'As it stands, it means nothing on its own. But it may link up with some other bits and pieces of information. Thanks for telling me.'

Henry Allen, perspiration beading his forehead, came into the office as he spoke. 'Ah, Chief Inspector! Two more for finger-printing? I just popped in . . . I've only got a minute to spare . . . the sale displays are getting out of hand on the ground

149

floor. Er . . . it's not my turn, but do you think I could be granted a special dispensation and be taken right away?'

'Of course,' agreed Thane. 'How about you two?' he asked Watford and the girl.

'We're in this next batch,' said Watford. 'Come on, Henry, we'll all go through together.'

.   .   .   .   .

The buzz of talk, the shuffle of feet, the fingerprinting continued. At the end of an hour and a half the first fifty of the store had been "processed" and the pace was quickening. But to Thane, sitting chain-smoking on a vacant desk-edge, waiting, wondering, growing more excited by the minute, more exasperated with the slowness of time, without knowing the real cause for either emotion, it seemed an interminable drag. He jumped to his feet when the phone rang, and seized the receiver.

'It's MacLeod again, sir, at the observation post. The Hillman furniture van left twenty minutes ago. I've been having another natter with that pump attendant . . . said we wanted another kettle of water. This van comes every morning, it seems. The driver's a cousin of the garage owner, a fellow called Jack Waddie. He and his mate pull in for a cup of tea, stay for about twenty minutes or so, then shove off again. The pump man says they pull the van in off the road in case any of the Hillman bosses spot it . . . Waddie'd get his books on the spot.'

'What happens on a Thursday . . . does he know?'

'He says the van calls as usual . . . he's gone past the place on his day off, and seen the van parked round the back.'

'Any more pictures?'

'Yes, sir. Jenkins caught the van going . . . he says if he's lucky he should have a shot of the cab showing both driver and his mate. Want us to hang on, sir?'

'Stay put,' said Thane. 'I wish to God we could tap that garage telephone line . . . but after all the stink there's been, hell, it's almost Cabinet-level stuff to suggest it. Keep that camera ready, and take a shot of anyone who does anything

150

more than buy petrol. If anyone goes into that garage or talks to Buchan I want his picture. How's the wire repairing going?'

There was a faint chuckle over the wire. 'The G.P.O. bloke we've got along is doing his nut. He's sitting here playing with a blow-lamp and solder . . . says he's never worked so hard in his life looking busy doing nothing. I'll phone back as soon as anything happens, sir.'

The line went dead, and Thane hung up. Lifting the internal phone lying beside the other instrument he dialled Charles Farringdon's number . . . 01. The managing director's bark answered immediately.

'Thane here. Are you alone just now, Mr. Farringdon?'

'No, but I will be in a minute. I'm just finishing dictating some memos. Why?'

Speaking quietly but clearly, Thane told him 'I want you to get the transport manager to come up, under any pretext you like. And I want you to ask him some questions . . . questions I don't want him to realize the police are asking. You can cloak them with some business detail.'

'I follow,' said Farringdon. 'Just a minute . . .' over the line Thane could hear him gruffly dismissing the secretary. There was a pause, then Farringdon said, 'Right . . . I'm alone now. What sort of questions? And why the secrecy? Do you think my transport chief's mixed up in it all?'

'No. He's got nothing to do with it. But he might drop a hint that would upset my applecart. And coming from you, in the middle of ordinary business, he probably wouldn't think anything of it.'

'Go on,' rapped Farringdon. 'What questions?'

'Ask him who the regular driver of your furniture van is. Ask him if the driver is ever changed, and how long the driver's mate has been with him. And try to confirm, if you can, that the furniture van's registration number is HAG 327.'

'What's going on?' asked Farringdon.

'I'll tell you when I'm sure,' said Thane. 'Meantime if you'll ask the questions and phone me back . . .' even as he hung up, the managing director's outraged splutter floated down

151

to him. It was coming up for eleven a.m. on the wall clock of the office . . . time for his press conference in the store's publicity room. 'Back in fifteen minutes,' he told the detective sergeant, and strolled whistling from the room.

'Don't know what the hell he's so happy about,' grumbled the sergeant. 'Strewth, sometimes I'd swap my stripes for a nice steady job in the lost property section.'

.   .   .   .   .

The pressmen, too, noted Thane's cheerier air. Jock Mills made a mental decision to tip the *Hour's* subs desk that it might be worth while preparing for a late replate edition on the strength of the brisk way the chief inspector answered the broadside of questions he received within seconds of walking in the door . . . questions that ranged from such heavy-calibre posers as "Have you established a motive for Judith Marchand's murder" to a peppering of angle-seeking small shot along the line of "Have any precautions been taken to guard against more of the staff being attacked?"

Richards' death on the railway line kept the party going for another ten minutes, Thane manoeuvring, weaving, throwing out smokescreens with all the polished skill of a conference-scarred veteran. Then, he fired his own salvo . . . he gave the pressmen the release on the fingerprinting and interviewing that was in progress above their heads at that moment.

Jock Mills stayed silent. The mass interview line would be a handy second lead. But his story was already written, the type set, the plates locked on the giant presses. The *Hour* was hitting the street within the next half-hour, running a special early edition carrying the inside story of the Hillman robberies. A certain floor supervisor had taken a long chance, and had spilled the story to a relative who worked in the *Hour*'s circulation department from which it had been rushed to the reporters' desk.

Now, if they could cap it with an arrest announcement in the stop press . . . He let his thoughts wander in search of a bonus . . .

152

in his expenses, of course, the tax would kill it if it was on his payslip . . . then jerked back to the present as Thane closed the conference and left the room. It was time to find a phone. He hoped nobody had spotted the pin he'd driven between the call-box wires knocking it out of action until he needed it.

.   .   .   .   .

The Greenmantle shop in Napier Street was a small, double-window affair, but with its modern, black marble front and strip-lit interior gave every indication of being a prosperous little concern. A bell gave a quiet, two-tone chime as Phil Moss opened the plate-glass door and walked across the fitted carpeting to the main sales counter. A smart blonde sales assistant . . . about twenty-five and built on bust and bottom lines . . . greeted him with a smile straight from a toothpaste commercial.

She was wasting her time. Moss flipped his warrant card, and said 'Police . . . I'd like to see the manageress.'

'That's me,' said the girl in a throaty purr. 'Now what brings a nice policeman like you to see us?'

Moss fished in his inside pocket. 'Ever see her before?' he asked, laying a picture of Judith Marchand on the counter.

The blonde took a pair of fancy-framed spectacles from under the counter, put them on, and took a long look at the photograph. Then, taking the glasses off again, she said, 'Sorry . . . I've never seen her.'

'Anyone else in the shop?'

'Yes . . . just a moment.' The blonde wriggled across on her high-heeled shoes to a curtained doorway. 'Joaney . . . there's a policeman here who wants to see you. Have you been chasing men again?'

'Coming . . .' the curtains parted a moment later, and Moss blinked. A second blonde of almost identical statistics, looked out. 'Where . . . oh, hello,' she giggled.

'Ever seen this woman before?' asked Moss, pointing to the photograph, still lying on the counter.

153

Joaney undulated over, gave another little giggle, and picked up the picture. 'Oh, her,' she declared immediately. 'Yes, I remember her all right. She comes in window shopping about twice a week . . . since not long after the place opened about four months ago, in fact. Buys the odd thing now and again, too, you know the old nuisance I mean, Judy.'

Her companion peered at the picture again. 'Let me see . . . oh yes, it's her all right. I didn't recognize her at first.'

'It's those glasses,' said Joaney. 'If you don't get them changed soon, honey, you're going to land in trouble.'

'Do you know what's happened to her?' asked Moss.

'No . . . don't tell me she's been arrested for loitering,' giggled the manageress, Joaney joining in.

'That picture was in the morning papers,' said Moss. 'she was murdered at Hillman's store.'

'Oh . . .' the blonde "twins" were shocked into silence for a moment. 'We never read the papers,' explained Joaney. 'At least, not very often. It's a pretty busy little shop, Mr. Policeman, our prices are keen. And at night, well, we've other things to do.'

'I can imagine ' grunted Moss. 'Didn't you even know about the murder?'

'Oh, sure. I heard about it,' said Judy.

'Can you remember any of the things she bought here?' pressed Moss.

'She bought a couple of blouses once.' volunteered Joaney. 'You remember, Judy. Remember the quizzing she gave us about them.'

'What sort of quizzing?' demanded Moss.

'Oh, she wanted to see just about everything in the shop . . . then went right back and bought the first ones she'd seen. She was a terrible nuisance.'

Moss looked around. 'That must have been quite a job,' he sympathized. 'You seem to carry quite a stock. Do you girls do the buying?'

'Not us,' Judy shook her long blonde hair. 'Mr. Buchan, the boss does all that. We just let him know if we need anything

154

special, and he delivers most of the stuff himself . . . he keeps a lot in store at his garage.'

Moss, feigning disinterest, picked up the picture and put it away. 'Just a check-up,' he explained. 'Routine stuff, girls. There was a receipt for some purchase made here among her papers, and we wanted to see if she was perhaps a close friend. Oh . . . look, while I'm here, can you give me a pair of nylons?'

'You'd look cute in them,' giggled Joaney.

Moss reddened. 'I want them for a friend.'

'What size,' asked Judy, remembering her status as manageress and becoming more business-like.

'Nine,' said Moss.

'That's my size, too.' said Judy. 'What kind of shade would she like?'

'Uh . . . oh, just let me see what you've got.'

The blonde gathered a selection from the shelves behind her and spread them on the counter.

'What's new bronze?' asked Moss.

Joaney gave her toothpaste smile. 'You know a bit more about women than you pretend, Mr. Policeman. Here we are . . . it's our newest shade.'

'I'll take them,' spluttered Moss, pulling out his wallet.

He left the shop with a sigh of relief, the nylons in his pocket, and slid thankfully into the seat of the waiting police car.

'Control's been on, sir,' said the driver. 'will you pick up Professor McMaster at Millside before you go on to Hillman's store?'

'I've still the other two shops to do,' grumbled Moss. 'Never mind . . . we can't keep the Professor waiting. Head right back. I've got what we need anyway.'

. . . . .

It was just leaving eleven a.m. when the police Humber reached Hillman's. Moss and Professor McMaster got out, and as the car rolled away again, the Professor stalked into the store, Phil hurrying behind. McMaster kept up a running commentary

155

on modern ethics of merchandising. 'Sheer mass hypnotism,' he declared, striding along. 'Get people to come inside, show them things they don't need at prices they can't afford, and persuade them they can't do without them. Hire purchase and sales technique are the twin ills of our civilization,' he snapped, brushing past a startled customer.

'The lifts are over there,' suggested Moss. 'We want the sixth floor office.'

'Lifts? Pshaw. Use the stairs. Good for the liver. Keeps your muscles in trim . . . do you better than those pills you take. That's the trouble with people today . . . want to see the insides of some of the specimens I deal with . . . cut through layer upon layer of fatty tissue.' McMaster was already tramping up the stairway, two steps at a time, Moss struggling in his wake. By the time they reached the sixth floor, Phil felt almost on his knees—but old McMaster was as brisk as when he had started.

Thane was in the interviewing room, standing by the sergeant's desk. The two policemen were talking to a small, unhappy looking man in oil-stained dungarees. Thane looked up, and gestured to them to come over.

'This is Willie Laing,' he said. 'Willie's just been telling us a few things. Start at the beginning again, Willie, and remember, we'll square it with the firm for you . . . so there's nothing to worry about.'

Willie gulped, looked around the four faces, shuffled his feet. 'I didn't think I was doing anything really wrong,' he began. 'I was only helping a pal . . .' he stopped, seeking sympathy, found none visible, swallowed hard again, and went on. 'Like I said, it was to help Jack Waddie. He's one of the transport drivers. Jack goes out of town every Wednesday night, to visit his ma down in Troon. Well, we're due to start at eight in the morning in the transport department, and there isn't a train that really suits him. You see, Jack likes to stay overnight, and come back up in the morning from Troon . . his ma's getting on in years. There's a train that gets in about eight fifteen at St. Enoch station. So I punch his card for him at the same time as my own every Thursday morning.'

156

'But I thought there was a check on people coming through after starting time,' interrupted Moss. Thane silenced him with a wave.

'That's right, mister,' said Laing. 'But you see, Jack just comes round to the garage entrance, slips in beside the vans and goes straight to work. If anyone catches him, he just says he had nipped out for a paper. Nobody really watches the time-clock at that hour of the morning . . . so it's easy.'

'Does anybody else know about this?' asked Thane softly.

'His mate, Danny McBain,' said Willie. 'But that's all . . . less that knows these wee fiddles the better.'

'That's the way to leave it,' said Thane. 'Jack Waddie is out just now. He'll be back pretty soon, though. Can you keep your mouth shut, Willie?'

The little man nodded earnestly. 'I didn't mean to do anything wrong, mister. I was just helping a pal. But when the polis started asking me about clocking in, well, I thought I'd better come clean.'

'All right, Willie.' Thane looked him straight in the eyes. 'When Waddie comes back, say nothing, do nothing to let him know we've had this talk.'

He towered over the little man. 'If you do, Willie, there'll be big trouble in store for you, I promise. Off you go, now . . . and remember.'

The little man scurried away.

9

McMASTER and the two detectives moved to a quiet corner of the room. 'I presume that touching example of employee integrity has quite a bearing on your case, Thane,' remarked the tall, lean medical man.

'It certainly has,' said Thane. 'It completes one half of the whole affair. And I'm hoping that the rest is about to fall into place. What's your latest contribution, sir?'

'The P.M. report on Judith Marchand,' said McMaster, pulling several closely-typed sheets of quarto paper from his inside jacket pocket and handing them to Thane. 'Briefly, Judith Marchand was a well-nourished, healthy woman. Examination of the body and stomach contents shows she died shortly after one p.m. on Tuesday. Considerable force in the strangulation, of course . . . but she was also hit in the stomach with considerable force . . . probably by a knee. That would "wind" her sufficiently to reduce her ability to struggle.'

'Did she struggle . . . I mean, effectively?' queried Thane.

The professor nodded slowly. 'We found traces of blood and skin tissue under two fingernails . . . not enough blood to enable us to group it, I'm afraid. Just enough to answer the benzedrine test. But at least you can take it she scratched her attacker.'

'On the face?' asked Phil.

'My good man, how should I know?' protested McMaster. 'I'm a scientist, not a magician. All I can say is we found skin tissue and blood. It could be from any part of the body, pleasant or otherwise, for all I know.'

158

He glanced at his watch. 'Well, time I was going. I've got Richards' body to tackle next.' A frosty little smile quivered on his lips. 'By the way, Thane, I've got a golf engagement tomorrow. Be a good chap and don't produce any fresh bodies till I've finished my round.'

'The old . . .' Phil Moss grinned broadly as McMaster stalked away.

Thane wrinkled his face ruefully. 'He's a downy old bird, McMaster. How'd your end go, Phil?'

Moss gave the thumbs up sign. 'Couldn't be better.' He leaned back against the office wall and scratched the top of his nose with a forefinger.

'Get on with it, then,' said Thane in friendly impatience.

'Right. First, I phoned the stocking company. Just as Birmingham reported, the firm supply a few small stores in addition to Hillman's, and one of them is Greenmantle. But Mr. Buchan and his pals made a slip, Colin . . . a real corker! I described the stockings over the phone, code markings and all. And the makers say that they're a new shade, not long on the market . . . and that the only supply they've made has gone exclusively to Hillman's. No one else has that shade . . . new bronze . . . in stock yet. Definitely not Greenmantle.'

Colin Thane's eyes narrowed. He gave a low, soft whistle. 'So they were definitely stolen,' he murmured.

'As definitely as this pair,' said Moss, pulling the small parcel from his pocket and opening it with all the bland confidence of a magician. 'I bought them in Greenmantle's an hour ago! You should see the set-up there, Colin . . . two blonde pieces of homework that look as though they've strayed from Hollywood . . . or Sauchiehall Street on a Saturday night.'

Running the nylons through his hands, Thane was jubilant. His hunch did make sense—here was the proof. Quickly, he told Moss of the report from the observation crew watching the garage, of the Hillman van, its driver, and the obvious implications.

'This character Waddie "punches out" of the store on a Wednesday evening, nips round to the garage again, walks in the door, and goes to earth. Once the routine search of the store is over, out he comes, like a fox from his burrow. He helps load the selected stolen material into his furniture van, shoving it into the drawers, inside the wardrobe, anywhere. But he can't leave the store again, even if the other man can. So when the job's done he nips back into his burrow again and waits till morning. Then all he has to do is reappear within the building. His time-card's been punched and as far as everybody's concerned . . . even the fellow who punched the card for him . . . he's arrived at the store for the first time that day.'

'Aye, sounds all right,' agreed Moss. 'But what about the other fellow . . . you said that Waddie helped someone else. Does the other man hide? And who is he?'

'Joe Deacon, the night commissionaire, holds the answer to that,' said Thane. 'I'm trying to lay hands on him right now. If he confirms what I think he will, then we've got them all.'

'On circumstantial evidence most of the way,' warned Moss. 'Theft, okay. But murder?'

'Someone's bound to crack,' said Thane. 'This is a hanging job, despite the new law. If a little talk will keep someone's head out of a noose, I reckon he'll talk. And besides, Judith Marchand scratched the man who attacked her. We find a man with scratch marks, add a few other hunks of evidence, and there's an ample case for any jury worth their salt.'

'Look who's lining up for fingerprinting,' said Moss softly, glancing over Thane's shoulder at the continued bustle of activity in the interviewing room. 'It's our pal Rosey, the store 'tec.'

'Don't worry about Rose,' said Thane, shaking his head. 'He's not our man. He's a nasty little character in many ways, yet, you know, he's only landed in a jam because he allowed his personal feelings to get mixed up with his anxiety over his job. In fact, he's darned lucky he isn't body number three. I reckon if we hadn't been hiding up in Farringdon's penthouse on Wednesday night and hadn't come down when we did, Mr. Rose would be lying in a box now while the staff paid out on a wreath "sheet".'

160

He turned, watched the white-faced store 'tec go through the formality of fingerprinting, questioning. Rose left the room in a few minutes, giving a brief, bitter nod in their direction.

Phil Moss broke a tea-biscuit in his pocket, took out a portion, and began quietly munching. 'That means that whoever hit me on the head was . . .'

'Was either the driver, or, much more likely, the killer himself . . . I believe they're two separate individuals, for very good reasons. I've been riding Rose pretty hard, but quite deliberately. I wanted to lull someone else into a feeling of security.'

'What happens next, then?' asked Moss. 'Do we raid this garage?'

'We do,' agreed his chief. 'But first of all, we have lunch. Then we wait until that Hillman van has left the store with its afternoon load. Once it gets a little way away from the store, we stop it, arrest the crew, and get a plain-clothes man to drive it under cover. Then we take the crew along with us to Rook Road and enter the garage. I've made an application for a search warrant, and we should have it in plenty of time. There's always a chance, too, that we may get something more from the observation van before zero hour.'

They left the "processing" team still on duty, continuing their monotonous round of interviews. By turning up the man who faked Waddie's time-clock entries they had already more than earned their keep, but the job must continue, in the hope that yet another new fact might be uncovered. The team, and the observation crew at the garage, were not the only men still at work on the case. Thane knew only too well the many widely-varied duties being carried out at that moment—McMaster at his grisly task down in the City Mortuary, Lanarkshire men continuing to seek some local lead in the case of Andy Richards, Millside officers delving into Richards' past and at the same time trying to discover more detail about Judith Marchand and the Greenmantle shops. For Thane, however, his job was to wait, and he might as well wait over a decent meal.

Hillman's restaurant was three flights of stairs down, on

the third floor. But he felt like a change of scenery. Leaving word with the detective sergeant where they would be found, Thane and Moss went out into Sauchiehall Street, crossed it, and went up a side-road into a quiet little pub. It had a first-floor restaurant which, like most pubs, served a meal which for cheapness and plain, good cooking took a lot of beating.

Two ice-cold beers at their elbows, they took their time over the food. Phil had trouble with a main course, and finally settled for soup and a double-portion of semolina—though his face grew a little gaunt as he saw the medium-rare steak that was placed before Colin Thane. Coffee—in a thick, man-sized cup—and a cigarette completed the meal. Finally, they rose, split the check, then walked back along the street and across to the department store.

Back on the sixth floor, the interview team were contenting themselves with a sandwich meal, and continuing their work while they ate. Nothing more had turned up, reported the detective sergeant.

It was one thirty. Thane sent out for the evening papers, cursed the *Hour's* story linking the store thefts with the murder—and its broad hints that Richards' death was almost certainly part and parcel of the same affair—and grinned sympathetically at the rival evening paper's, by comparison, pedestrian story. It had been a good lunch—he was almost asleep in his chair when the phone rang. Phil answered, nodded, and tossed the receiver across the desk.

Thane caught it neatly. Sergeant MacLeod, from the observation van, was the caller. He spoke quickly, obviously excited yet, disciplined by his training, not wasting a word. 'I think we've got it, sir. Buchan's just had a visitor. Drove up in the car you suggested, got out, and went straight inside. He's there now . . . hold on, sir . . .' The line went silent for a long minute, then, just as Thane caught the sound of an engine coming through the phone earpiece, MacLeod spoke again. 'He's just come out. Spoke to Buchan at the office entrance, then got in his car and is driving off.'

'Pictures?' snapped Thane.

162

'I'll check.' Silence again, for a longer period, then, 'Yes. Jenkins says they're in the bag. Want us to pack up now?'

Thane hesitated. 'I want those pictures quickly. But . . . no, Jenkins can stay where he is. You take his plates and walk down towards Dumbarton Road. I'll have a car pick you up there in five minutes. Go straight to Headquarters. They'll be waiting on the plates, and will rush prints through. Then go straight back to the garage with them. We'll probably be there by that time. Okay?'

'Okay,' agreed MacLeod. 'Though I hope I get back in time. I'd like to see the fun.'

.   .   .   .   .

Thane fixed the car, and warned Headquarters laboratory to have their darkroom ready to develop the photographs. If they really rushed, the job should take about twenty minutes from start to final print. Then he left the office, and climbed the private stairway to Farringdon's penthouse.

'If you expect me to play detective again without knowing what the hell it's about you're up a gum-tree,' barked Farringdon the moment Thane entered the managing director's office. 'You'd think I was on your ruddy suspect list . . . hey, I don't suppose I could be?'

'You're not,' grinned Thane. 'We checked your alibi.'

'My alibi?' grunted Farringdon, raising his eyebrows. 'But I never gave one.'

'We checked it anyway,' shrugged Thane. 'No, this time I want you to come on a car trip. Not a long one, just within the city. And I'd like you to bring Pat Miller with you.'

'The girl? What for?'

'To show you something interesting,' sparred Thane. 'But as usual, keep quiet about it, even to Pat. Just say you're going to the police station.'

'And where are we really bound for?' asked Farringdon shrewdly.

'The driver knows the way,' said Thane, backing to the door.

163

'He'll call for you in half an hour . . .' and he made a quick getaway.

.   .   .   .   .

Jack Waddie climbed into the cab of the big Morris Commercial, and glanced at the dashboard clock. It was two fifteen p.m. Young Danny McBain, his mate, climbed into the seat beside him a moment later, slammed the door, and pulled a *Noon Record* from the dashboard pocket.

'Goin' to the White City the night,' he said, chewing busily on a piece of gum. 'The girl's on holiday at Rothesay, an' ma second string's on the night shift . . . not a damn thing else to do. Ah've seen the flicks, and it's old-time night at the jiggin'.'

'Fancy anything?' asked Waddie, switching on the engine and stamping on the floor-mounted self-starter button. As the furniture van came hoarsely to life Danny nodded wisely.

'There's a new Irish dug. Pal of mine says it's a cert. Dunno what the bookies'll give on it, though. It's no tipped, but still . . .'

'Shove a quid on it for me,' said Waddie.

'Can you no come yoursel'?'

Waddie was too busy steering the van out of the Hillman garage entrance and into the narrow street beyond to be able to reply immediately. 'Busy tonight,' he replied, belching as his canteen meal settled. 'Got to give my cousin a hand at the garage. Lot of work piling up.'

'Ah could use a bit o' extra money masel',' hinted the lad.

Waddie shook his head. 'Sorry, Danny. Nothing doing.'

Danny flushed a little, then resumed his rhythmic chewing and concentrated on the *Noon* dog-cards. The van rumbled its way through the streets out of the city, its interior crammed with furniture to be delivered to a dozen different addresses. They were going out along Pollokshaws Road when Waddie suddenly swore and threw the engine down into third gear. Danny glanced up. A police patrol car was just ahead of their bonnet, the driver's white-gauntleted arm waving them down.

'Jeeze, what's up?' he said. 'You been going too fast again, Jack?'

164

Waddie muttered sulphurically. 'Fast my backside. The baskets probably haven't anything better to do. Probably want to see the log.' He drew into the kerb, stopped, switched off the engine, and sat back, his small eyes glittering angrily. The police car had stopped a few yards ahead, but now reversed until its tail was only a couple of feet from the van's radiator. 'Sods are too lazy to walk,' grunted Waddie, fumbling in the dash pocket for the log sheet which listed his journeys and times as required by law.

But the men in the patrol car didn't get out. Instead, a tall figure in civilian clothes appeared at the driver's side of the lorry cab, flashing a warrant card. Waddie went suddenly white, switched the engine on again and banged the starter. But the the big man outside had the door open—and another figure had suddenly yanked open the other door and was diving in.

'Don't do it,' barked Colin Thane. 'There's another car right behind you, Waddie. You can't move the van.'

'What the hell's goin' on?' protested Danny. 'Here, take your elbow out of ma guts.'

'Sorry, son,' said Phil Moss, ripping the ignition key from the dash. The two patrolmen had left the leading car now, and were standing one on either side of the cab.

'Come out of it, Waddie.' said Thane. 'Slowly. You too, son.'

'What for?' demanded the driver, eyes darting desperately about, his face suddenly pasty.

'You're wanted at the station,' said Thane. 'But first we're taking you for a little run. Come on now . . . move.'

Waddie turned in the driver's seat, sighed, and moved to climb down. Then, like a flash, he swept his hand under the seat, and swung his arm up again, a tyre lever cutting through the air. Thane dodged the blow, and seized the man's wrist as the heavy bar whistled past. He twisted hard, and Waddie screamed as the metacarpus bones in his wrist cracked. The driver came out of the van as if catapulted, the tyre lever clanking on the roadway. Thane and the uniform man grabbed him, a pair of handcuffs clicked round his wrist. A very frightened Danny came out of the van, and shivered at the sight.

'Behave yourself, son, or you'll get the same,' warned Thane.

'Don't worry, mister . . . don't worry,' the boy quickly assured him.

They were marched back to the rear of the van, where a big police Humber sat, its nose only a yard from the Morris's tail.

'In the front, lad,' said Thane, not unkindly. Danny slid in obediently beside the waiting driver. A plain-clothes man, standing ready, took the van's ignition key from Moss and headed back towards the cab. Waddie watched him go, a dawning mixture of fear and comprehension on his face.

'The back for you, Waddie,' ordered Thane. The van driver entered the Humber, Thane and Moss one on either side of him in the big back seat. The patrol car in front moved off. Then the furniture van, its new driver at the wheel, drove away. And finally, the Humber started off, leaving a small crowd of curious onlookers standing at the pavement's edge. The Humber turned down into Nicholson Street and headed back towards the river, and the north side of the city.

.   .   .   .   .

Four other cars and a patrol van were waiting at the foot of Rook Road. As Thane's Humber appeared they fell in behind. The convoy purred up the road, then, as the garage came into sight, accelerated a little. The G.P.O. van was still parked there.

Then the cars split, following a pre-arranged plan. Two swept into the garage, one blocking the forecourt exit, another stopping at the main office doorway. The patrol van skidded to a halt at the pavement's edge, and a dozen uniform men piled from its rear and sprinted to encircle the block. Another car waited beside it, engine running, while the fourth, Thane's Humber hard on its heels, roared straight through the open gates leading into the garage yard.

The growl of engines and the squealing of tyres had hardly died away before the officers had saturated the garage buildings. The pump attendant watched, bewildered, while the two mechanics were led out to the patrol van. He was even more

166

bewildered when he joined them a moment later, two constables coming in with him then shutting the van door behind them.

'Just sit quiet, boys,' said the older of the two officers. 'This doesn't concern you.'

. . . . . .

Jumping from the Humber almost before it had stopped, Colin Thane ran into the main garage, two uniform men hard on his heels. While the constables collected the mechanics, he went on towards a side door set in one wall of the gloomy, oil-stained garage, close beside the greasing ramp. He threw the door open, and found himself in a small corridor, with another door at its end. The second door was locked. He stood back, and all his fourteen stone went into the kick his size twelve shoe placed on the door-edge. It flew open with a splintering of wood. An office lay beyond—and was empty. A cigarette was lying on the desk still burning, a faint pillar of smoke climbing ceilingwards. There was another door leading from the room—presumably towards the front office. As he turned to it, other footsteps rang from beyond it, the handle rattled, a voice swore. The key was still in the lock—he turned it, and swung the door open, just before a brawny uniform sergeant put his shoulder to it. A constable stood beside him.

'Nothing out front,' said the sergeant. 'Oh . . . another door. Maybe he got out that way, sir.'

'It was locked too—maybe he did it from the other side,' agreed Thane. But there had been no key. Sudden comprehension dawned. He put a finger to his lips, nodded towards the desk, with its plush front, the chair lying just behind it, and gestured silently. The other two grinned in understanding. Suddenly, all three pounced on the desk, and with a tremendous heave sent it sliding back to the wall. The chair, jammed as the desk swept back, hit the wall first and slid into the kneehole even as the desk itself crashed against the plaster. A muffled scream of pain and fear came from underneath. The three policemen

167

pulled the desk away from the wall again, to expose a moaning, huddled figure. They had found John Buchan.

Thane jerked the man upright. 'John Buchan. I have a warrant to search your premises on suspicion of housing stolen property. I must ask you to remain here while this is executed.' He released his grip, and as Buchan slumped to the floor again told the sergeant, 'Hold him. And bring the others in.'

.   .   .   .   .

It didn't take long to find the stolen Hillman stock—or most of it, anyway. The bulk of it was in a brick lock-up at the rear of the garage. Some more, including several thousand cigarettes still in their corrugated cardboard cartons—were in a big metal cupboard in the main garage. Both were double-locked. Both were opened in a matter of seconds with a bunch of keys found in one drawer of Buchan's desk.

Thane went back to the little inner office, now crammed with people. Waddie and Buchan were there, both handcuffed, standing side-by-side under the vigilant guard of two uniform men. Danny the vanboy, still chewing gum in a slow, desperate attempt to retain composure, was finding the situation like a Hollywood movie come to life—and discovering that it was better to watch the silver screen than to be involved in real life drama. Farringdon and Pat Miller, both unsure but expectant, waited in the opposite corner beside Phil Moss. And Sergeant MacLeod was there, still in his borrowed G.P.O. overalls, a large manilla envelope in one hand.

Thane took the envelope, glanced at its contents, and said something that brought a smile of pleasure to MacLeod's face. Then he went over to Farringdon and the girl.

'Want to see what we've found? You'll find it interesting,' he declared. Obediently, they followed him from the office and into the lock-up. 'Have a look at some of that stuff,' he invited. 'See if it means anything to you.'

Farringdon pounced on the nearest bundle—a collection of men's shirts. He gave a bear-like growl as he pawed through

168

them. Pat was examining the labels on a collection of frocks. Shoes—underwear—coats—hats, men's, women's, children's wear. Some still had price tags attached.

'Now over here,' said Thane, and led them across the concrete floor of the garage to the big cupboard. Once more the girl and her boss poked and prodded at a wide assortment of articles. It was Farringson who broke the silence first.

'It's all ours, as far as I can make out, Thane. It's only a fraction of the stuff, of course, but by God, it's good to see it. So you've cracked the case, eh? A damn good piece of work.'

'And these men back in the office . . . they're the men who killed Judith?' asked Pat, her hazel eyes suddenly hard and bright.

'I don't think so,' said Thane. 'They played their part. But we've still to get their boss, the man who strangled Judith and probably murdered Richards the doorman.'

'You know who he is?' pressed Farringdon, hands in his pockets, his face granite-grey with emotion.

'We'll have him within the hour,' said Thane. 'Come back to the office, if you want to hear his name.'

.   .   .   .   .

In the hushed tension of the garage's little office the slightest sound or movement seemed magnified to almost unbearable prominence. Buchan and Waddie still stood against one wall, exchanging sidelong glances. Young Danny was perched on the edge of the desk, still slowly chewing the now tasteless gum as he watched Phil Moss methodically checking through the desk drawers. Thane pulled the chair over for Pat Miller, and as the girl sat down jerked his head in a motion that sent Danny scuttling. He took over the lad's perch, and sat there a moment, one leg swinging—backwards—forwards—backwards—forwards.

He cleared his throat, and, as eyes riveted on him, began to talk softly, almost sadly.

'A lot of stolen property has been found in your garage, Buchan. Other property, definitely stolen, has been sold in your Greenmantle shop. I know how you took it out of Hillman's.

169

I know about Waddie's Thursday morning calls. It was a pretty clever setup. But that's not the end. I'm investigating two murders, Buchan. Judith Marchand, strangled. Andrew Richards, murdered by train. Both discovered too much about the Hillman thefts. You know what that means? And you know that murder in the furtherance of theft is still a hanging charge?' He stopped, and sat there, leg swinging idly again, waiting.

Buchan licked his lips, glanced at Waddie, standing dejectedly, handcuffed wrists hanging slack, and tried to bluster. 'Can you prove these goods are stolen? I run a legitimate business. I've accounts with every single firm whose goods are out there. I'll show you their invoices if you want.'

'Probably you can,' agreed Thane. 'Having a cover account is all part of the scheme, isn't it? But if we get down to matching the quantity of stock you hold against the invoices you've received, what then? And how is it that your shop is selling a style of nylon that it hasn't had delivered yet . . . a style that only Hillman's could show, until some were stolen a couple of weeks back? Think again, Buchan. You've got a record. Judith Marchand was investigating your shop, found the stolen goods . . . and you strangled her.'

'It wasn't me,' Buchan broke down in a babble of words. 'I didn't know it was going to happen . . . I wouldn't have let it happen, I swear.'

'But you knew Richards was going to die,' whip-cracked Thane. 'You could have stopped that. You helped to murder him.'

'He . . . he said we were in too deep. I only hit Richards over the head, knocked him out like I was told to, I didn't kill him. Ask Waddie . . . he was there.'

With a hoarse snarl and a jingle of his handcuffs, Waddie suddenly came to life and swung at his fellow-prisoner. But the two uniform men grabbed him, and whirled him round again. One of them clipped the jaws of a fresh handcuff on to Waddie's wrist, then clamped the other section on his own arm, completely anchoring the driver.

'So you were there, Waddie,' mused Thane. 'Your time-clock

170

dodge won't get you out of this. What was it like when the train wheels chopped Richards head?'

Waddie stood silent, truculent.

'Think you're tough, Waddie? Tough enough to stand a murder rap?'

'There's nothing to pin on me,' grunted the driver.

'You have an alibi, then?' said Thane softly. 'Just tell us where you were, and who can prove it, and of course, you're in the clear. Only don't inflict that old story on us about being with your mother at Troon.'

Waddie licked his lips. 'I was in the store, in hiding,' he finally declared. 'You cops were all round the place. How could I have got out?'

'Difficult to prove, though, isn't it?' mused Thane.

'There's a lump on your pal's skull to prove it,' said the driver, fighting a rear-guard action. 'And I'd have stove his skull in if I'd been able to get a clearer chance, you interfering shower.'

'All right, you were in the store. You were going to help move Judith Marchand's body that night, weren't you?'

Waddie nodded. 'But that's all,' he declared. 'I didn't kill her . . . and as for Richards, maybe they took care of the wrong man.' He glared again at the trembling Buchan.

'Did the lad here know anything about what was going on?'

The driver shook his head. 'I used to chase him off on Thursdays, as soon as we stopped at the garage. I said I had business to discuss with my . . . cousin' he mouthed the word as if admitting the relationship left a bad taste.

'That's right, mister,' said Danny with great earnestness. 'I always went down the road to a wee café for half an hour. Ask them at the café . . . they know ma face.'

Thane gestured to Sergeant MacLeod. The "linesman" handed over the envelope again. 'We took some pictures today,' said Thane. 'These are prints. Here's your van at the garage, Waddie . . . another of the van . . . and there's a closeup of you leaving.' He stopped, looked round the room, then slowly drew

171

out the last print. 'And here's another picture, one that will especially interest you, Buchan.'

He threw the print on the desk-top. Buchan looked, and, below his little pencil moustache his mouth quivered. His face was ashen. Charles Farringdon lumbered forward, and stared at the photograph, surprise, disbelief, growing amazement mirrored one after the other on his heavy, jowled face. The picture, an enlarged section of the original plate, showed Buchan standing at the entrance to the garage's main office—ushering Henry Allen, the Hillman head buyer, into the building.

'Allen,' nodded Thane. 'We've got other pictures. He's the nigger in this particular woodpile, isn't he, Buchan,' he demanded.

Buchan didn't answer for a long moment. Then he nodded. 'Allen did it . . . he killed Judith Marchand. He's the boss of the show. It wasn't till afterwards I heard about it. He was going to get the body out the next night, but when you appeared, he had to abandon it.'

'And Richards? You were the man with the moustache he met near Hillman's on the Wednesday night,' said Thane.

Buchan wearily agreed. 'I took him to the garage. He was to wait for Allen there . . . he'd found out somehow that Allen was behind the whole business. When I got him here, I gave him a drink then slugged him with a rubber cosh when his back was turned. It knocked him out cold and I gave him another dose whenever he came to. Allen turned up about eleven that night, and packed Richards into a wee van I've got. He came back about a couple of hours later, collected his own car from the garage and drove away again.'

'And that fake suicide note? Who wrote it?' pressed Thane, grim-faced as he regarded the broken man before him, seeming to hear the swish of that cosh, its dull thud against a defenceless man's skull.

'I wrote the note,' admitted Buchan. 'It was another of Allen's ideas . . . he thought that at the least it might confuse you for a spell, at the best it might throw the whole load on to Richards. I tried copying his signature straight from paper at first, but it was no use. So I used tracing paper finally, and got

172

a pretty smooth copy at the fifth try. Transferring it was simple.'

'It was a reasonable fake,' agreed Thane. 'It's doubtful whether we could definitely disprove it in a court . . . but you made your mistake in writing the suicide note with a ball-point. You should have used Richards' pen . . . the ink was a different colour, to start with. But never mind that. All that you've told us means that as your friend Waddie was, by his own admission, still playing hide-and-seek with us at the store, the only man who can vouch for your story is Allen.'

Buchan bit his lip. All his fears of the past few days had become hard, solid fact in the last half-hour. All the easy visions of quick, almost risk-free money that Henry Allen's plan had raised had faded—and in their place remained only the factual nightmare of the dock at the High Court. He wasn't scared of a stretch—he could do that standing on his head. But my God, the rope. . . .

'I want to make a statement,' he declared. 'I'll tell you all I know.'

'You're playing it wise,' said Thane, hiding the jubilation he felt. 'We'll get it from you later. Jack Waddie, James Buchan, I arrest you on charges of theft, assault on a police officer and being involved in the murders of Judith Marchand and Andrew Richards. I must warn you that anything you say will be taken down and may be used in evidence. Have you any reply to make, Waddie?'

'Get. . . .' snarled the driver. 'I want my lawyer.'

'Buchan?'

The garage proprietor said shakily, 'I didn't know about the woman's murder. And I had to help with Richards . . . I was forced to.'

'I'll see you both later,' said Thane. 'In the meantime, just keep remembering, it will help your case to co-operate with us.'

.   .   .   .   .

The two prisoners had been bundled into a police car and driven away to Millside Police Station for a further formal caution and charging. Then their personal possessions would be taken from them, along with ties, belts and, in fact, any other article which could lend itself to suicide—a standard precaution in a murder arrest.

Thane and Moss stood outside the garage with Farringdon and Pat. Behind them, officers were still searching the garage on the off-chance that other goods remained hidden. The two mechanics and the pump attendant had been sent home for the day.

'And now for Allen, I presume,' said Farringdon. 'My God, that milk-and-water mouse of a man. The last person I'd cast as a double murderer. You going to pick him up straight away, Thane? I suppose that means arresting him in the store itself?'

'Now for Allen,' confirmed Thane. 'But there's one last call to make first, to explain a final part of this whole affair. Want to come along?'

'I wouldn't miss it,' said Farringdon grimly. 'The little swine, with his "yes sir—no sir, three bags full sir". I always marked him as a frightened little twerp. You know what I mean, good enough at his job, but scared stiff in case he put a foot wrong. Huh—some fool he's made of a lot of us.'

'He—he always seemed so quiet, almost timid,' said Pat, toying nervously with the strap of her handbag. 'Yet he could strangle Judith, and then act so . . . so distressed about it all.'

'He's cold-blooded enough,' agreed Thane. 'Cold enough to probably stand and watch until a train killed Richards . . . for he'd never take the chance of leaving him alive on that line. Richards was marked for death from the moment he tried to put the squeeze on Allen. It was probably that mild exterior that made Richards think he'd get away with blackmail. Instead, he ended on a mortuary slab.

'But don't worry about Allen. He's clever and dangerous to a degree, but there's no chance of him getting away. I've got two men on every door leading out of Hillman's. They've been there since Allen returned to the store after lunch. If he

174

leaves, they've got orders to shadow him . . . and if they miss
him then they know they'll be back on the beat tomorrow.'

He shepherded them towards the waiting car.

.   .   .   .   .

It was three twenty when the police Humber drew up
outside Joe Deacon's home in Possilpark. Thane rang the
doorbell, and a small, plump, middle-aged woman opened the
door to them. 'Come in,' she invited. 'Joe's in the sitting-room
with a constable. He's been waiting on you.'

Deacon rose to his feet as they entered. There was a worried
look on his tired face. 'Hello, Mr. Thane . . . oh, Mr. Farringdon,
didn't expect you, sir. I'm sorry I was out this morning. When
I got back I wanted to phone right away, but the policeman said
I was just to wait.'

'That's what we wanted, Joe,' said Thane. 'Mind if we sit
down?'

'Please do, all of you.' The night commissionaire and his
wife bustled around finding seats for them. 'Would you like a
cup of tea?' asked Mrs. Deacon.

'No, thanks,' smiled Thane. 'We won't be here more than a
few minutes.' He turned back to Deacon, who was sitting
anxiously forward on the edge of his chair.

'Remember Wednesday night, Joe, when we searched the
store?'

'I'm not likely to forget it, sir,' the man half-smiled.

'And remember Mr. Allen coming in afterwards?'

'Aye.' Deacon nodded, obviously wondering where the
questions were leading.

'When did you first see him, Joe?'

'Why, when he came in, sir.'

'Take your time to this one, Joe. Did you actually see him
come in the door . . . or did you see him just inside it?'

Deacon flushed scarlet.

'Which was it, Joe?'

'Just inside the door,' he finally admitted. 'What with all the
excitement, I locked the door and nipped into the gents' for a

175

minute . . . it's just a couple of yards away from the entrance, almost opposite the box in fact. Mr. Allen was just inside the door when I came out again.'

'So you can't really say whether he was coming in . . . or had been trying to go out and had turned round when he heard you?'

The night commissionaire shook his balding head. 'I couldn't say, sir.'

'Let's try it again, Joe. You went into the gents'. How long were you?'

'A couple of minutes, Mr. Thane, no more.'

'And you locked the outside door?'

'Definitely. Mr. Allen could have opened it, though. He has a key.'

'Was it locked when you let him out again?'

Deacon nodded slowly.

'I don't think it was ever unlocked, Joe. He was in the store, watching you. When you nipped into the toilet he sneaked past the commissionaire's box . . . Inspector Moss and I were too busy grilling Rose the store 'tec to see him go. He was going to unlock the door and slip out . . . but you came back too quickly for him.

'Think back, Joe. Has he ever come in late like that before?'

'Now and again,' agreed Deacon. 'Sometimes he works late, too.'

'Usually on a Wednesday night?'

Deacon nodded, more and more puzzled.

'Do you always know when he's working late?'

'No . . . no, I couldn't say that, sir. But then, if Mr. Farringdon doesn't mind me saying so, the bosses are usually a bit slack when it comes to observing routine things like notifying us. And Mr. Allen's a keen wee man. Like I was saying, sometimes he stays late without telling anyone.'

'He does, Joe. He certainly does. More often than you know.' Thane took out his cigarettes, tapped one absently on his thumbnail, then used it as a pointer to emphasize his next words. 'He hides in the store, Joe, along with a pal, or just stays "working late". Then, when you've all settled in the box playing

176

cards . . . you play cards a lot, Joe, don't you, maybe more than you should?' Deacon's shamefaced glance at his boss was confirmation. 'When you've all settled in the box he does what he wants . . . loads clothing, shoes, just about everything you can think of, into the furniture van down in the garage. He's picked the stuff beforehand, hidden some of it, but left the rest on the racks or on stands, knowing just what he wants to collect. The loading's always on a Wednesday night, to fit in with his plan. The van drives out in the morning, the stuff hidden in the furniture it's carrying. Then all that stolen material, hundreds of pounds worth each time, is unloaded at a garage where the staff always get Thursday off.

'There's nothing left to chance, Joe. When he's finished, on a Wednesday night he comes down to the back door of the store. He makes sure you're not watching, and then he lets himself out with his keys. If you see him, well, he says he's coming in . . . not going out. If it's too obvious, well, he just happens to have been working late, and he's surprised you didn't see him when you made your nightly check of the building. But it's a quiet lock on the door, Joe, and it's only now and again you see him.' Thane stopped, gave a slow shrug of his shoulders, and fumbled in his pocket for a match. Phil Moss snapped his lighter, and the cigarette tip glowed red. Slowly, luxuriantly, Thane inhaled the smoke and let it trickle down his nostrils. He felt an exhilarating surge of confidence, a lightness of mind.

Little Henry Allen might still have to be tried and convicted by a jury. But in Thane's mind he had already been found guilty. Henry Allen, who had been running his own chain of shops using Buchan as a front. Who had been feeding them with stolen goods, covering the reset stock with small, genuine orders from the same manufacturers who dealt with Hillman's . . . and who better than the head buyer to take care of that detail?

His shops were booming . . . they couldn't do otherwise with a one hundred per cent profit on probably three out of every four things they sold. And Judith Marchand had found out . . . found out, yet, because of her debt to Allen's wife, who had helped her and her baby in their time of need, had been unable to go to the police and tell what she knew. Maybe that last letter had been a final effort to put her conscience before her feeling of gratitude to the thief's wife.

Definitely, Allen must have found out what she knew. Perhaps she warned him to stop, or she'd tell. Definitely, too, she hadn't mentioned the letter. And then that blow in her stomach, the retching pain . . . the tightening, biting suffocating scarf . . . Thane shivered.

Richards? Richards had been a blackmailer. But blackmailer or not, he had been murdered in fiendish fashion. Allen, the dormouse, sleepy, frightened of the boss, Allen had driven out of Bishopbriggs, the drugged form by his side. He had parked off the road on the vacant lot, dragged Richards to the line, and laid the still breathing man's neck on the metal rail. The train acted as executioner—and he had returned to his Bearsden home, to probably make faint protest to his wife about the long hours he had to work. His wife would be so sorry for poor, dear Henry. Would she be so sorry, he wondered, if she knew about the two blondes that Phil Moss had discovered?

He took another drag at the cigarette. 'We'll "lift" him now, Phil,' he said quietly. 'His time's run out.'

THE dull, infuriatingly monotonous ringing tone came loud over the line. Henry Allen pursed his lips, waited another few seconds, then replaced the receiver. For the third time running he had dialled John Buchan's garage—and for the third time running there had been no reply. He lifted the phone again, dialled "0", and tapped his signet ring impatiently on the edge of the mouthpiece. The operator answered at last.

'Look, miss, I've been trying to dial Partick 6116 . . . Buchan's garage. I can get no reply, and there should be somebody there.'

'Just one minute, sir, I'll try to get through.' There was almost a minute's silence, then the girl's voice came back on the line. 'Hello, sir. I'm afraid the number must be out of order. We've a linesman working in the area, so perhaps if you'd like to try later. . . .'

'Thanks,' grunted Allen, and hung up, doubts crowding in on him.

The whole situation seemed wrong. First, when he had come back from lunch about an hour before, he had found Farringdon and the Miller girl had left the store, going off in a police car on some mysterious errand. Then, bumping into the transport manager on the ground floor, he had been given fresh cause to worry.

'Don't ask me what's going on,' the transport man had shrugged. 'But the boss was pumping me about the men's duties, and then I find my staff seem to be top priority on this damned fingerprint list.'

179

And now Buchan wouldn't—or couldn't—answer his telephone.

Just jitters? It could be, he knew. The plump little man let his eyes flit round the office room—old-fashioned, finicky, moulded to fit the fussy, rather nervous personality that he had created for himself over the last score of years. Only once before had he had this kind of premonition . . . yes, that was the word for it, premonition. To be exact, it had been in 1932 a couple of hours before he and two companions had broken into an office block in Liverpool, hoping for easy pickings. He had hung back a little, without really knowing why. They'd been unaware of the new-fangled burglar alarm system installed in one of the offices . . . until the police had come charging into the building. The other two were caught red-handed, their booty ready-packed in a suitcase. But Allen the only one of the trio without a record, had got away.

There was then, at any rate, some honour left among thieves. His frantic dash to escape, ending with him climbing at breakneck pace down a twenty foot rone-pipe, would have been useless if either of his companions had talked. But they had taken a stiff sentence without a mention of their mystery friend's identity. And Henry Allen, the young drapery clerk, watched impassively in the public gallery as they were led from the court to the cells.

They had been a good team. For three years they had worked together, pulling jobs throughout the Midlands by night, respectable citizens by day. Allen, a product of the Manchester slums, was the junior of the trio. But he already had a long, fairly successful career in petty crime behind him, plus a two-year term in Borstal for an attack on an old woman who had put up a struggle for her handbag when he had tried to snatch it one night when he was short of ready cash.

But in Borstal, as elsewhere, that deceptively shy exterior had paid off . . . his action was openly regarded as a momentary slip on the part of a pleasant young man who had fallen on hard times.

Now here he was in Hillman's . . . with that same feeling again. The first tendril of doubt had been when he heard from

180

Gwynneth that Thane had been out at their house. Not that his wife could have told the policeman anything. She was as ignorant of his past and present as everyone else. Funny, looking back, the way they had met.

After his friends had been sentenced, Allen had quickly headed for London to let things cool down. He bumped into Gwynneth in a hotel cocktail bar. She was on holiday from Glasgow with two girl-friends, and entering the bar on their own was, for those days, quite an act of bravado for the girls from the north. Allen caught the rainbow flash of her diamond earrings, her pleasant but not over-intelligent face. His draper's instinct summed up the quality of her clothes . . . and he moved in, the shy, nervous young Englishman who spoke vaguely about his business background. Gwynneth's family had money . . . not enough to make her an heiress, but sufficient to smooth the path of life. Allen remembered that night of fear in the office block, decided to retire . . . and, bowing to the inevitable, Gwynneth's parents gave them the house at Bearsden as a wedding gift. Another family friend pulled strings, and the bridegroom found himself back in drapery again . . . though this time as an assistant buyer in the growing Hillman organization. Life was easy. His quick brain, turned to legitimate channels for the first time in years, brought him promotion.

The old hunger for excitement and easy money remained, and often he slipped off "sick" for the odd day at the races. But on the whole, for a while he had grown fat, contented, a tolerated, rather patronized member of society. In the quiet moments, he sometimes hated this new life. And Gwynneth in steady doses drove him nearly crazy. But she was still his main meal-ticket, and so, winter sale, summer sale, the years slipped by.

That swine Farringdon moved to the top, slave-driving his way to bigger profits and quickly earning Allen's undying hatred. Hillman's head buyer took to "working late" more often, trying his indifferent luck at the dogtracks, drinking at out-of-town bars where he was known as a deceptive little character with a roving eye. But he was always the tired, willing company servant when he finally got home to Gwynneth again—and it would have rocked Hillman's to its foundations to know of his other life.

Bumping into Buchan had been sheer chance. The fan-belt had whirled off Allen's car outside the Rook Road garage, and he had gone in looking for a new one. Then, some nights later, they'd found themselves side-by-side at a dogtrack. They met a few more times, and Buchan told him about his cousin who was a driver at Hillman's. Some drinks later, the garageman had boasted about his police record.

Still it hadn't meant anything, until the day Farringdon gave him a particularly vicious bawling out for a piece of unlucky buying. His brain still clouded at the memory. He could show the fat swine . . . he'd never liked to knuckle under to anyone. But Allen hadn't the money to cut adrift. If he had, he would have cut free from Gwynneth too. He was getting too old and heavy to start from scratch again. Then he had thought of Buchan, of Waddie the driver . . . and remembered an old trick he had once heard being worked in the bakery business.

Sixty, twenty, twenty was the split they had decided on. He mortgaged all he owned without Gwynneth's knowledge, and Buchan took a loan on the garage to rent and outfit the three shops.

'One is small-time, two just adequate, three being sensible,' he had insisted to the garageman. Duplicate accounts with makers and wholesalers who supplied Hillman's, small genuine orders—and then the real stock, straight off the department store pegs, had begun to fill the Greenmantle shops, while Buchan fronted as owner.

Four thousand pounds in three months, they had cleared. Over three hundred a week, tax-free, plus the genuine sales. They had installed the two blondes in the main shop right at the start. Joan and Judy had a flat, where Buchan in theory paid the rent and Allen was merely a close friend . . . close enough to have a key. A year he'd wanted. A year in which to build a bankroll big enough to either launch out on his own or to clear out altogether. Of course, the police had to come into it sooner or later. That hadn't worried him. Allen deliberately kept the robberies down in quantity to a point where they could have been just due to shoplifting . . . he had been near enough to the top to be sure of knowing what was going on.

Judith Marchand, though . . . when she had given him twenty-four hours to clear out before she told what she knew, he had been shaken. After that, killing her had been an obvious necessity, a task that could not be delayed.

Richards hadn't been such a surprise. Allen had been conscious of the leer on the ex-cop's face for days, almost weeks, before he had suddenly asked for a thousand pounds to keep his mouth shut. It was funny, in a way . . . Richards had died still believing that Judith was "in" on the deal and was hiding.

But Buchan had gone windy now . . . the two killings had shown him as a small-timer without the stomach to press for success. Allen knew that only his veiled threats and iron will was holding the garage man from running.

But perhaps that had now changed. Perhaps Buchan's fear of arrest had finally proved the stronger. Was that the reason for there being no reply from the garage? Buchan had been obviously uncomfortable when Allen had looked in on his way back to the store after lunch. It would do no harm to check . . . He lifted the phone again, got a line from the Hillman switchboard operator, and dialled rapidly.

Judy, the blonde manageress, answered from the Greenmantle shop.

'It's Harry, Judy,' he said. 'Your boss been in today at all?'

'Harry, honey! No, we haven't seen him here. Nobody but customers and a silly old policeman who was in this morning. Why don't you look over yourself and cheer me up?'

'Maybe, maybe,' he said impatiently. 'What did the police want?'

'It was awfully exciting,' giggled the girl, 'One of our customers, an annoying old girl, has been murdered . . . it's been in all the papers, fancy!'

'What's that got to do with the shop?' snapped Allen.

'Nothing . . . nothing at all. The policeman said they were

183

just making inquiries to see if they could find people who knew her. He was quite a lamb, actually. He bought a pair of nylons before he left.'

Allen replaced the phone, and sat staring at the instrument, his mind working furiously. The whole situation shrieked danger.

The best thing to do would be to go round to Buchan's garage and find out exactly what was going on. But first . . . he flipped open his desk diary, found the number he wanted, and once more dialled rapidly.

'I want to book a sleeper berth on tonight's train to London,' he told the Central Station reservation clerk who answered. 'I'll want to join at Motherwell, not Glasgow . . . and I want a first-class if possible.'

'We can manage, sir. There have been one or two cancellations. How about the 10.20 p.m.? She stops at Motherwell okay. Your name, sir?'

'Munro . . . Joseph Munro,' replied Allen. 'I'll pick up the ticket within half an hour.' He sat back with a sigh, the phone back on its cradle. Stage one of his escape route was open, if necessary. The Lanarkshire police would be quieter and less likely to be watching. . . .

Sliding open the bottom drawer of his desk, he pulled it completely off its runners and reached into the space behind. His hand closed on a small tin box—his "emergency kit". Five hundred pounds in cash, and a tiny wash-leather pouch containing half-a-dozen diamonds worth another five hundred. There was more money lying in a bank under a "cover" name. With luck, he'd collect that too. Shoving the tin into his jacket pocket, he hesitated, then pulled open the middle drawer. This time he scooped up a heavy jack-knife, and fumbled with it, swearing under his breath as he levered the blade open. Now the marlin spike at the other end . . . he held the knife in his hand, a vicious weapon, needle-tipped spike at one end, the sharp, broad blade at the other. Carefully, he slid the opened knife into his right-hand trouser pocket, took his brown Homburg hat from the peg, then pressed the buzzer at the side of his desk.

'I've just had an urgent phone message,' he told his secretary

184

when she answered. 'I'll have to go out for a spell . . . I should be back in about an hour.'

.   .   .   .   .

Sunlight danced and glittered on the department store's broad colour-packed display windows as the two police cars slid to a halt at the pavement's edge. Quietly, a C.I.D. man left the first car and walked round the building, alerting the guards watching each of the four doors. Not until he returned did the other occupants alight from the cars. Thane in the lead, followed by Moss and three other officers, they crossed the crowded pavement, Farringdon and Pat Miller close behind. The doorman drew himself erect as he recognized the store boss, and snapped a smart salute.

'Seen Mr. Allen?'   demanded Farringdon.

'No, sir. Not since just after lunch, sir.'

The hot, stale smell of the store hit Thane's nostrils. He looked round the busy counters, the slow-moving masses of customers. In the wall above his head a huge air-conditioning fan was at work, but its efforts were making little impression on the heavy atmosphere. He could feel the first beads of perspiration already forming on his forehead. Detailing one man to watch each of the two stairways, the chief inspector headed towards the bank of lifts, the others close behind him. They were about fifteen yards off when a "Down" cage reached the ground floor. Its gates sighed open, and a froth of people . . . women, children, a couple of harassed husbands, some staff . . . came out, mixing with others moving forward to get aboard. The cage was packed before Thane's party could reach the gates. He gestured the others to wait, and Phil Moss jerked a thumb to the left, where, two lift-gates along, the sign was already flashing the arrival of another cage.

Again the gates sighed open. The half-dozen people aboard stepped out . . . and even as Thane moved forward, almost shoulder-to-shoulder with Farringdon, he saw Allen among those leaving, chatting to Jerry Watford, who was at his elbow. The

185

recognition was mutual and simultaneous. Allen's gaze swept from Thane across to Farringdon, saw the expression in the managing director's face . . and knew. He took a step backwards towards the lift, hesitated, then, as Thane thrust forward, he turned, shouldered Watford aside, and began to sprint through the crowd towards the nearest exit.

The detectives took off after him, and Watford, after a bewildered moment, followed. Shouts, then screams, filled the air as Allen barged head-on into a girl, sent her sprawling, then threw a savage punch into the stomach of a young airman who tried to grab him. He ran on, the police closing the gap . . . and a lane opened before him as the groups of customers shrank back from the small, wild-eyed figure in the charcoal grey business suit.

Allen was only a few yards from the door leading into Main Street when the two plain-clothes men posted there charged at him. He came to a sudden stop, gripping the counter with one hand to maintain his balance . . . and an array of glassware went crashing. His right hand leapt into his trouser pocket and the knife flashed free. The two policemen made their bid. He sidestepped one, and the knife-blade ripped a bloodied gash down the hand of the other. The wounded man staggered back with an involuntary grunt of pain . . . and Allen, the doorway barred, Thane pounding towards him, fled up the other angle of the counter, back into the store, towards the stairs. A dog, its lead dragging free, barked excitedly and lunged at him . . . he lashed out with a foot, and the dog tumbled back with a yelp of surprise. One of the detectives who had been following Thane had doubled back round the counters. Now he dived forward. But even as he grabbed Allen's knife-wrist his quarry grabbed a crystal fruit bowl from the counter beside him with his free hand and smashed it into the man's unprotected face. He was free again . . . the man, his mouth smashed, his nose broken, fell back against the counter.

On the stairs now . . . he sprinted up, dodging the customers who seemed frozen where they stood, so swift was his passage. Colin Thane was close behind, close enough for his pounding feet to be heard, with Phil Moss and Watford only a few steps to the rear. None of them shouted. There was no time, no energy

186

to be spared. But below them a police whistle was shrilling, calling the other men from their posts.

Allen burst into the first floor at the hardware section, only a couple of yards ahead of Thane. A girl assistant, shock and fear on her blanched face, stood right in his path, unable to move. With a stroke of his left arm he spun her round and threw her straight into the chief inspector. Thane stumbled, almost tripped. The girl fell to the floor, screaming but unhurt, while Thane and Moss took up the chase again. Other police were coming up the stairway and fanning-out behind them.

It was the moment James Rose had dreamed of for long years . . . his chance to be a hero. He had been walking through the hardware department when the chase stormed in in all its fury. And now Allen, his face glistening with sweat, was running straight towards the store 'tec, running with a blind disregard for anyone but the men pursuing him. Rose's thin features suddenly flushed. He glanced desperately around for a weapon, and grabbed one of the score of firewood hatchets lying on a counter only feet away. He raised the hatchet, and jumped into Allen's path. He shouted, though excitement made his high-pitched words an incoherent babble.

And Henry Allen swept under the upraised arm and pumped his knife-hand up-down in a deadly two-way blow. The marlin spike, held uppermost, sunk its sharp, round length into the soft flesh under the store 'tec's exposed chin, then tugged free for the return down-stroke, the blade ripping through Rose's shirt at the second top button and tearing a long, deep, razor-like gash that stopped just short of the man's belt. Rose gave a gurgling shriek of pure agony. The axe clattered backwards to the floor, and Rose fell against the counter, his body ablaze with pain.

Gasping for breath, wiping the blinding sweat from his eyes, his legs incapable of carrying him another yard, Allen turned at bay while the police closed in. There were five of them . . . Thane, Moss, Jerry Watford and two plain-clothes men. They moved forward warily, realizing the injury, disfigurement, or even death that their quarry was so willing and capable of dealing.

A strained, sudden hush had descended, broken only by the

187

quivering moans from the huddled form so close to Allen's feet. A widening pool of blood was covering the rubber floor.

'Drop the knife, Allen,' said Thane softly. 'Your number's up. Play it sensibly, man.'

Allen's limbs felt like lead. His heart was thumping. But he shook his head between rasping breaths. His eyes stared round, his mouth hung open. He would have been a pathetic sight, but for the glinting knife in his hand.

Watford made a tentative move, but the blond assistant manager stopped as Thane placed a restraining hand on his arm. Slowly, very slowly, Phil Moss began to move his hand towards his hip pocket. Thane saw the action from the corner of one eye, and stepped forward boldly, talking quietly as he went. 'You're in a tough enough spot already, Allen. We've got Buchan and the driver . . . and Buchan's talking as fast as he can.'

The Hillman buyer, incredibly, sneered. 'Then I'll just have to take you with me, Thane, and go out in a blaze of glory,' he countered. The knife hand came forward threateningly. And at the same second Phil Moss slid his baton from his hip pocket and, his arm a blurr of speed, threw the short heavy stick with a skill and accuracy that was almost inbred. The baton took Allen on the left temple with stunning force. Before the smaller man could recover from the surprise, Thane had pounced on him. There was no time for finesse. His left hand grabbed Allen's knife-wrist his right the man's other arm. Simultaneously, he used one of the Glasgow ned's dirtiest, most effective fighting tricks. Up went his knee, hard into Allen's stomach, while his head hit the man square in the face.

.   .   .   .   .

They had the 'cuffs on Allen ten seconds later, a suddenly quiet Allen who walked obediently towards the lift between two detectives, starting on the first stage of a journey that would end weeks later in the dock of the High Court.

.   .   .   .   .

188

It took time for things to settle down again. But finally, after Rose was placed on a stretcher and, temporarily bandaged, had been rushed to the Royal Infirmary for an emergency operation, Thane went over to where Pat Miller was helping Doc. Williams, the police surgeon, to patch up the two injured C.I.D. men.

'I've called another ambulance for these two characters,' said Williams. 'Never mind, boys, you'll get a nice spell of sick leave out of this. Nurses flocking round the heroes, the chief inspector bringing you black grapes and comic books . . . what more do you want?'

The man with the smashed face mumbled a blistering reply. But the twisted, painful grin took the venom from it.

'Any likelihood of more business, Colin?' asked the doctor, neatly pinning a final roll of bandage round the other man's arm.

'That's the lot, Doc,' said Thane thankfully. 'What do you think of Rose's chances?'

'He'll be okay,' said Williams. 'He was damned lucky, though. If that spike had hit him a bit further back, or gone just a little deeper, he'd have had his lot. As it is, he'll have an interesting scar on his chest, and some embroidery under his chin . . . nothing more. Must have hurt like hell, of course, but pain isn't everything.'

'We'll look after him, and do anything we can for your two men into the bargain,' said Farringdon's gruff voice. The managing director beamed almost affectionately at them. 'Funny, the way Rose stood up to Allen. I'd have almost banked on him running.'

'That's how it sometimes goes,' said Thane thoughtfully. 'At first, I thought Rose might be involved pretty deeply. Even when I decided I was wrong, I kept on using him to make the real culprit feel more secure. It was dirty, but necessary. Some people might say that he felt in such a spot he just had to stand up to Allen the way he did, to prove himself. Between his manner, and the chip he's been carrying on his shoulder, he's not exactly an endearing character. But I'd prefer to think that he just has natural guts, even though he probably never knew it himself.' He grinned. 'Finding out may make quite a change in him.'

'One thing about Allen's scheme still puzzles me.' said Farringdon. 'You told us in the car that the telephone in my bedroom rang while you were waiting that night. Yet at the time it did, Allen was already in the store. Who made the call? Buchan? And how could he warn Allen if he discovered that I was still in the building?'

'Allen made the call himself,' said Thane. 'Remember telling me that yours was a private phone, a direct outside line, and that the switchboard was unattended? All Allen had to do was go to your switchboard room, plug in a line and dial your number. If you answered, well, he was just someone who'd got a wrong number . . . and he'd think twice about moving stuff down to the furniture van. If there was no reply, they went full steam ahead. Don't blame Deacon, the night commissionaire, too much, by the way. He did his job to the letter. Allen was as clever as they come . . . and anyway, he was one of the last people Deacon or anyone else for that matter would really suspect.'

'When did you first think that it might be Allen?' asked Pat Miller, accepting a cigarette as Farringdon handed round his gold case.

Thane waited until he had lit up. 'I'm not very sure myself,' he confessed. 'Probably when I went to his home to try and get a picture of Judith Marchand, and got an eyeful of the house and garden. It just didn't fit in with his job, somehow. I don't know what you paid him, Mr. Farringdon, but it pointed to more money than he earned . . . either money from his wife, or from some outside activity. Then there was the fact that Judith Marchand owed Mrs. Allen quite a load of gratitude, the motive I'd been seeking for her silence.'

The store chief heaved a deep sigh of relief. 'And now it's all over. Thank the Lord. Now we can tackle the summer sale without having all this hanging over us. Tomorrow's our big day, Thane.'

'Tomorrow. . . .' Colin Thane blinked as a sudden thought struck him. 'Look, I'm afraid I'll need to move. I'll . . . I'll see you later. Come on, Phil.'

190

'What's the rush?' asked Moss as they sped down the stairs to the ground floor of the store.

'Rush? Heck, it's half past four. I'll need to get back to Millside before the super's clerk stops paying out. Mary's waiting on my pay to get the rest of the cash she needs for that new carpet. She's coming here first thing in the morning to grab it.'

'And you wonder why I stay single,' said Moss sarcastically as they hurried towards the door.

.   .   .   .   .

At the High Court of Justiciary, sitting in Glasgow, Henry Allen was found guilty of murder . . . murder in the furtherance of theft.

They hanged him at eight o'clock on a dull Friday morning. He screamed all the way to the gallows.